ADVENTURE TIME COMICS

VOLUME
①

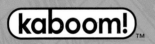

ADVENTURE TIME COMICS Volume One, February 2017.
Published by KaBOOM!, a division of Boom Entertainment, Inc.
ADVENTURE TIME, CARTOON NETWORK, the logos, and all related
characters and elements are trademarks of and © Cartoon Network.
(S17) Originally published in single magazine form as ADVENTURE
TIME COMICS No. 1-4. © Cartoon Network. (S16) All rights reserved.
KaBOOM!™ and the KaBOOM! logo are trademarks of Boom
Entertainment, Inc., registered in various countries and categories.
All characters, events, and institutions depicted herein are fictional.
Any similarity between any of the names, characters, persons, events,
and/or institutions in this publication to actual names, characters,
and persons, whether living or dead, events, and/or institutions is
unintended and purely coincidental. KaBOOM! does not read or
accept unsolicited submissions of ideas, stories, or artwork.

For information regarding the CPSIA on this printed material, call: (203)
595-3636 and provide reference #RICH – 724676.

BOOM! Studios, 5670 Wilshire Boulevard, Suite 450, Los Angeles, CA
90036-5679. Printed in USA. First Printing.

ISBN: 978-1-60886-934-3, eISBN: 978-1-61398-605-9

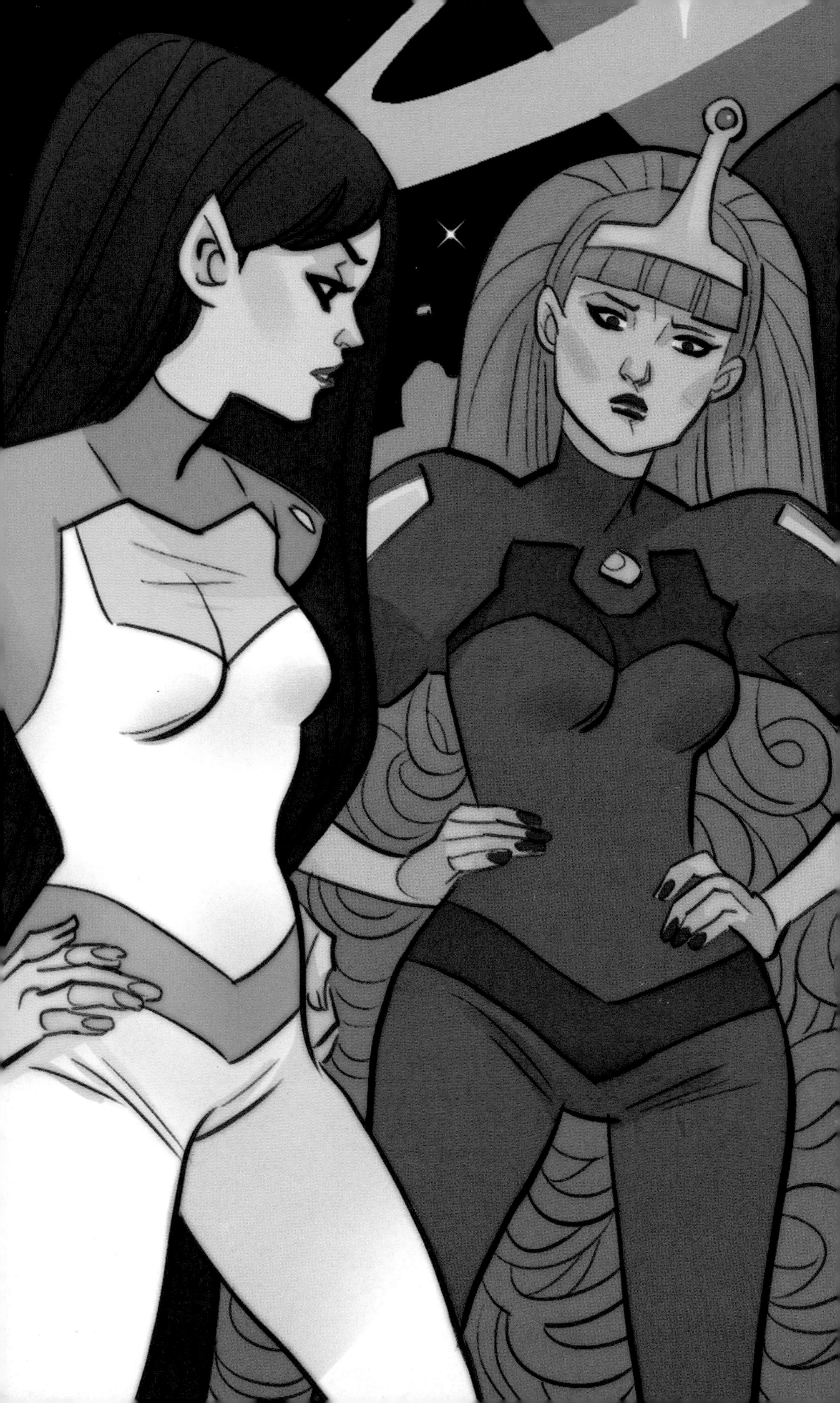

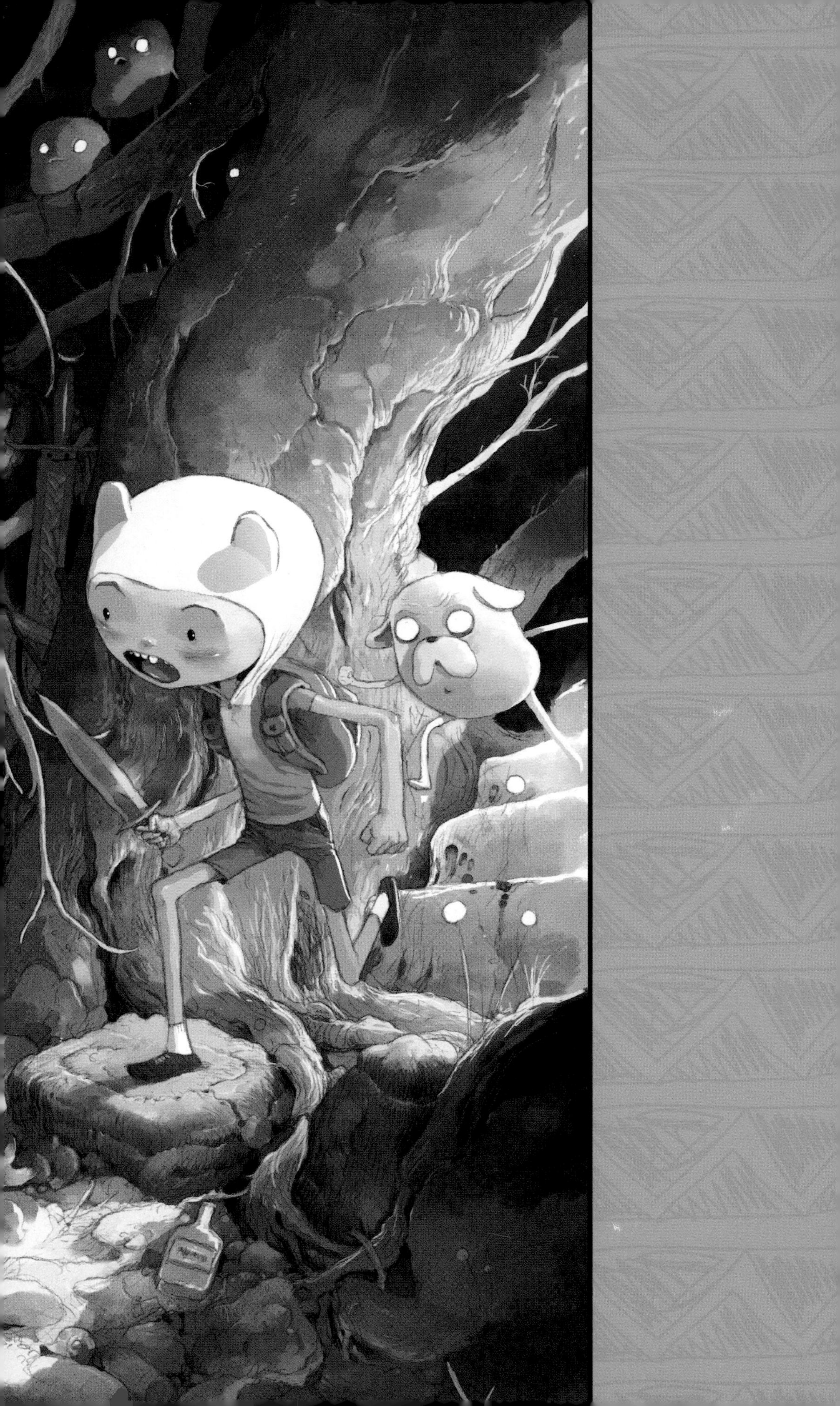

ADVENTURE TIME™
Created by **PENDLETON WARD**

"TOOTHPASTE FAIRY"
Written & Illustrated by
ART BALTAZAR

"STAND NEXT TO ME"
Written & Illustrated by
KATIE COOK

"OLIAD GETS A BREAK"
Written & Illustrated by
TONY MILLIONAIRE

"GOOD SHELF"
Written & Illustrated by
KAT LEYH

"DIRTY DUNGEON"
Written & Illustrated by
BOX BROWN

"THE GREATEST WARRIOR
EVER"
Written & Illustrated by
GREG SMALLWOOD

"RIVIERA REVERIE"
Written & Illustrated by
SOPHIA FOSTER-DIMINO

"FINN'S LULLABY"
Written & Illustrated by
EVGENY YAKOVLEV

"BMO DELUXE"
Written by
KELLY THOMPSON
Illustrated by
SAVANNA GANUCHEAU
Letters by
COREY BREEN

"FINDERS KEEPERS"
Written & Illustrated by
VERONICA FISH

"ECHOES"
Written & Illustrated by
S. M. VIDAURRI

"LOST IN SPACE"
Written & Illustrated by
MARGUERITE SAUVAGE

"IT'S ALL FUN AND GAMES"
Written by
JIM ZUB
Illustrated by
DEREK CHARM

"MOON BEAM"
Written & Illustrated by
AATMAJA PANDYA

"TICKED OFF"
Illustrated by
JAMES LLOYD
Colors by
MAARTA LAIHO

"TO THE NORTH"
Written by
NICOLE ANDELFINGER
Illustrated by
ANISSA ESPINOSA

Cover by
NICK PITARRA

Designer
MICHELLE ANKLEY

Associate Editor
ALEX GALER

Editors
**SHANNON WATTERS &
WHITNEY LEOPARD**

With Special Thanks to Marisa Marionakis, Janet No, Curtis Lelash, Conrad
Montgomery, Meghan Bradley, Kelly Crews, Scott Malchus, Adam Muto
and the wonderful folks at Cartoon Network.

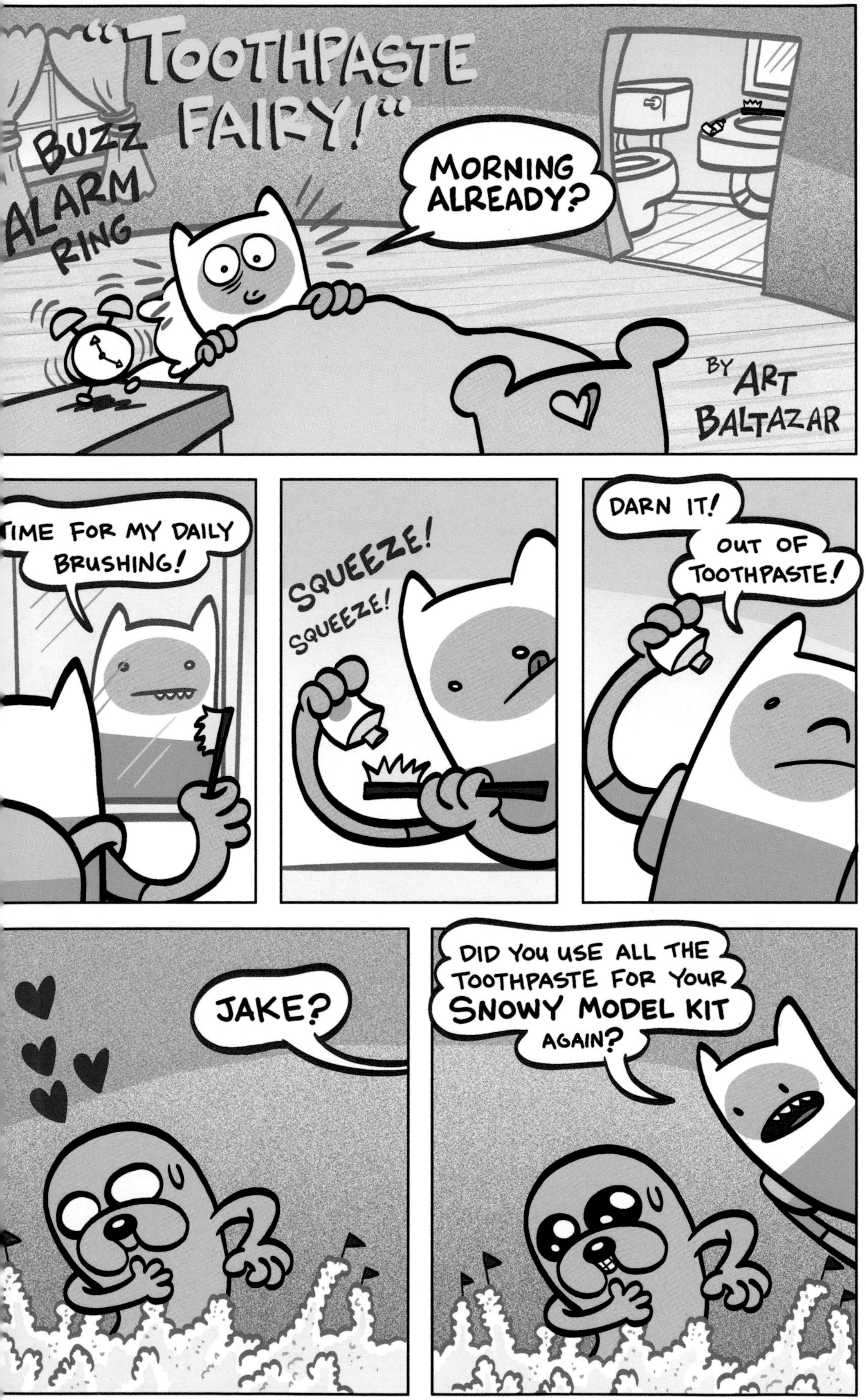
"TOOTHPASTE FAIRY!"
BUZZ
ALARM
RING
MORNING ALREADY?
BY ART BALTAZAR
TIME FOR MY DAILY BRUSHING!
SQUEEZE!
SQUEEZE!
DARN IT!
OUT OF TOOTHPASTE!
JAKE?
DID YOU USE ALL THE TOOTHPASTE FOR YOUR SNOWY MODEL KIT AGAIN?

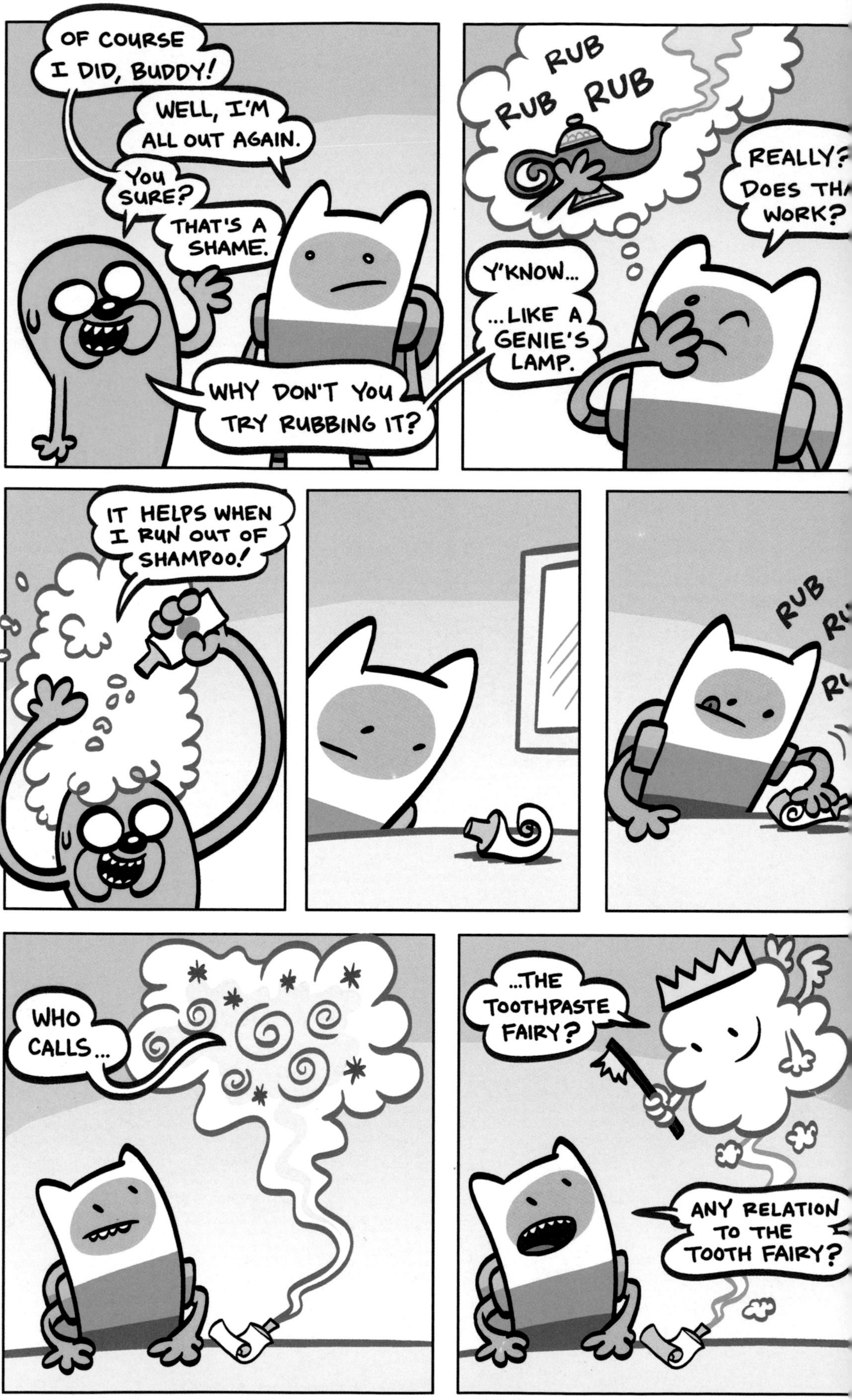
OF COURSE I DID, BUDDY!
WELL, I'M ALL OUT AGAIN.
YOU SURE?
THAT'S A SHAME.
WHY DON'T YOU TRY RUBBING IT?
Y'KNOW...
...LIKE A GENIE'S LAMP.
RUB
RUB RUB
REALLY? DOES THA
WORK?
IT HELPS WHEN I RUN OUT OF SHAMPOO!
RUB
WHO CALLS...
...THE TOOTHPASTE FAIRY?
ANY RELATION TO THE TOOTH FAIRY?

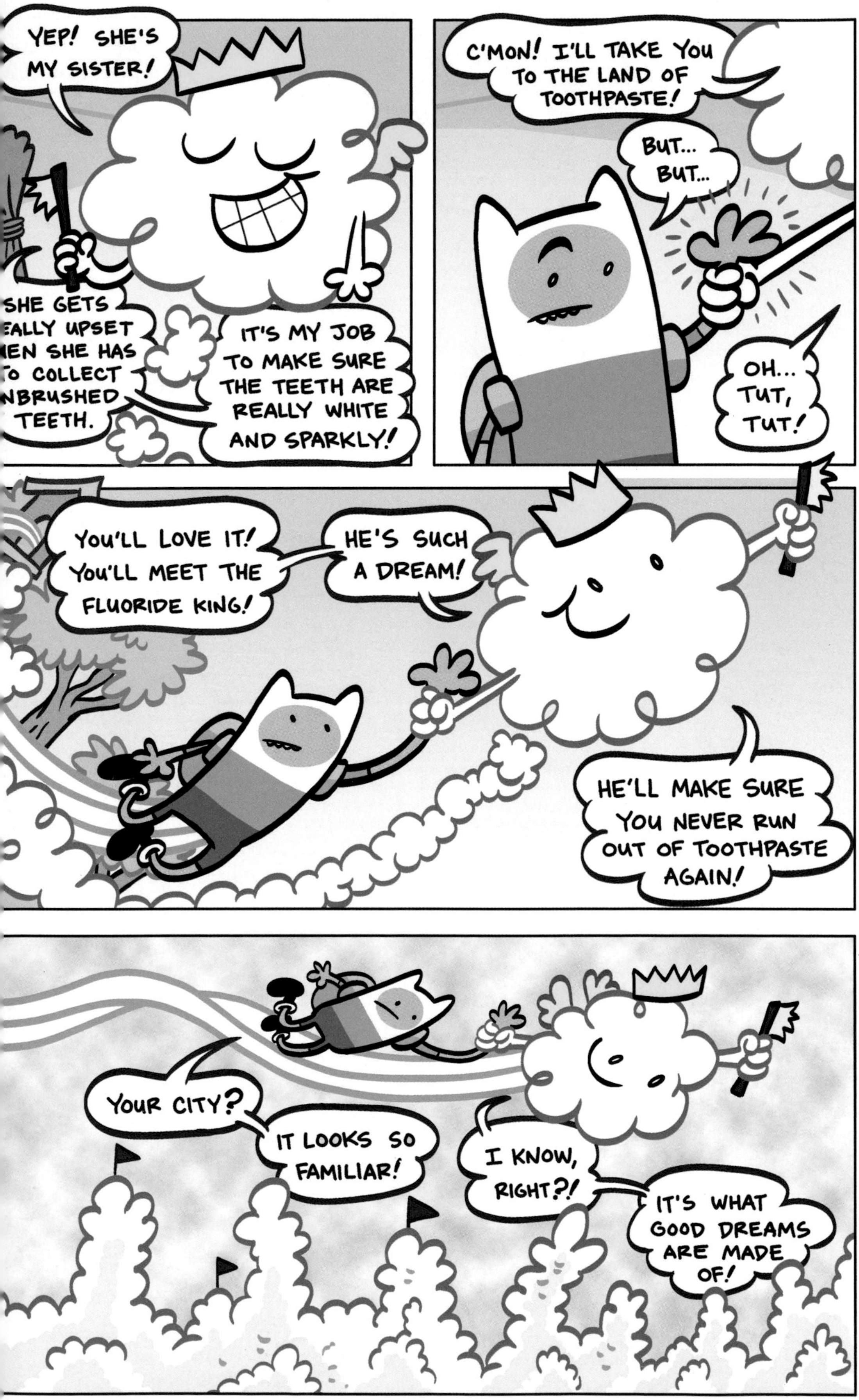
YEP! SHE'S MY SISTER!
SHE GETS ...EALLY UPSET ...EN SHE HAS ...O COLLECT ...NBRUSHED TEETH.
IT'S MY JOB TO MAKE SURE THE TEETH ARE REALLY WHITE AND SPARKLY!
C'MON! I'LL TAKE YOU TO THE LAND OF TOOTHPASTE!
BUT... BUT...
OH... TUT, TUT!
YOU'LL LOVE IT! YOU'LL MEET THE FLUORIDE KING!
HE'S SUCH A DREAM!
HE'LL MAKE SURE YOU NEVER RUN OUT OF TOOTHPASTE AGAIN!
YOUR CITY?
IT LOOKS SO FAMILIAR!
I KNOW, RIGHT?!
IT'S WHAT GOOD DREAMS ARE MADE OF!

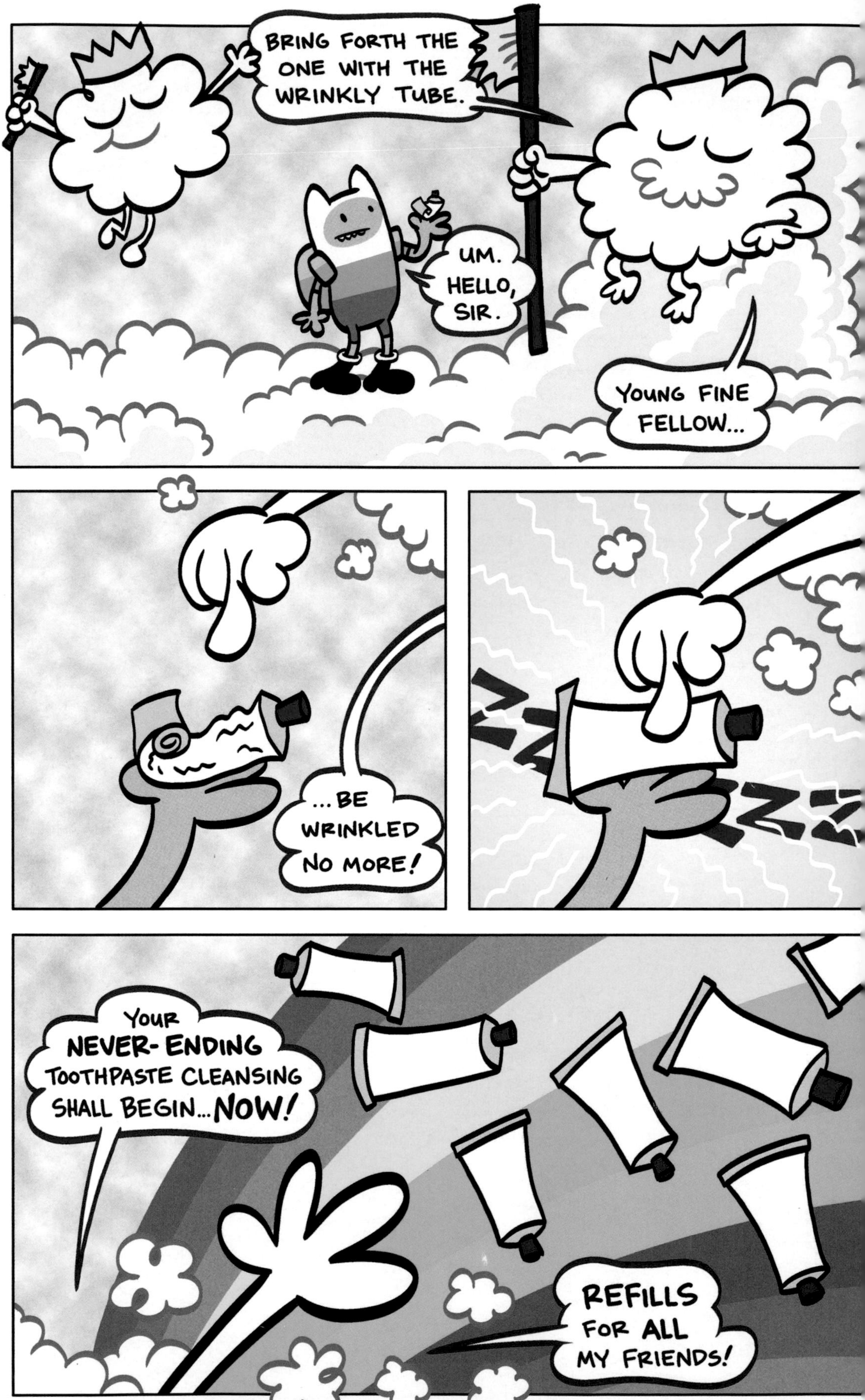
BRING FORTH THE ONE WITH THE WRINKLY TUBE.
UM. HELLO, SIR.
YOUNG FINE FELLOW...
...BE WRINKLED NO MORE!
YOUR NEVER-ENDING TOOTHPASTE CLEANSING SHALL BEGIN...NOW!
REFILLS FOR ALL MY FRIENDS!

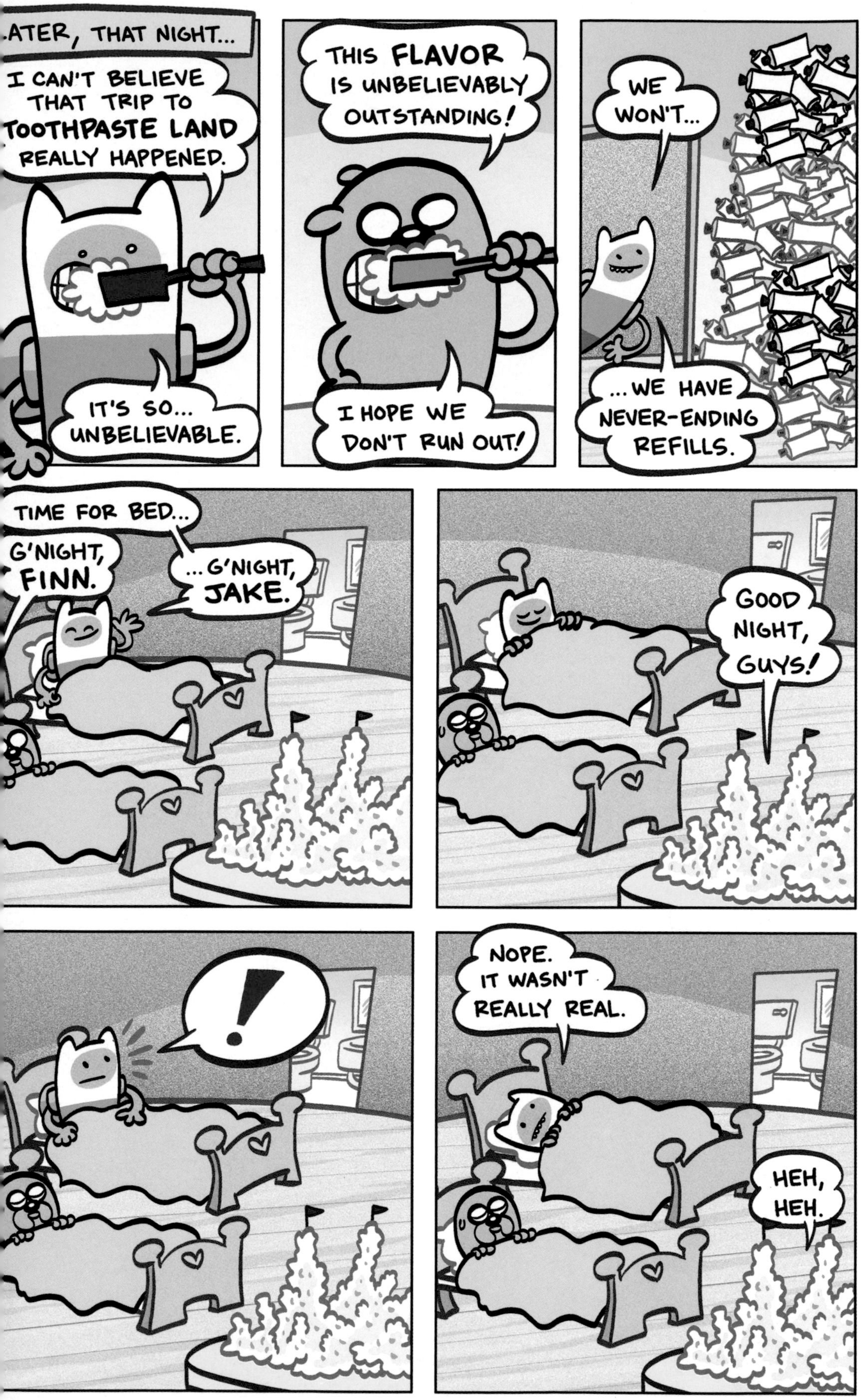
LATER, THAT NIGHT...
I CAN'T BELIEVE THAT TRIP TO TOOTHPASTE LAND REALLY HAPPENED.
IT'S SO... UNBELIEVABLE.
THIS FLAVOR IS UNBELIEVABLY OUTSTANDING!
I HOPE WE DON'T RUN OUT!
WE WON'T...
...WE HAVE NEVER-ENDING REFILLS.
TIME FOR BED...
G'NIGHT, FINN.
...G'NIGHT, JAKE.
GOOD NIGHT, GUYS!
!
NOPE. IT WASN'T REALLY REAL.
HEH, HEH.

-BRUSH YOUR TEETH.

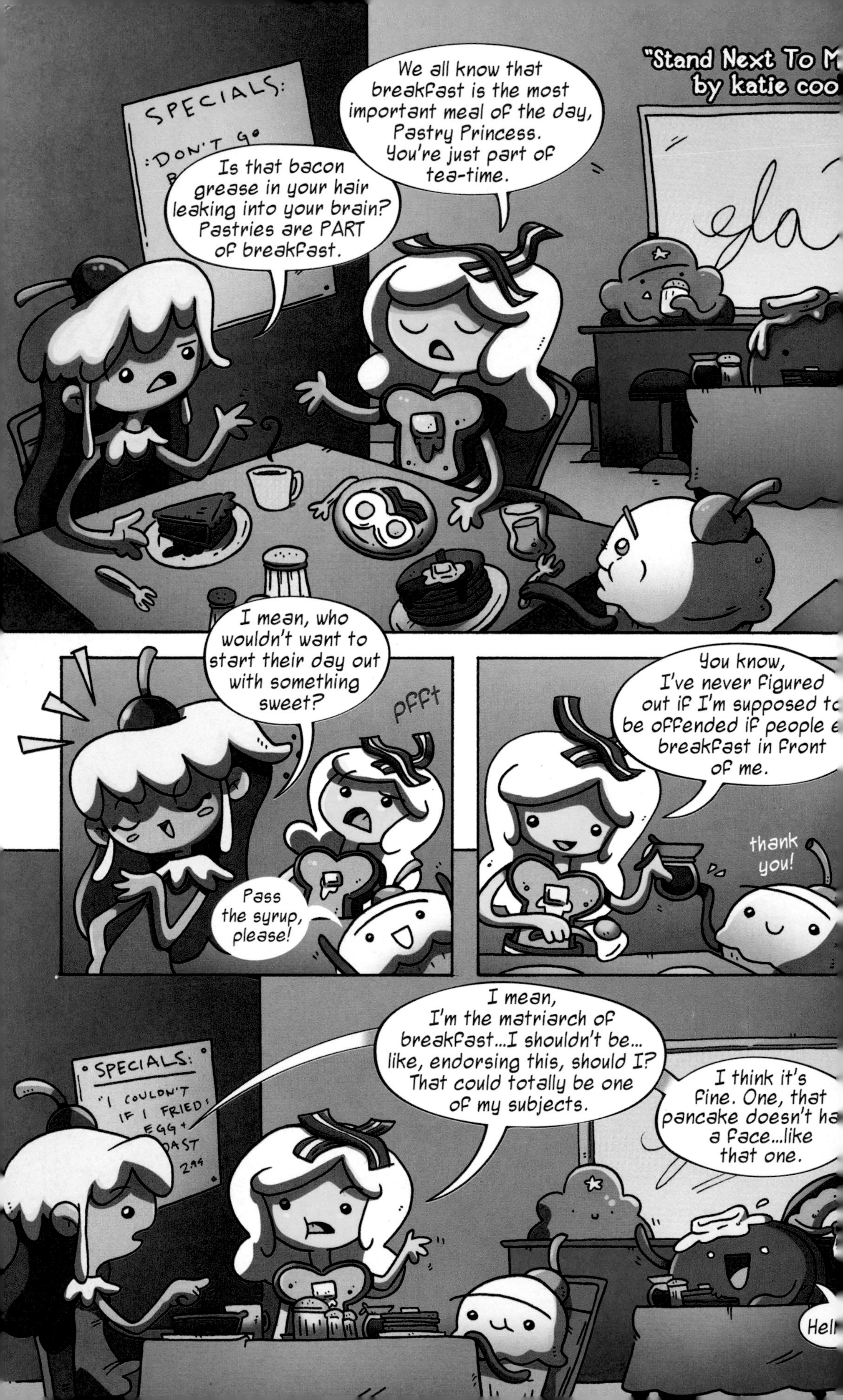

"Stand Next To M
by katie coo
SPECIALS:
:DON'T GO
We all know that breakfast is the most important meal of the day, Pastry Princess. You're just part of tea-time.
Is that bacon grease in your hair leaking into your brain? Pastries are PART of breakfast.
I mean, who wouldn't want to start their day out with something sweet?
pfft
Pass the syrup, please!
You know, I've never figured out if I'm supposed to be offended if people e breakfast in front of me.
thank you!
SPECIALS:
"I COULDN'T IF I FRIED: EGG + DAST 2.99
I mean, I'm the matriarch of breakfast...I shouldn't be... like, endorsing this, should I? That could totally be one of my subjects.
I think it's fine. One, that pancake doesn't ha a face...like that one.
Hel

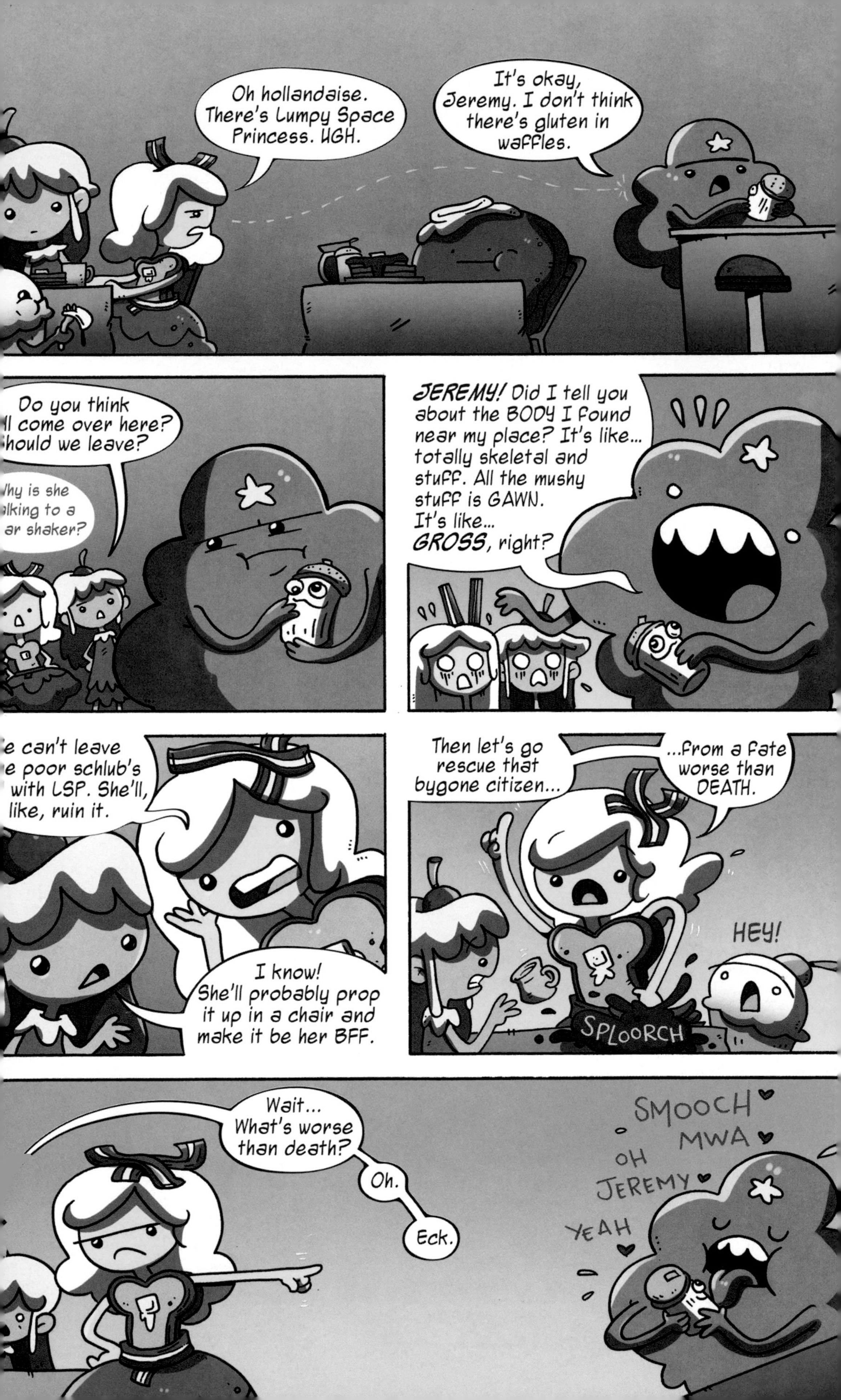

Oh hollandaise. There's Lumpy Space Princess. UGH.
It's okay, Jeremy. I don't think there's gluten in waffles.
Do you think ll come over here? hould we leave?
Vhy is she alking to a ar shaker?
JEREMY! Did I tell you about the BODY I found near my place? It's like... totally skeletal and stuff. All the mushy stuff is GAWN. It's like... GROSS, right?
e can't leave e poor schlub's with LSP. She'll, like, ruin it.
I know! She'll probably prop it up in a chair and make it be her BFF.
Then let's go rescue that bygone citizen...
...from a fate worse than DEATH.
HEY!
SPLOORCH
Wait... What's worse than death?
Oh.
Eck.
SMOOCH
MWA
OH JEREMY
YEAH

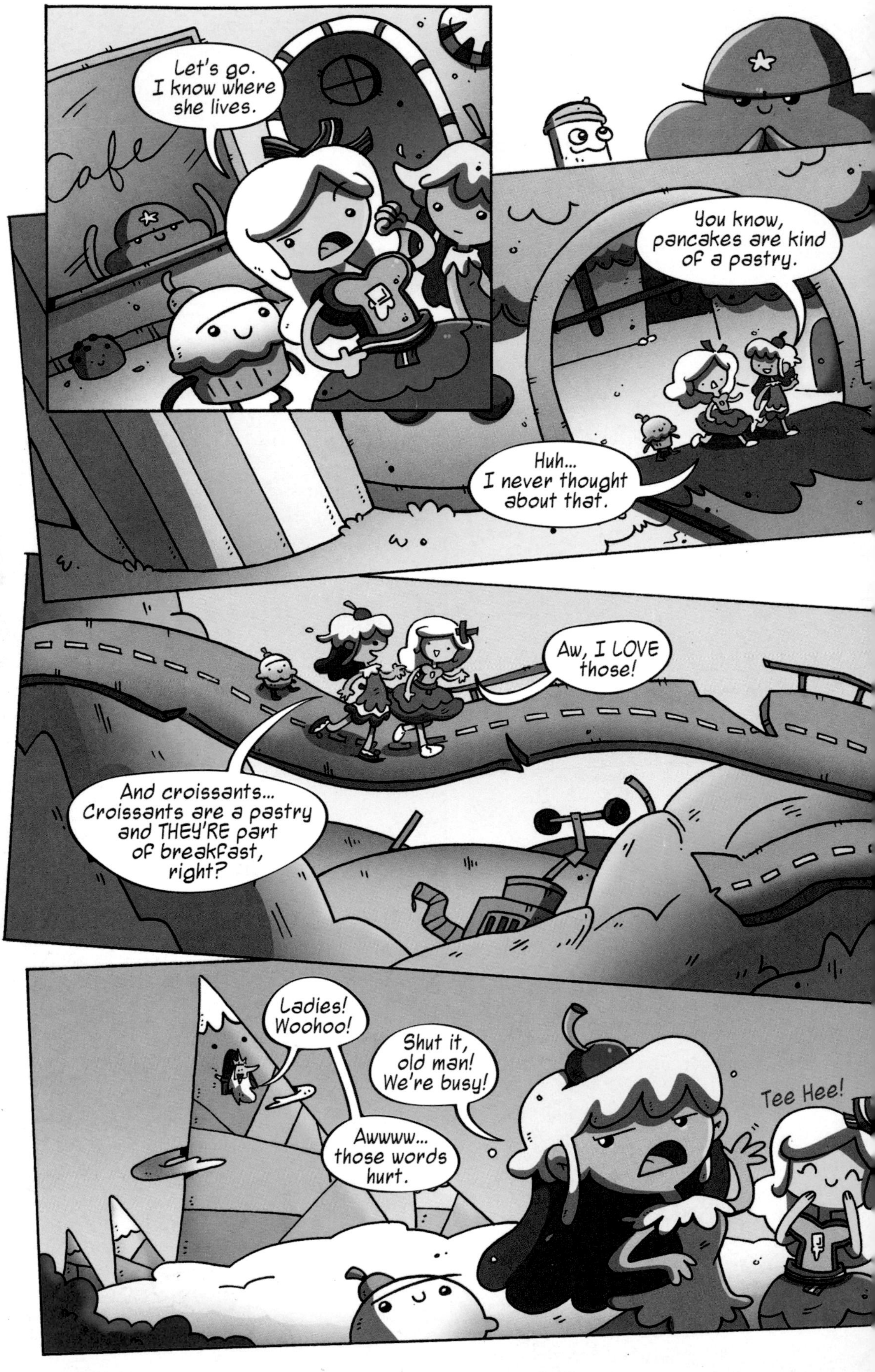

Let's go. I know where she lives.
Cafe
You know, pancakes are kind of a pastry.
Huh... I never thought about that.
Aw, I LOVE those!
And croissants... Croissants are a pastry and THEY'RE part of breakfast, right?
Ladies! Woohoo!
Shut it, old man! We're busy!
Awwww... those words hurt.
Tee Hee!

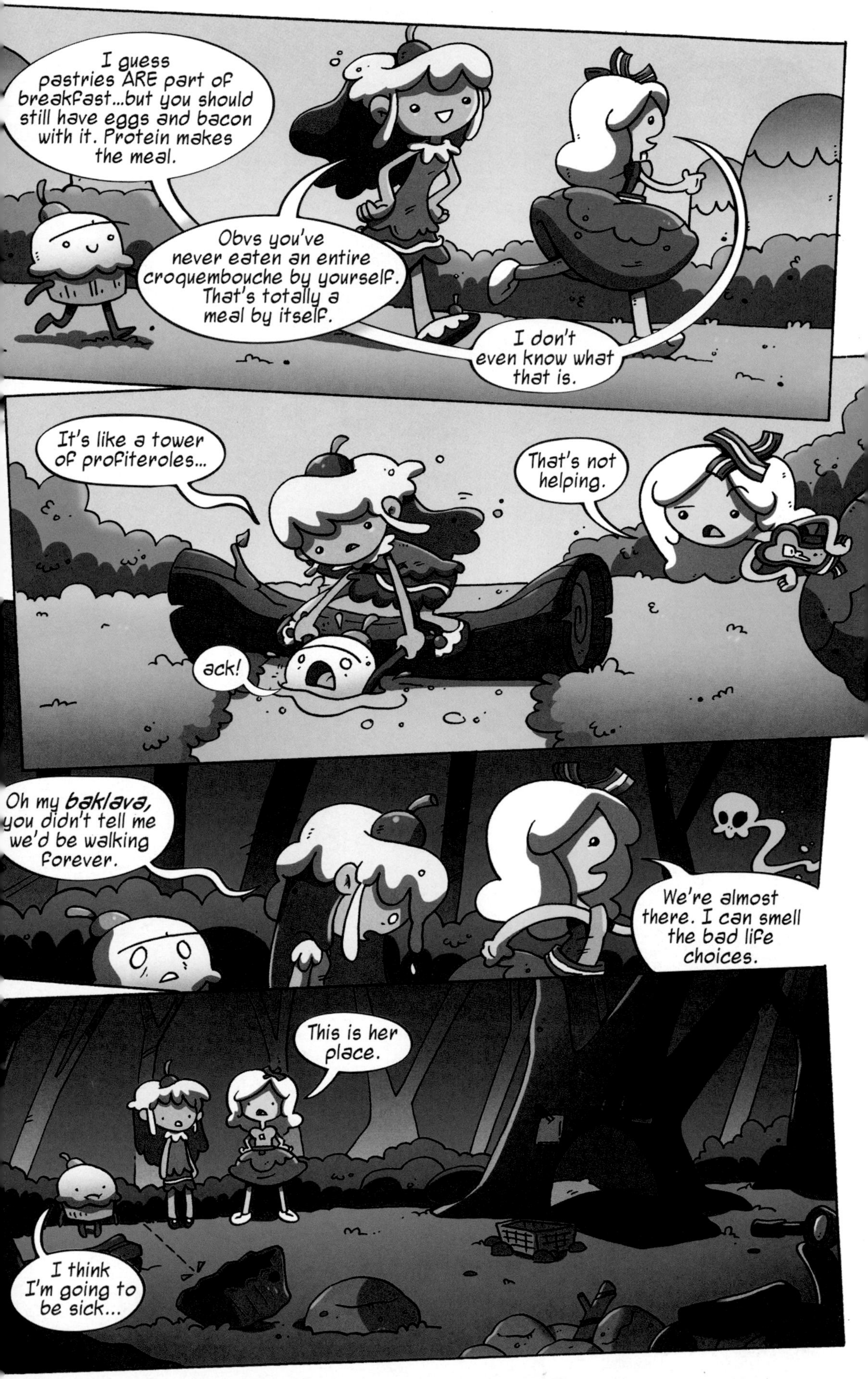

I guess pastries ARE part of breakfast...but you should still have eggs and bacon with it. Protein makes the meal.
Obvs you've never eaten an entire croquembouche by yourself. That's totally a meal by itself.
I don't even know what that is.
It's like a tower of profiteroles...
That's not helping.
ack!
Oh my *baklava,* you didn't tell me we'd be walking forever.
We're almost there. I can smell the bad life choices.
This is her place.
I think I'm going to be sick...

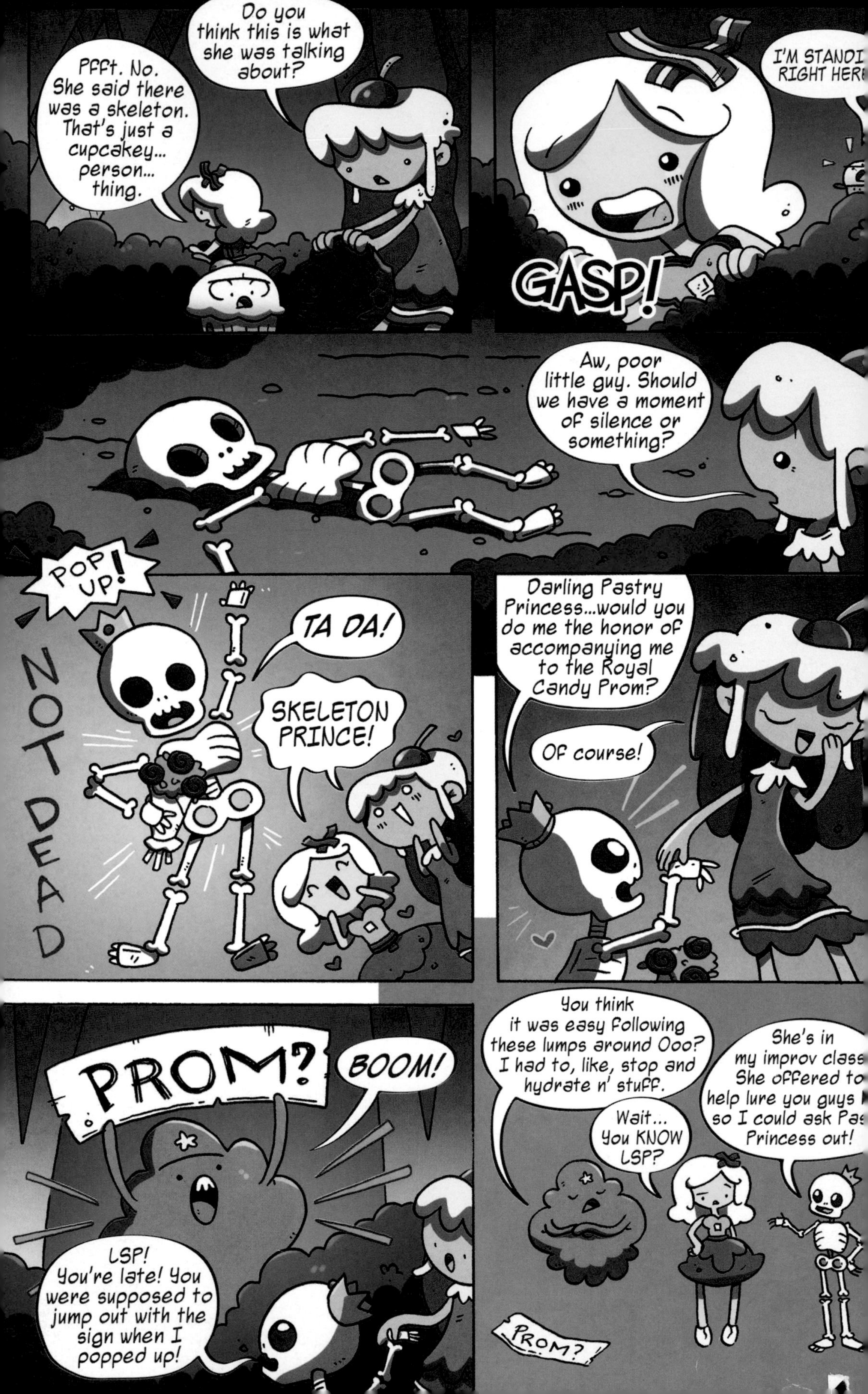
Do you think this is what she was talking about?
Pfft. No. She said there was a skeleton. That's just a cupcakey... person... thing.
I'M STANDI RIGHT HER
GASP!
Aw, poor little guy. Should we have a moment of silence or something?
POP UP!
NOT DEAD
TA DA!
SKELETON PRINCE!
Darling Pastry Princess...would you do me the honor of accompanying me to the Royal Candy Prom?
Of course!
PROM?
BOOM!
LSP! You're late! You were supposed to jump out with the sign when I popped up!
You think it was easy following these lumps around Ooo? I had to, like, stop and hydrate n' stuff.
Wait... You KNOW LSP?
She's in my improv class She offered to help lure you guys so I could ask Pas Princess out!
PROM?

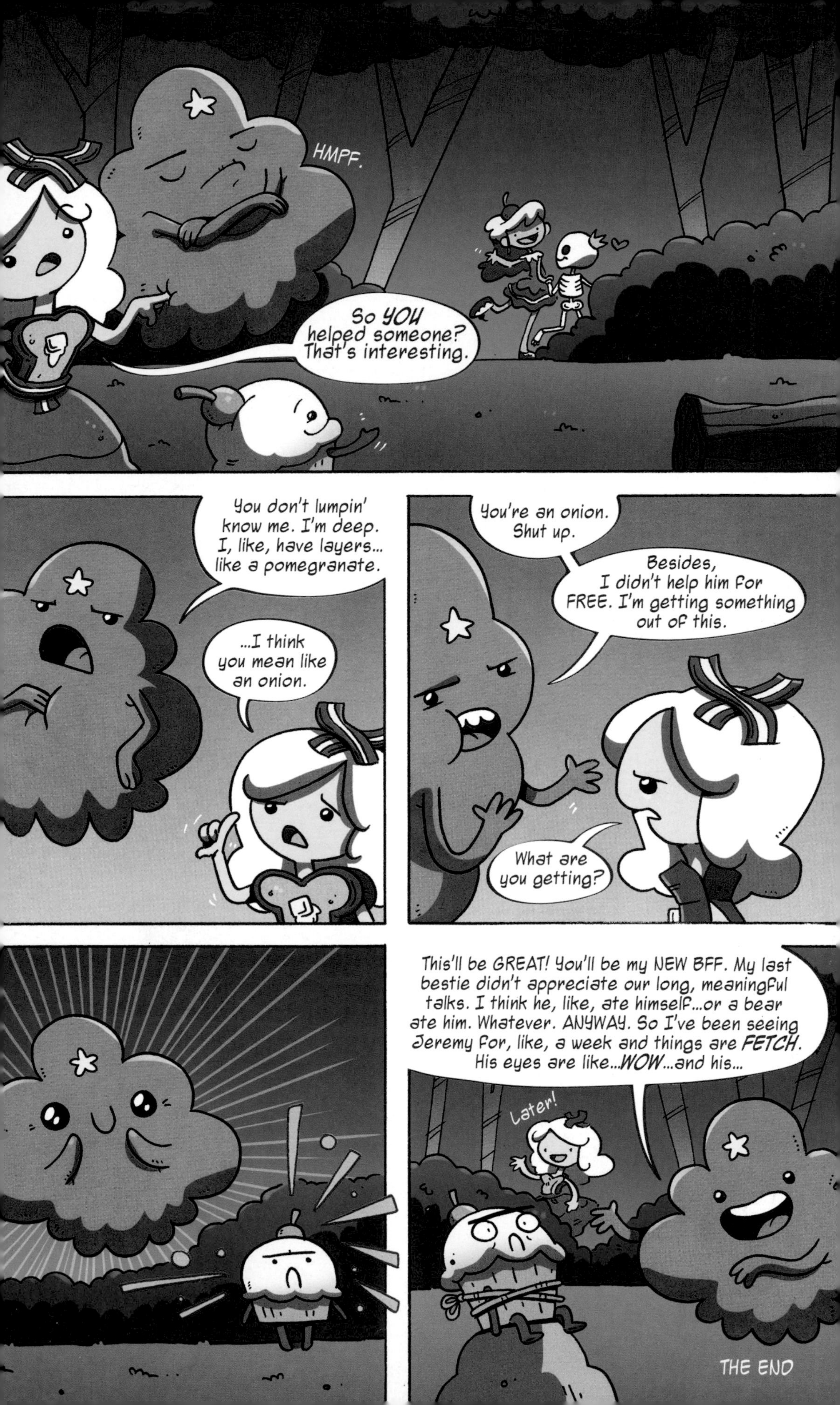
HMPF.
So YOU helped someone? That's interesting.
You don't lumpin' know me. I'm deep. I, like, have layers... like a pomegranate.
...I think you mean like an onion.
You're an onion. Shut up.
Besides, I didn't help him for FREE. I'm getting something out of this.
What are you getting?
This'll be GREAT! You'll be my NEW BFF. My last bestie didn't appreciate our long, meaningful talks. I think he, like, ate himself...or a bear ate him. Whatever. ANYWAY. So I've been seeing Jeremy for, like, a week and things are FETCH. His eyes are like...WOW...and his...
Later!
THE END

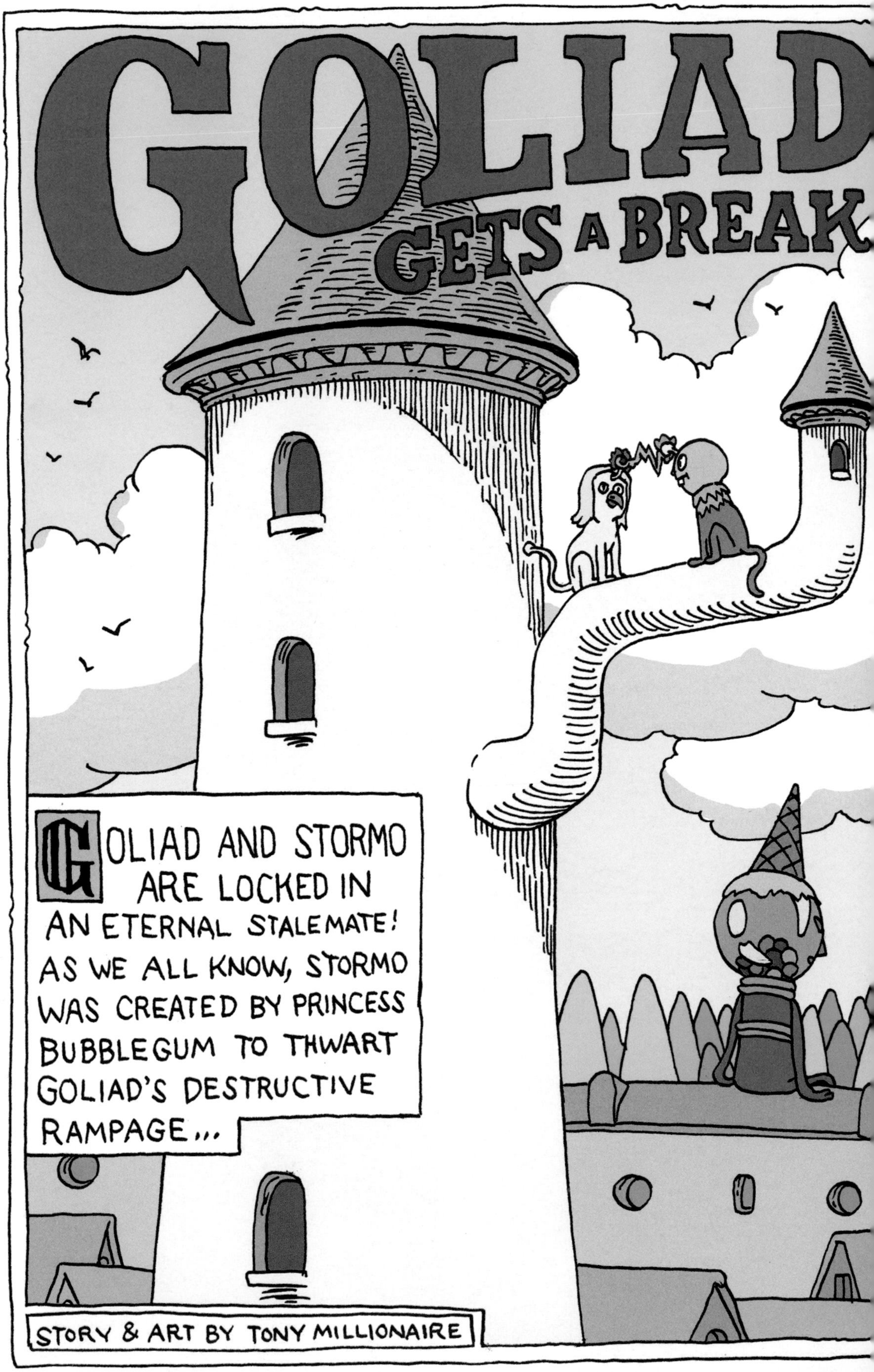
GOLIAD GETS A BREAK
GOLIAD AND STORMO ARE LOCKED IN AN ETERNAL STALEMATE! AS WE ALL KNOW, STORMO WAS CREATED BY PRINCESS BUBBLEGUM TO THWART GOLIAD'S DESTRUCTIVE RAMPAGE...
STORY & ART BY TONY MILLIONAIRE

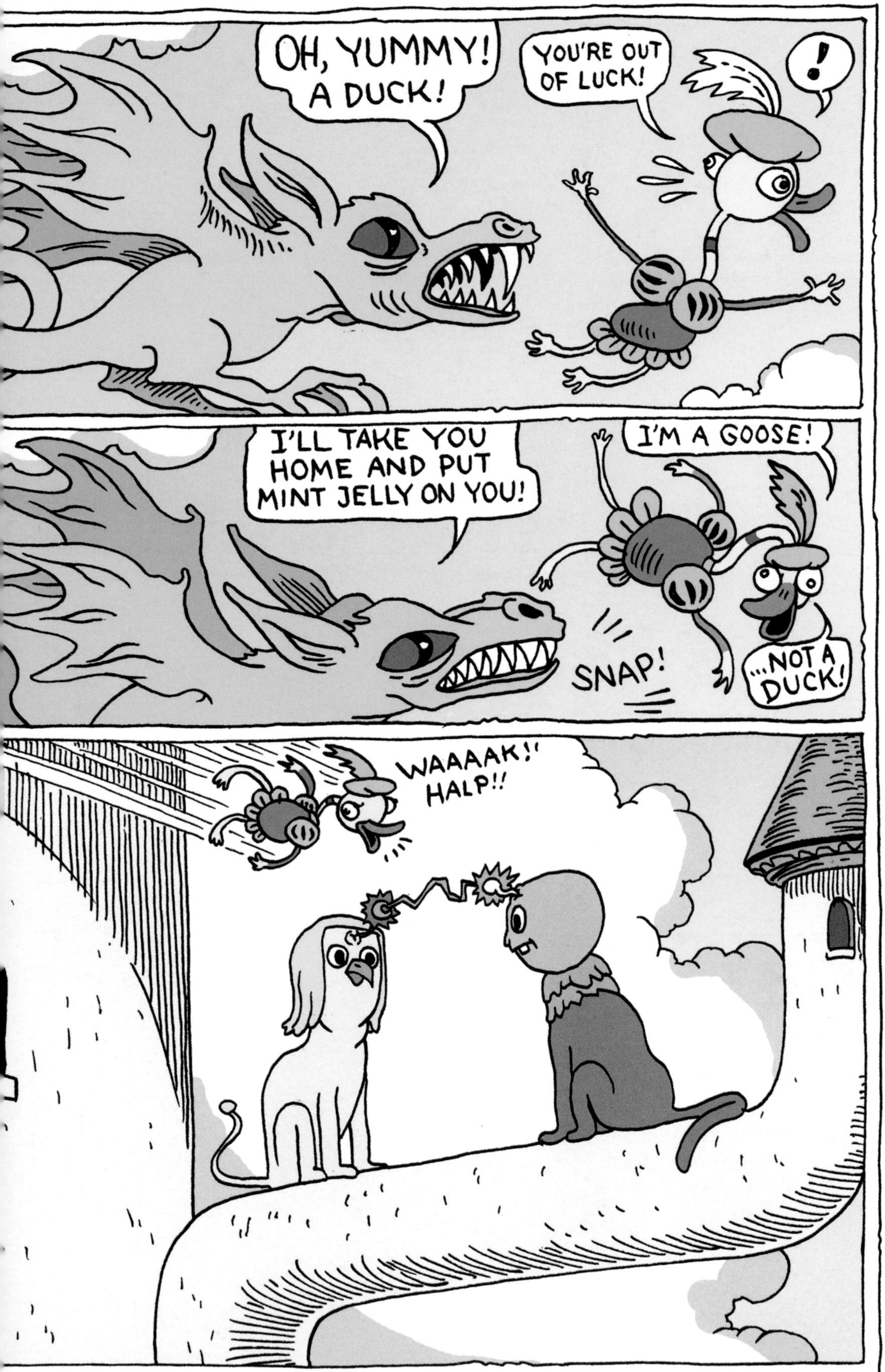
OH, YUMMY! A DUCK!
YOU'RE OUT OF LUCK!
!
I'LL TAKE YOU HOME AND PUT MINT JELLY ON YOU!
I'M A GOOSE!
SNAP!
...NOT A DUCK!
WAAAAK!! HALP!!

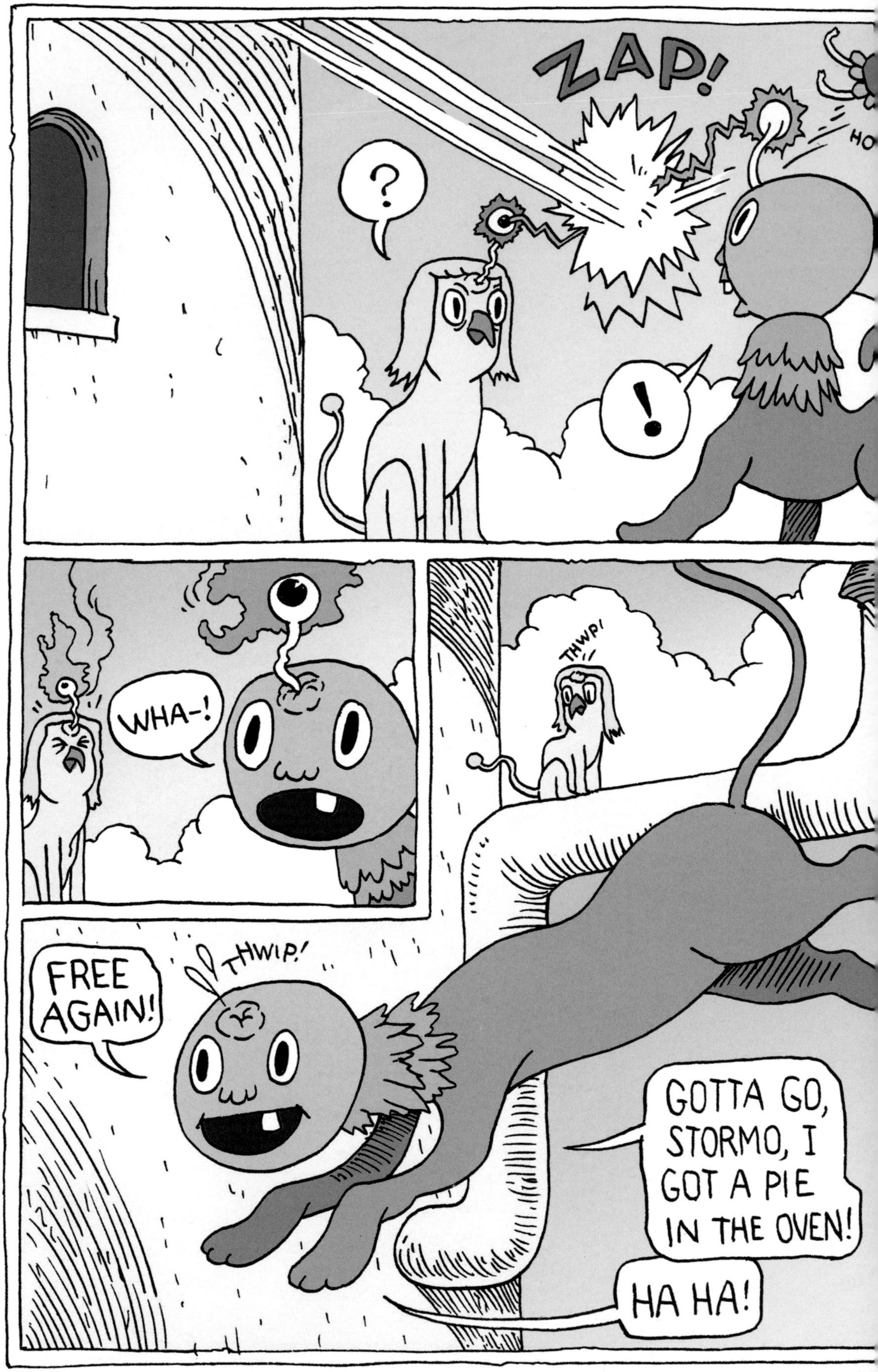
ZAP!
HO
?
!
WHA-!
THWP!
FREE AGAIN!
THWIP!
GOTTA GO, STORMO, I GOT A PIE IN THE OVEN!
HA HA!

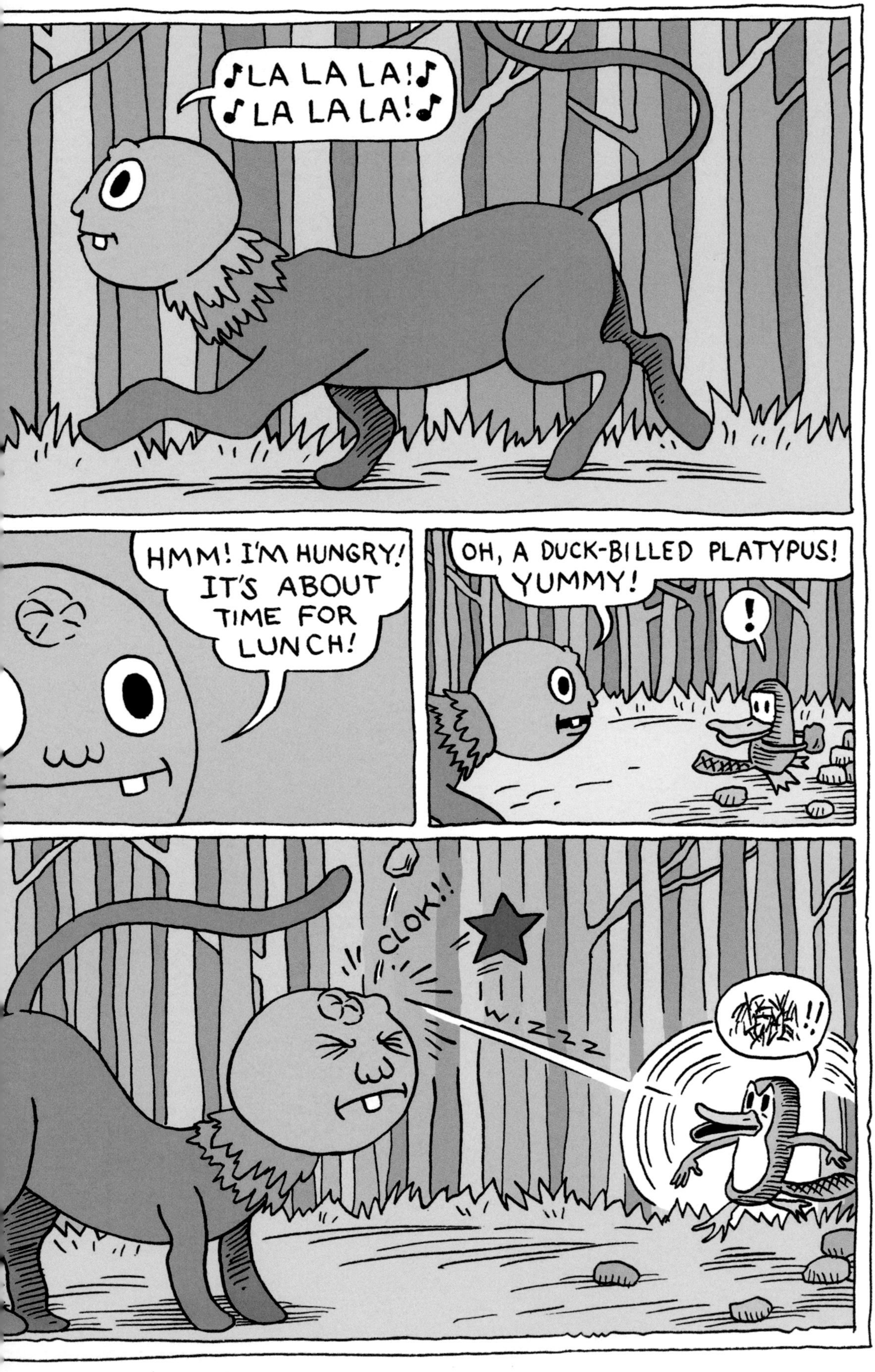
LA LA LA!
LA LA LA!
HMM! I'M HUNGRY! IT'S ABOUT TIME FOR LUNCH!
OH, A DUCK-BILLED PLATYPUS! YUMMY!
!
CLOK!!
WIZZZZ

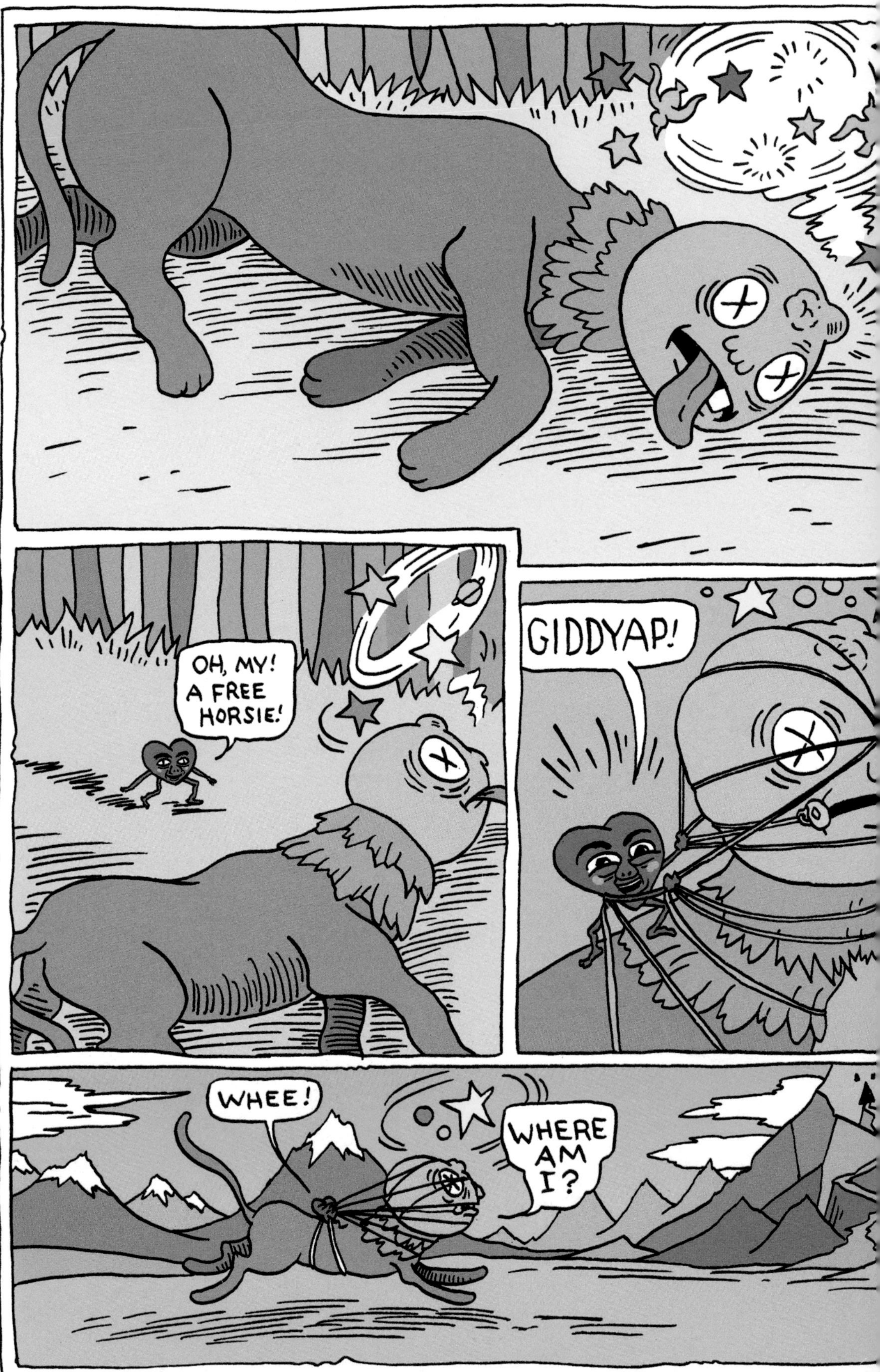
OH, MY! A FREE HORSIE!
GIDDYAP!
WHEE!
WHERE AM I?

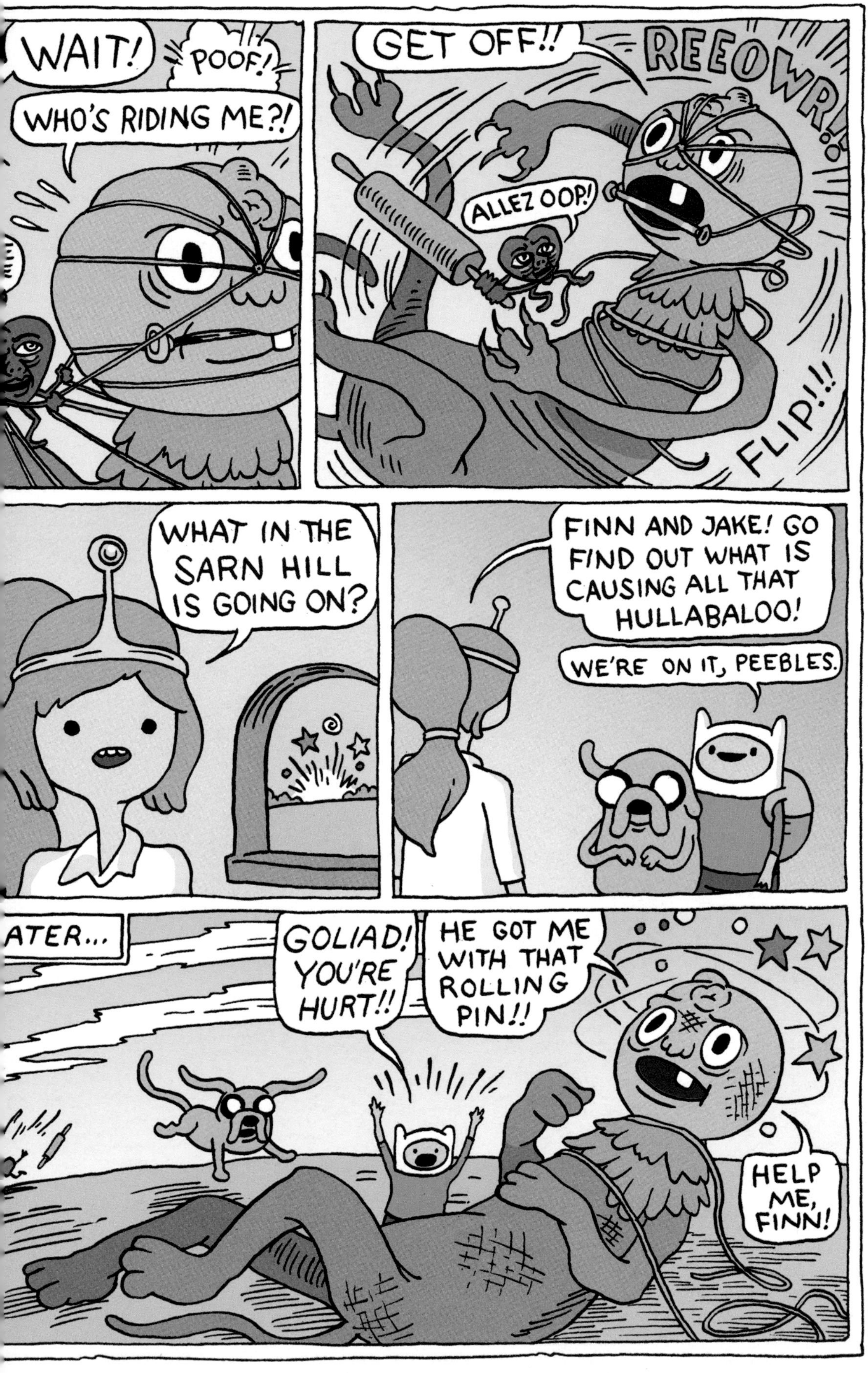

WAIT!
POOF!
WHO'S RIDING ME?!
GET OFF!!
REEEOWR!!
ALLEZ OOP!
FLIP!!!
WHAT IN THE SARN HILL IS GOING ON?
FINN AND JAKE! GO FIND OUT WHAT IS CAUSING ALL THAT HULLABALOO!
WE'RE ON IT, PEEBLES.
ATER...
GOLIAD! YOU'RE HURT!!
HE GOT ME WITH THAT ROLLING PIN!!
HELP ME, FINN!

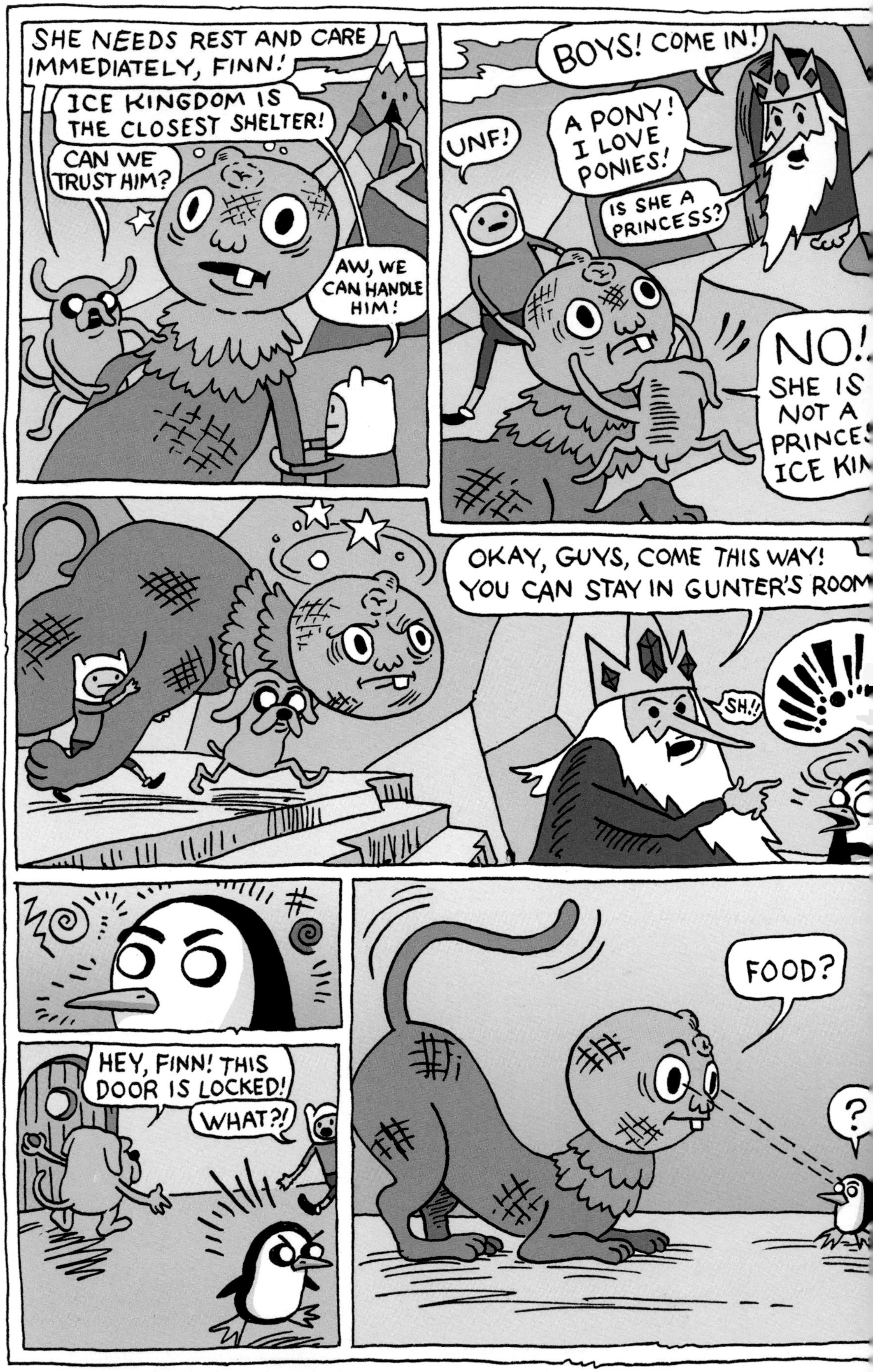

SHE NEEDS REST AND CARE IMMEDIATELY, FINN!
ICE KINGDOM IS THE CLOSEST SHELTER!
CAN WE TRUST HIM?
AW, WE CAN HANDLE HIM!
BOYS! COME IN!
UNF!
A PONY! I LOVE PONIES!
IS SHE A PRINCESS?
NO!
SHE IS NOT A PRINCE
ICE KI
OKAY, GUYS, COME THIS WAY! YOU CAN STAY IN GUNTER'S ROOM
SH!!
HEY, FINN! THIS DOOR IS LOCKED!
WHAT?!
FOOD?
?

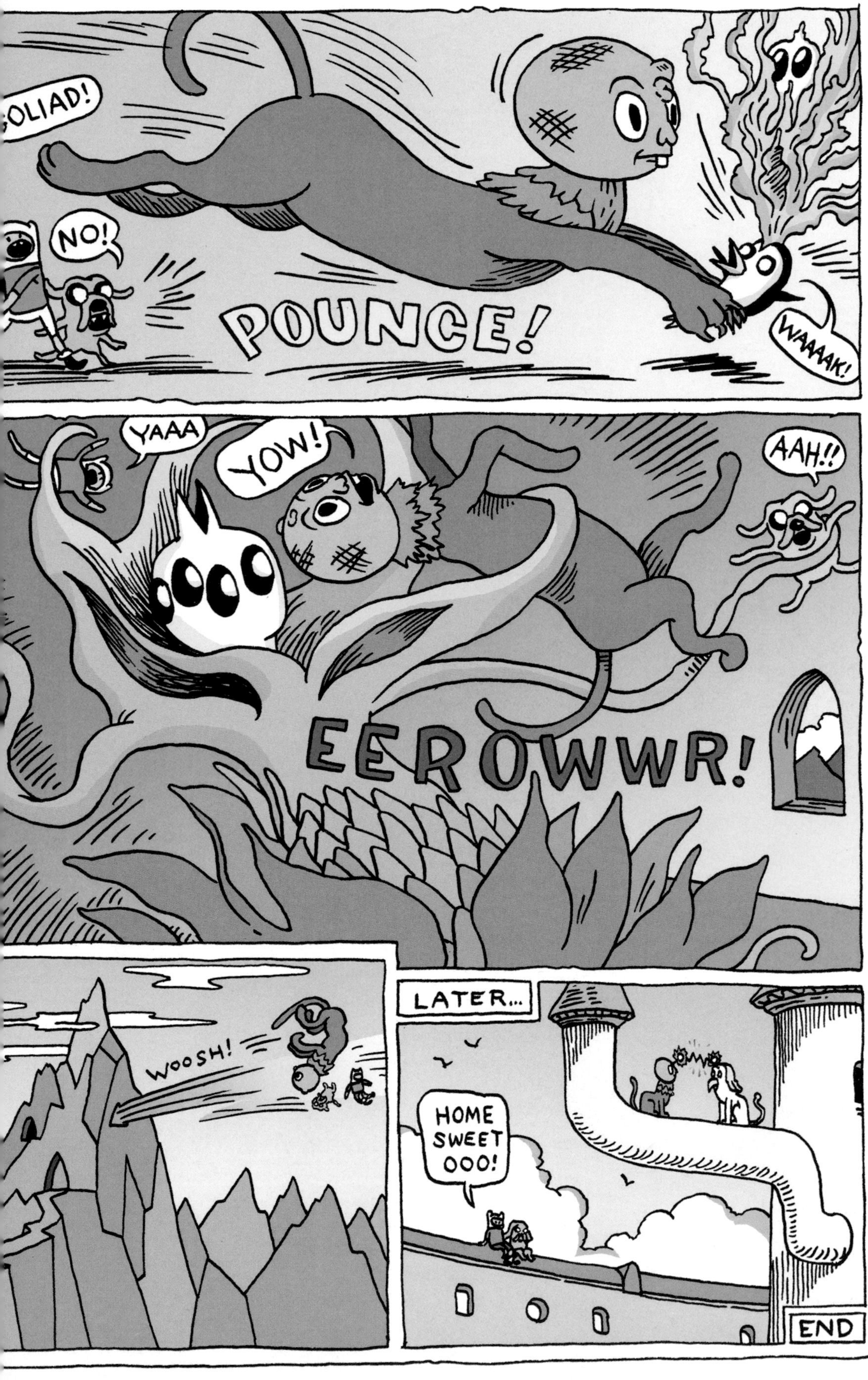

GOLIAD!
NO!
POUNCE!
WAAAAK!
YAAA
YOW!
AAH!!
EEROWWR!
WOOSH!
LATER...
HOME SWEET OOO!
END

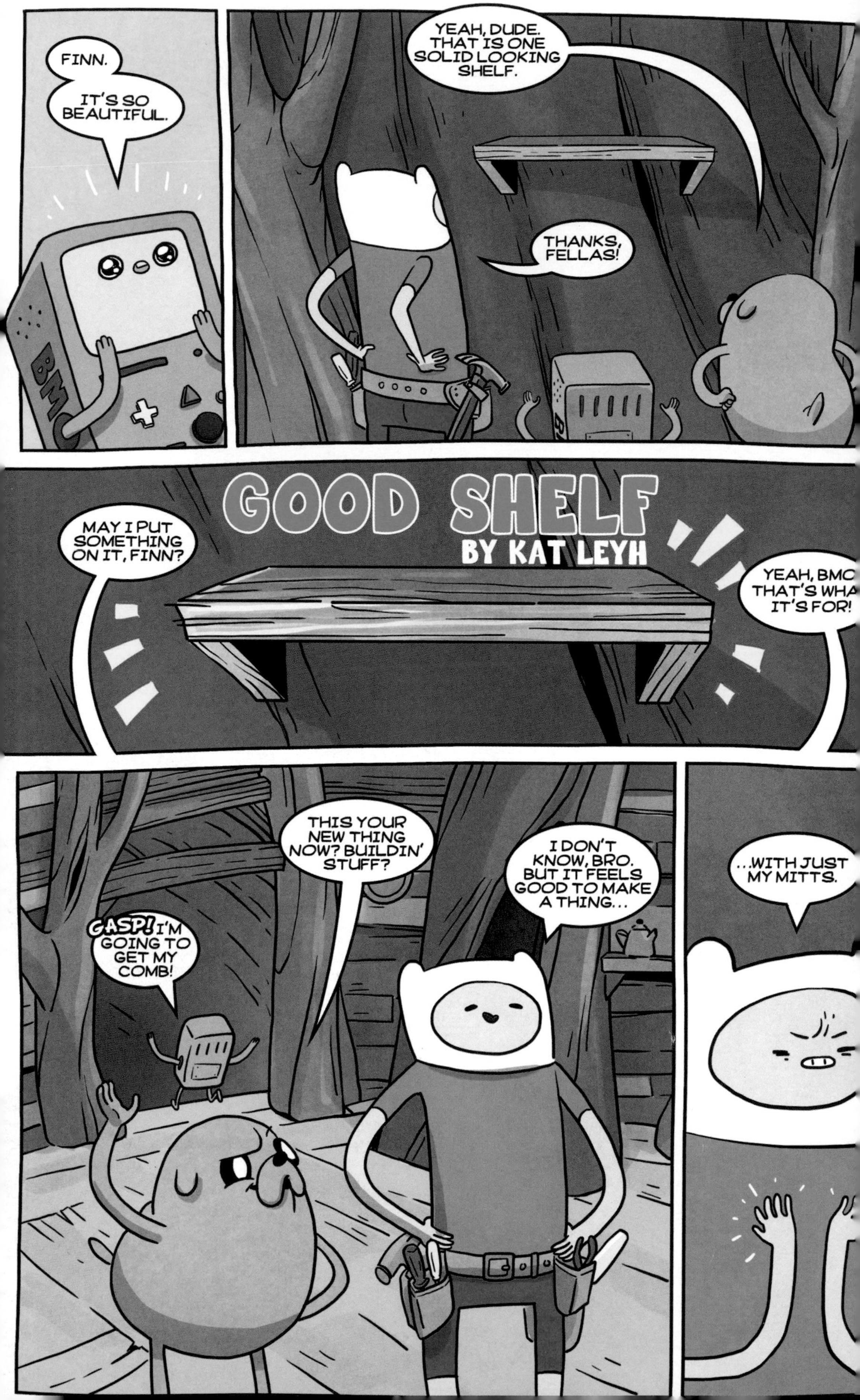
FINN.
IT'S SO BEAUTIFUL.
YEAH, DUDE. THAT IS ONE SOLID LOOKING SHELF.
THANKS, FELLAS!
GOOD SHELF
BY KAT LEYH
MAY I PUT SOMETHING ON IT, FINN?
YEAH, BMO THAT'S WHA IT'S FOR!
GASP! I'M GOING TO GET MY COMB!
THIS YOUR NEW THING NOW? BUILDIN' STUFF?
I DON'T KNOW, BRO. BUT IT FEELS GOOD TO MAKE A THING...
...WITH JUST MY MITTS.

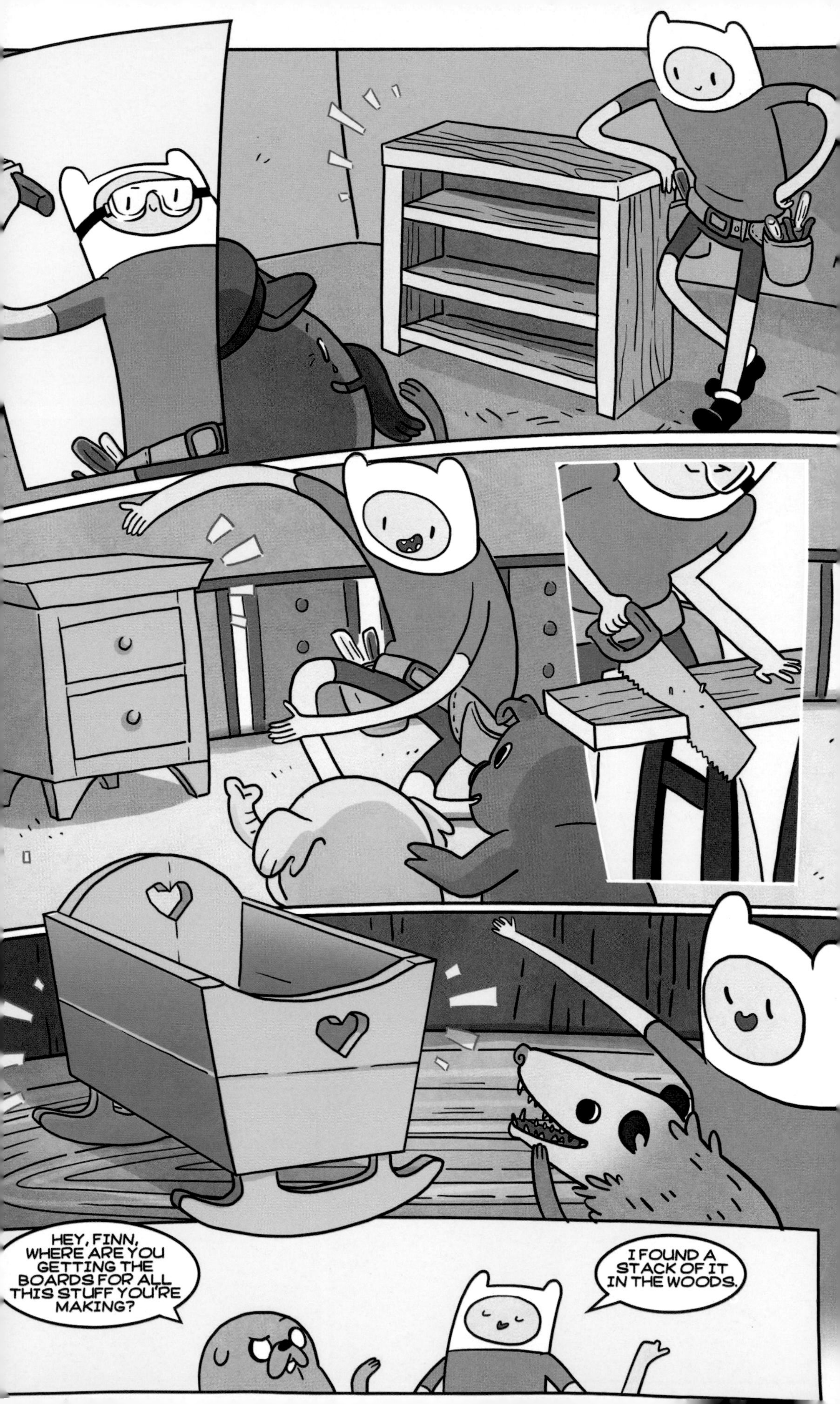

HEY, FINN, WHERE ARE YOU GETTING THE BOARDS FOR ALL THIS STUFF YOU'RE MAKING?
I FOUND A STACK OF IT IN THE WOODS.

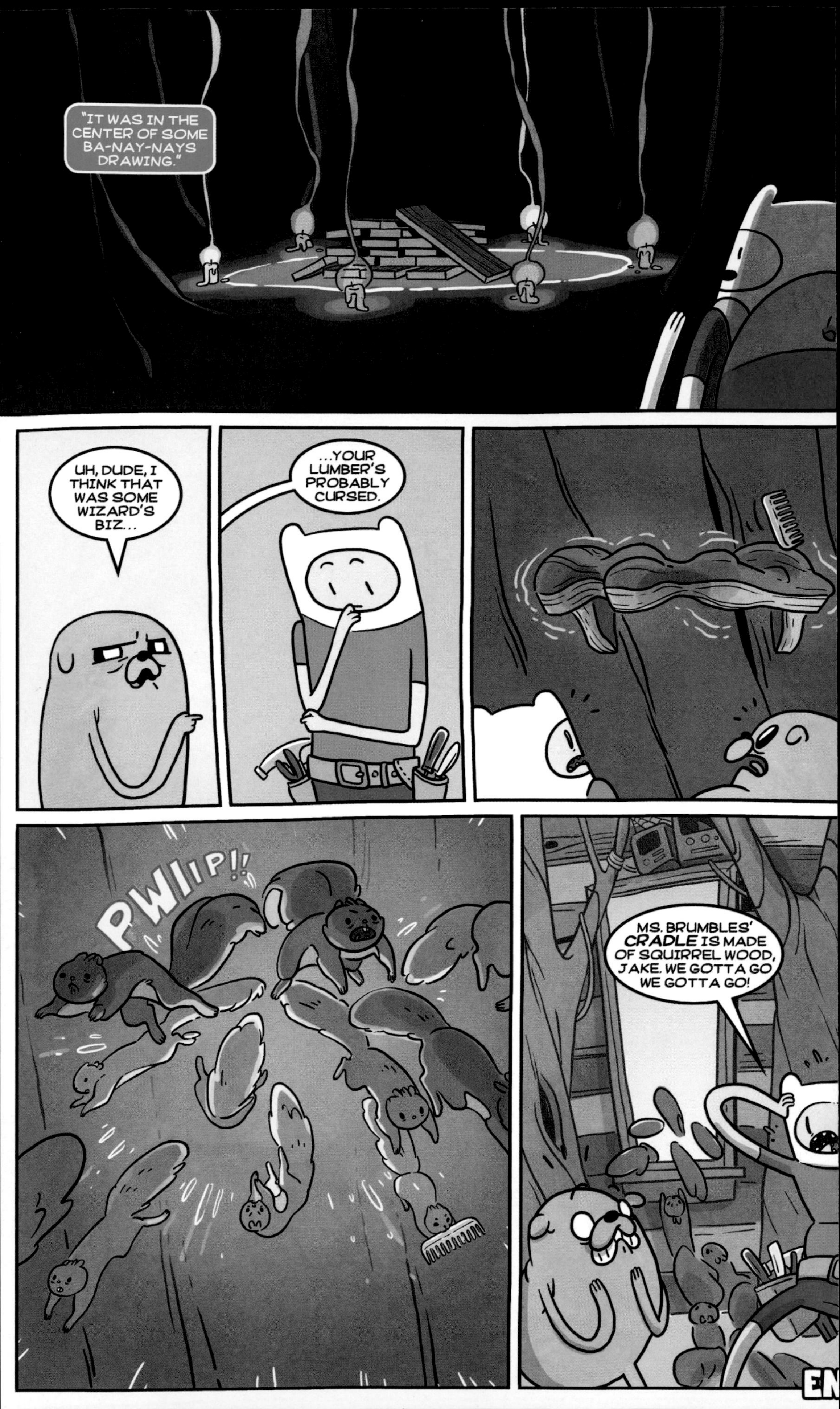
"IT WAS IN THE CENTER OF SOME BA-NAY-NAYS DRAWING."
UH, DUDE, I THINK THAT WAS SOME WIZARD'S BIZ...
...YOUR LUMBER'S PROBABLY CURSED.
PWIIP!!
MS. BRUMBLES' CRADLE IS MADE OF SQUIRREL WOOD, JAKE. WE GOTTA GO WE GOTTA GO!

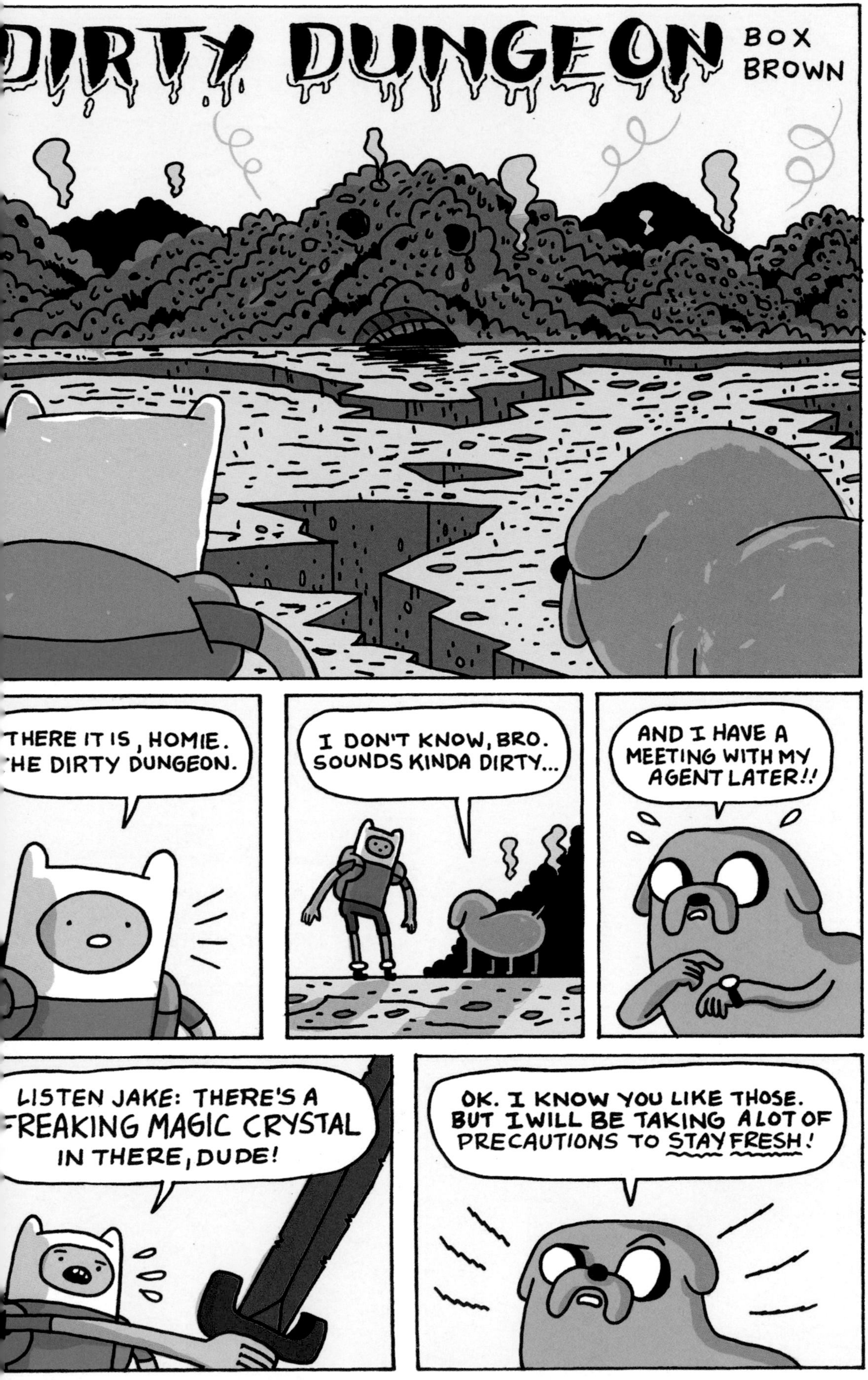
DIRTY DUNGEON
BOX BROWN
THERE IT IS, HOMIE. THE DIRTY DUNGEON.
I DON'T KNOW, BRO. SOUNDS KINDA DIRTY...
AND I HAVE A MEETING WITH MY AGENT LATER!!
LISTEN JAKE: THERE'S A FREAKING MAGIC CRYSTAL IN THERE, DUDE!
OK. I KNOW YOU LIKE THOSE. BUT I WILL BE TAKING A LOT OF PRECAUTIONS TO STAY FRESH!

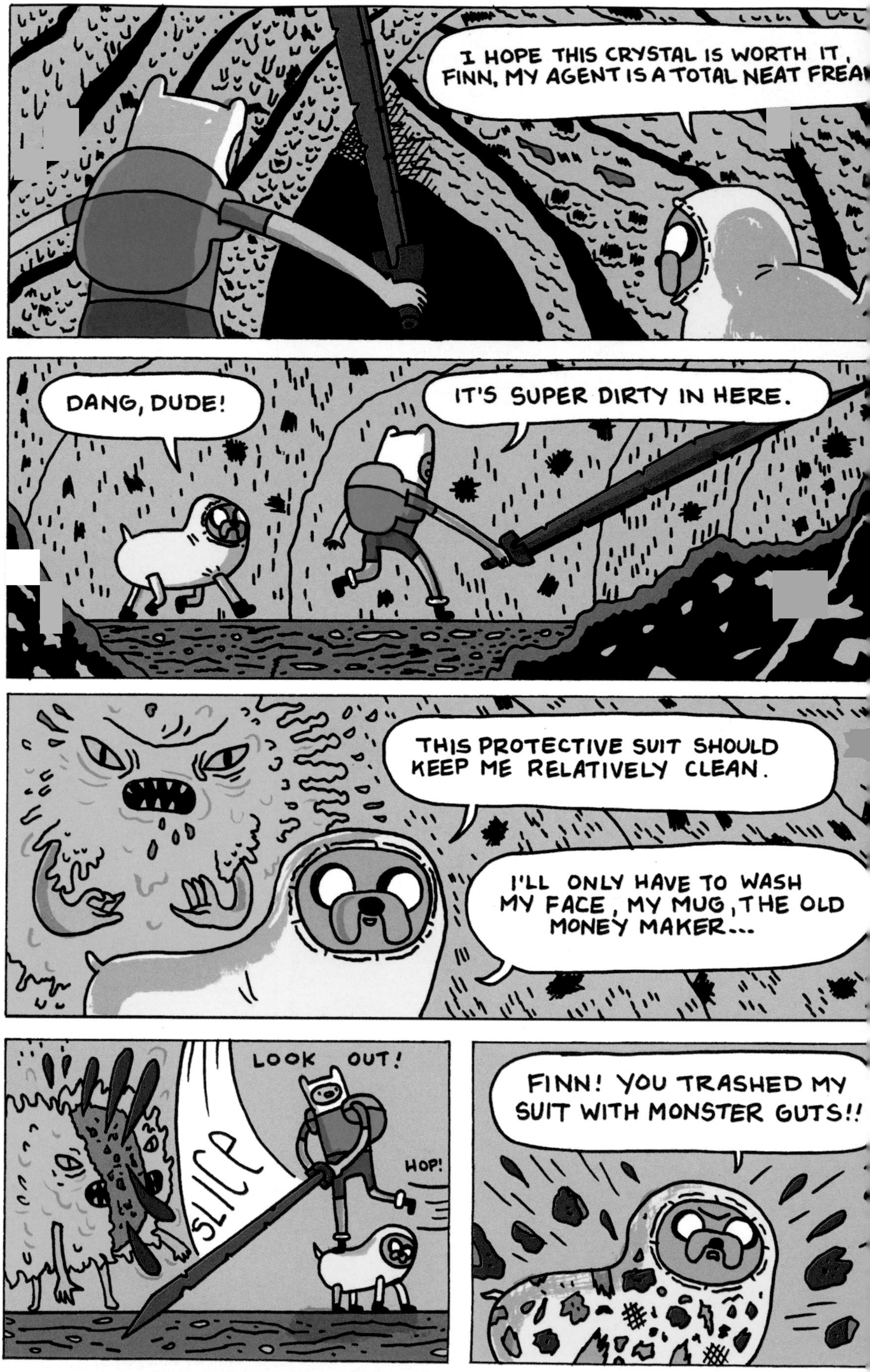

I HOPE THIS CRYSTAL IS WORTH IT, FINN. MY AGENT IS A TOTAL NEAT FREA
DANG, DUDE!
IT'S SUPER DIRTY IN HERE.
THIS PROTECTIVE SUIT SHOULD KEEP ME RELATIVELY CLEAN.
I'LL ONLY HAVE TO WASH MY FACE, MY MUG, THE OLD MONEY MAKER...
LOOK OUT!
SLICP
HOP!
FINN! YOU TRASHED MY SUIT WITH MONSTER GUTS!!

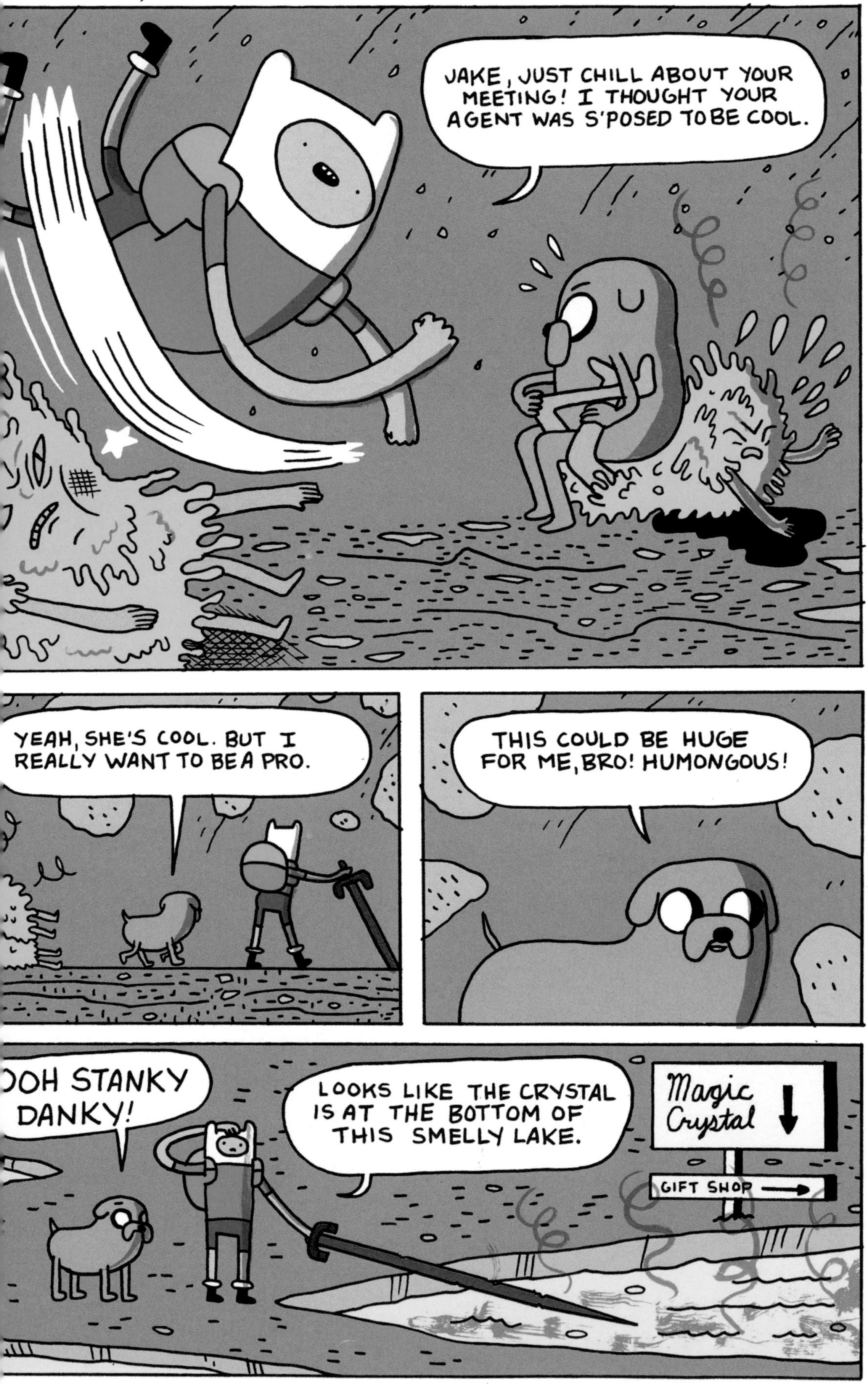
JAKE, JUST CHILL ABOUT YOUR MEETING! I THOUGHT YOUR AGENT WAS S'POSED TO BE COOL.
YEAH, SHE'S COOL. BUT I REALLY WANT TO BE A PRO.
THIS COULD BE HUGE FOR ME, BRO! HUMONGOUS!
OOH STANKY DANKY!
LOOKS LIKE THE CRYSTAL IS AT THE BOTTOM OF THIS SMELLY LAKE.
Magic Crystal
GIFT SHOP

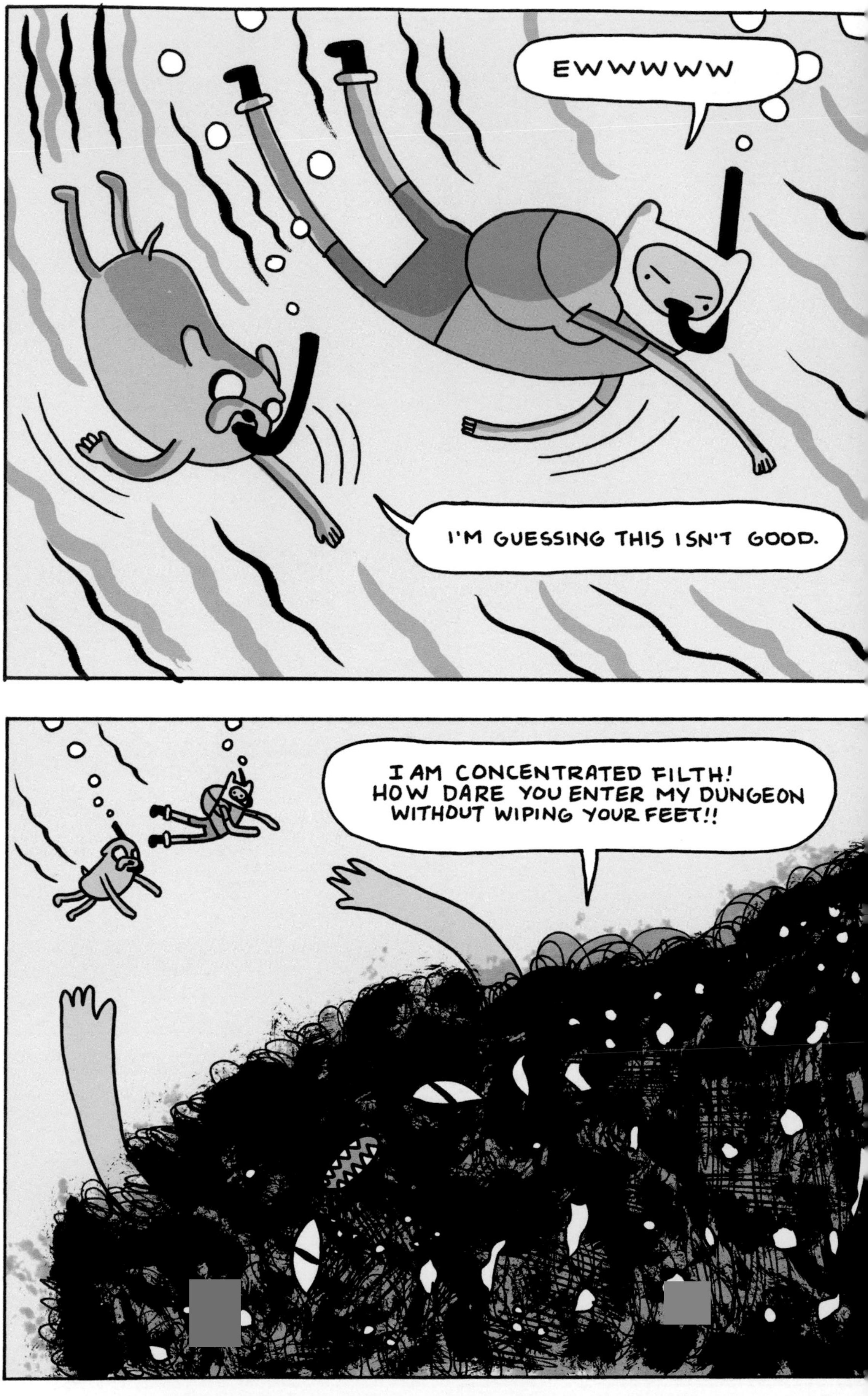
EWWWWW
I'M GUESSING THIS ISN'T GOOD.
I AM CONCENTRATED FILTH! HOW DARE YOU ENTER MY DUNGEON WITHOUT WIPING YOUR FEET!!

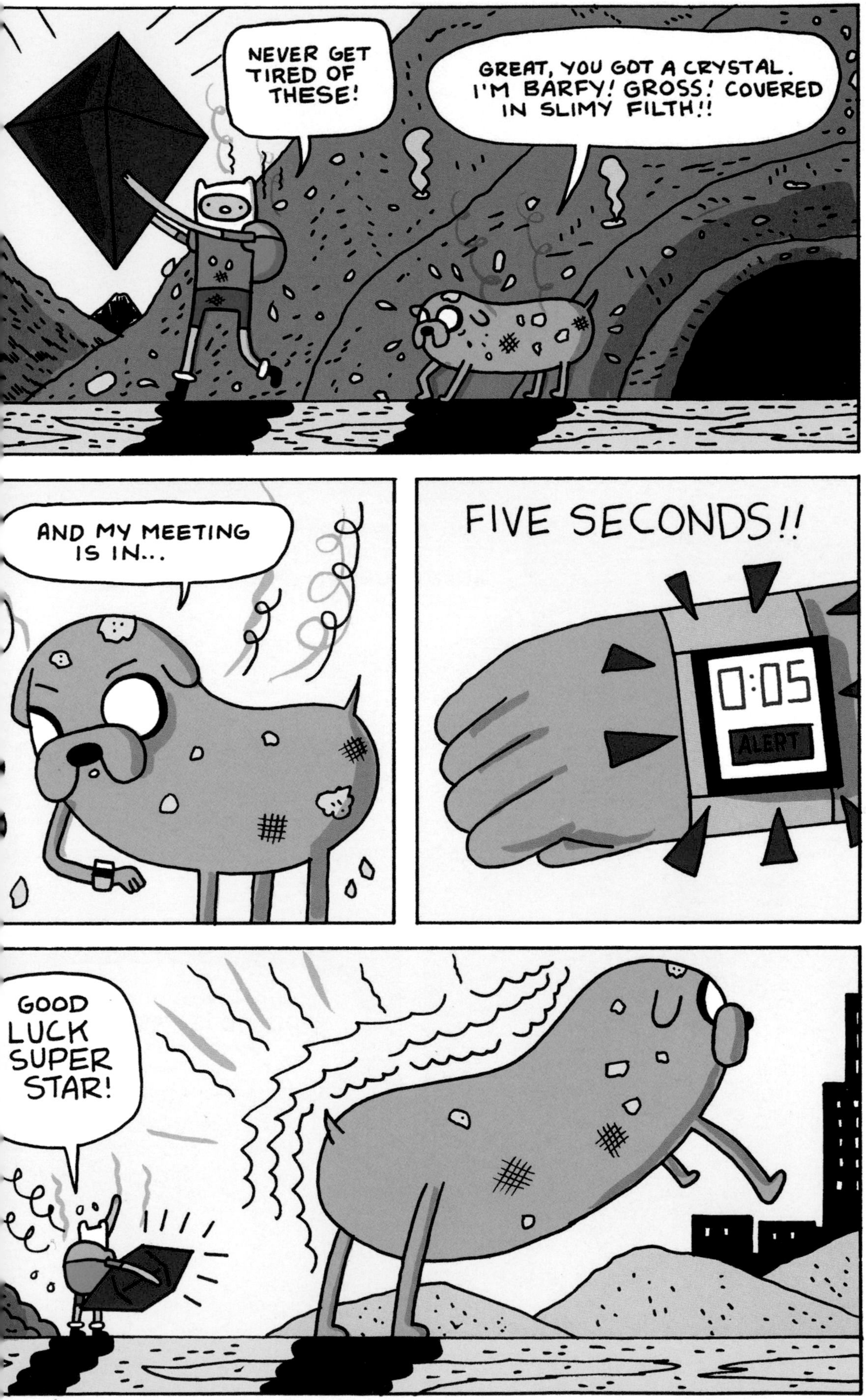
NEVER GET TIRED OF THESE!
GREAT, YOU GOT A CRYSTAL. I'M BARFY! GROSS! COVERED IN SLIMY FILTH!!
AND MY MEETING IS IN...
FIVE SECONDS!!
0:05
ALERT
GOOD LUCK SUPER STAR!

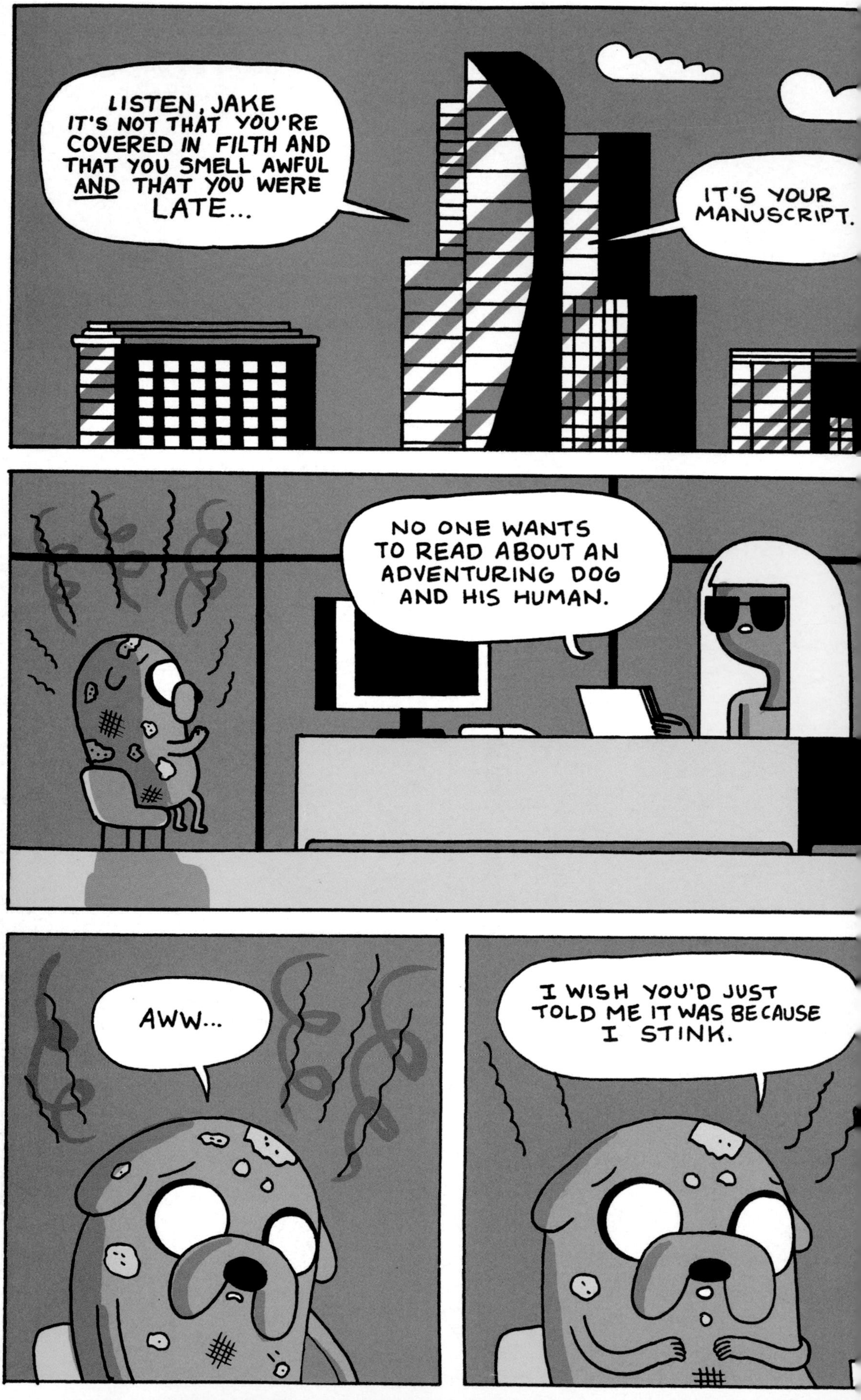
LISTEN, JAKE
IT'S NOT THAT YOU'RE COVERED IN FILTH AND THAT YOU SMELL AWFUL AND THAT YOU WERE LATE...
IT'S YOUR MANUSCRIPT.
NO ONE WANTS TO READ ABOUT AN ADVENTURING DOG AND HIS HUMAN.
AWW...
I WISH YOU'D JUST TOLD ME IT WAS BECAUSE I STINK.

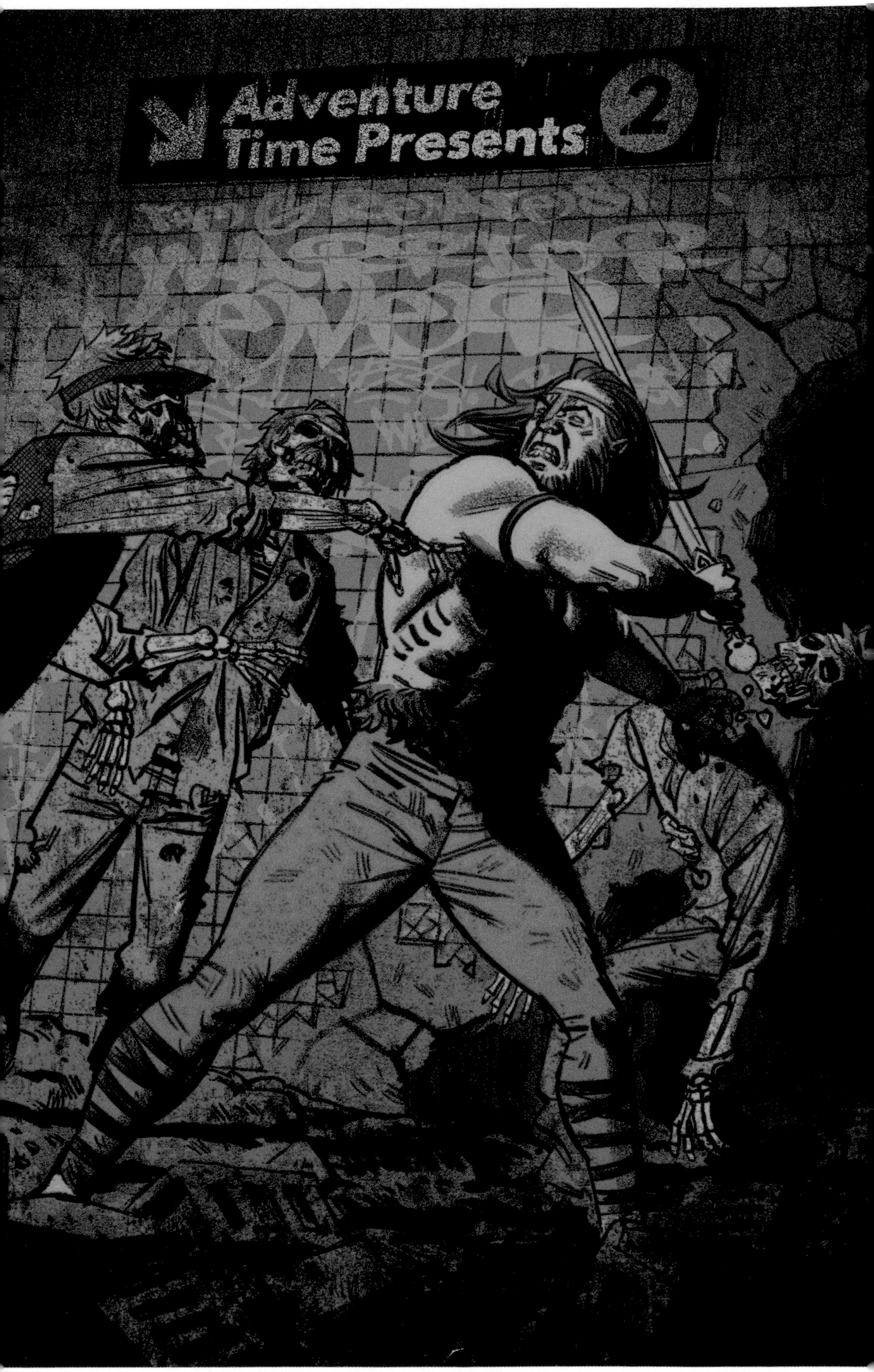
Adventure
Time Presents
2

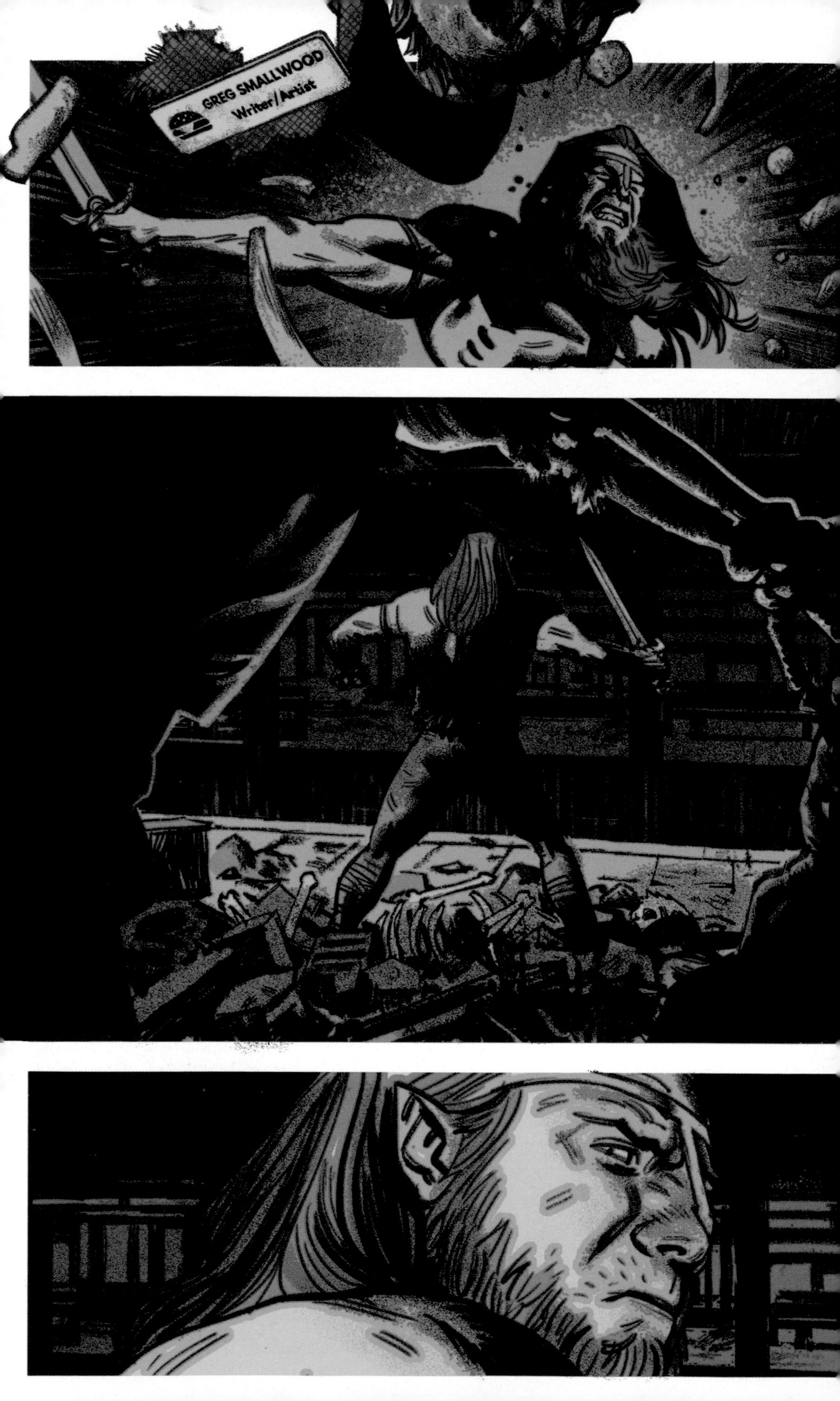
GREG SMALLWOOD
Writer/Artist

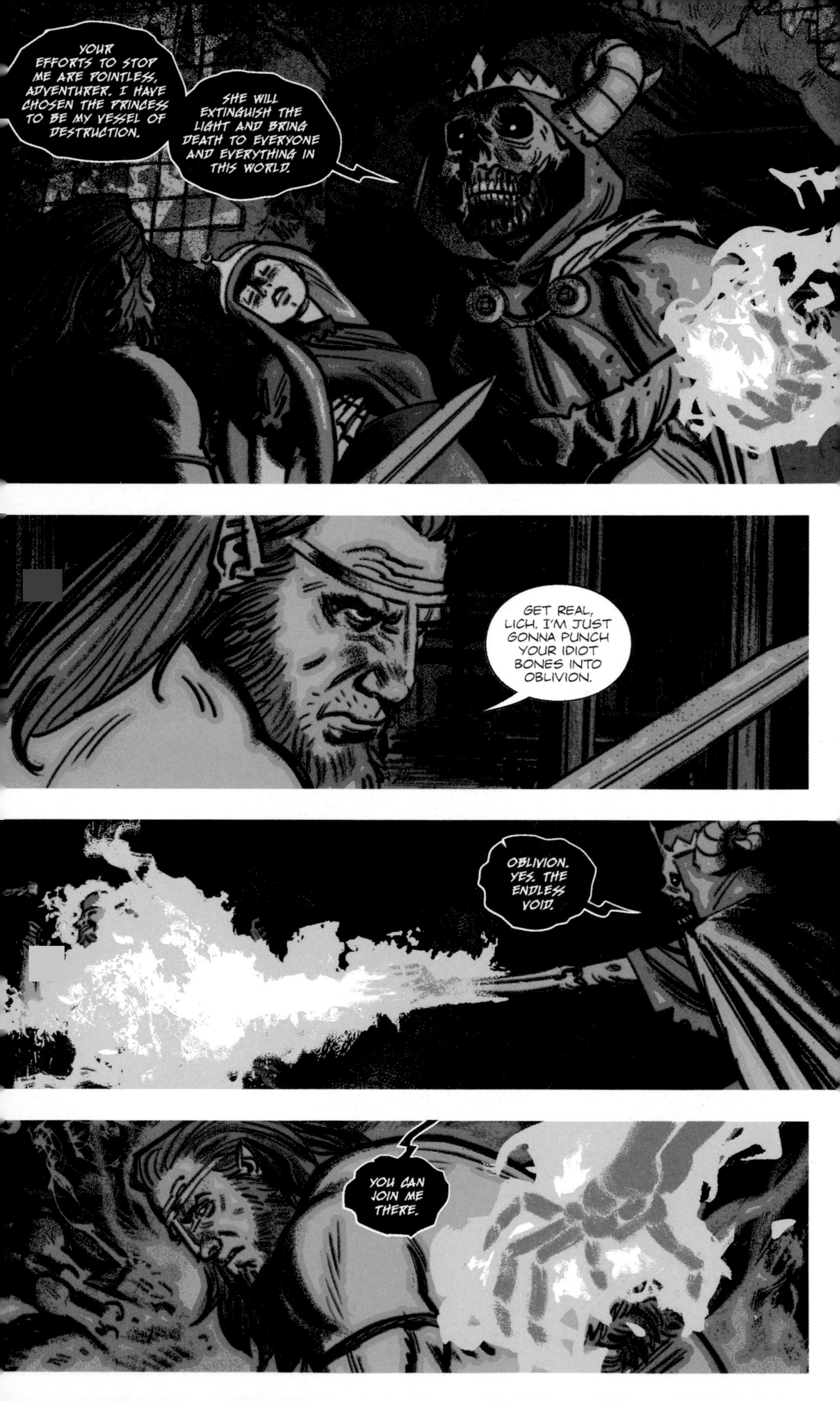
YOUR EFFORTS TO STOP ME ARE POINTLESS, ADVENTURER. I HAVE CHOSEN THE PRINCESS TO BE MY VESSEL OF DESTRUCTION.
SHE WILL EXTINGUISH THE LIGHT AND BRING DEATH TO EVERYONE AND EVERYTHING IN THIS WORLD.
GET REAL, LICH. I'M JUST GONNA PUNCH YOUR IDIOT BONES INTO OBLIVION.
OBLIVION. YES. THE ENDLESS VOID.
YOU CAN JOIN ME THERE.

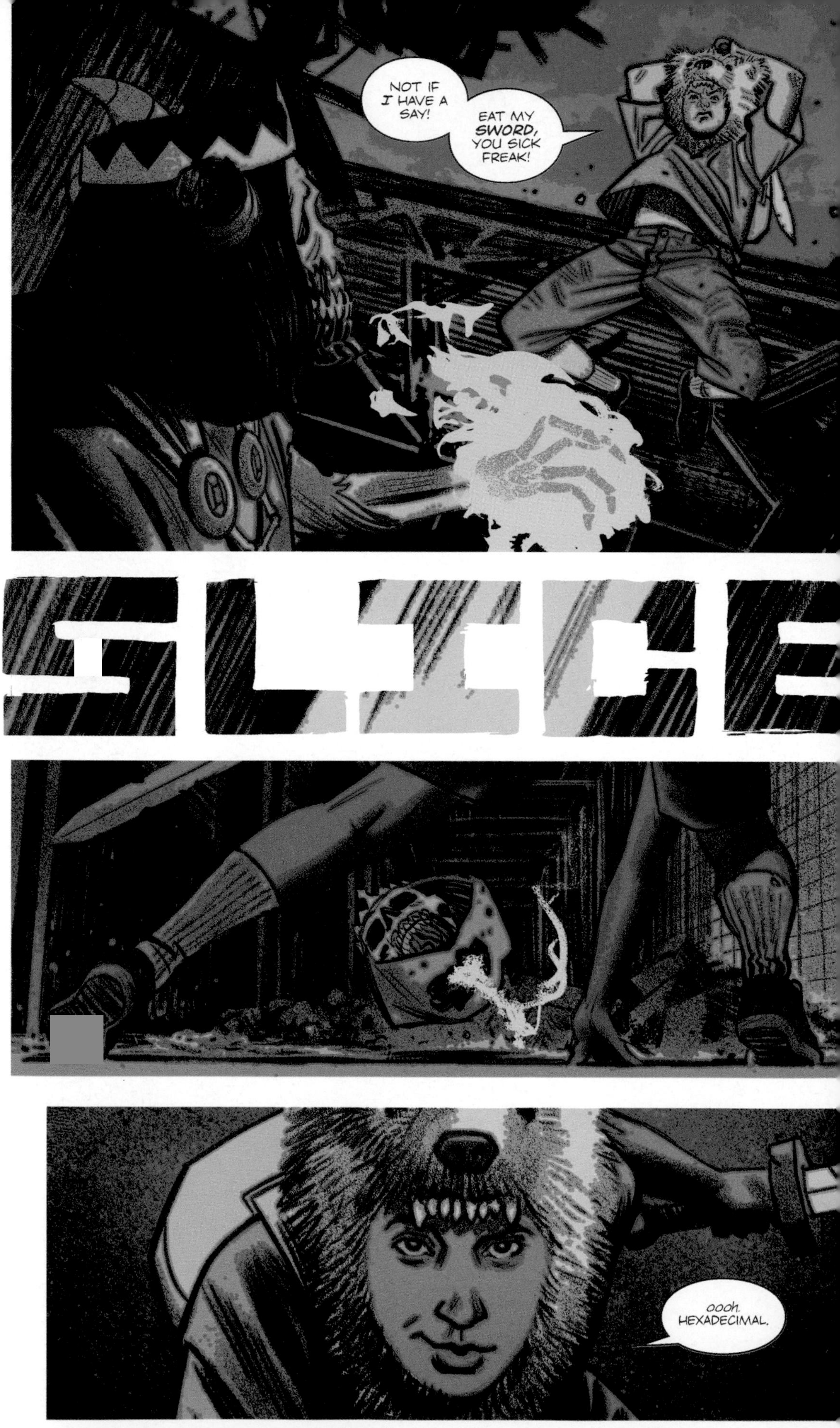
NOT IF I HAVE A SAY!
EAT MY SWORD, YOU SICK FREAK!
SLICE
oooh. HEXADECIMAL.

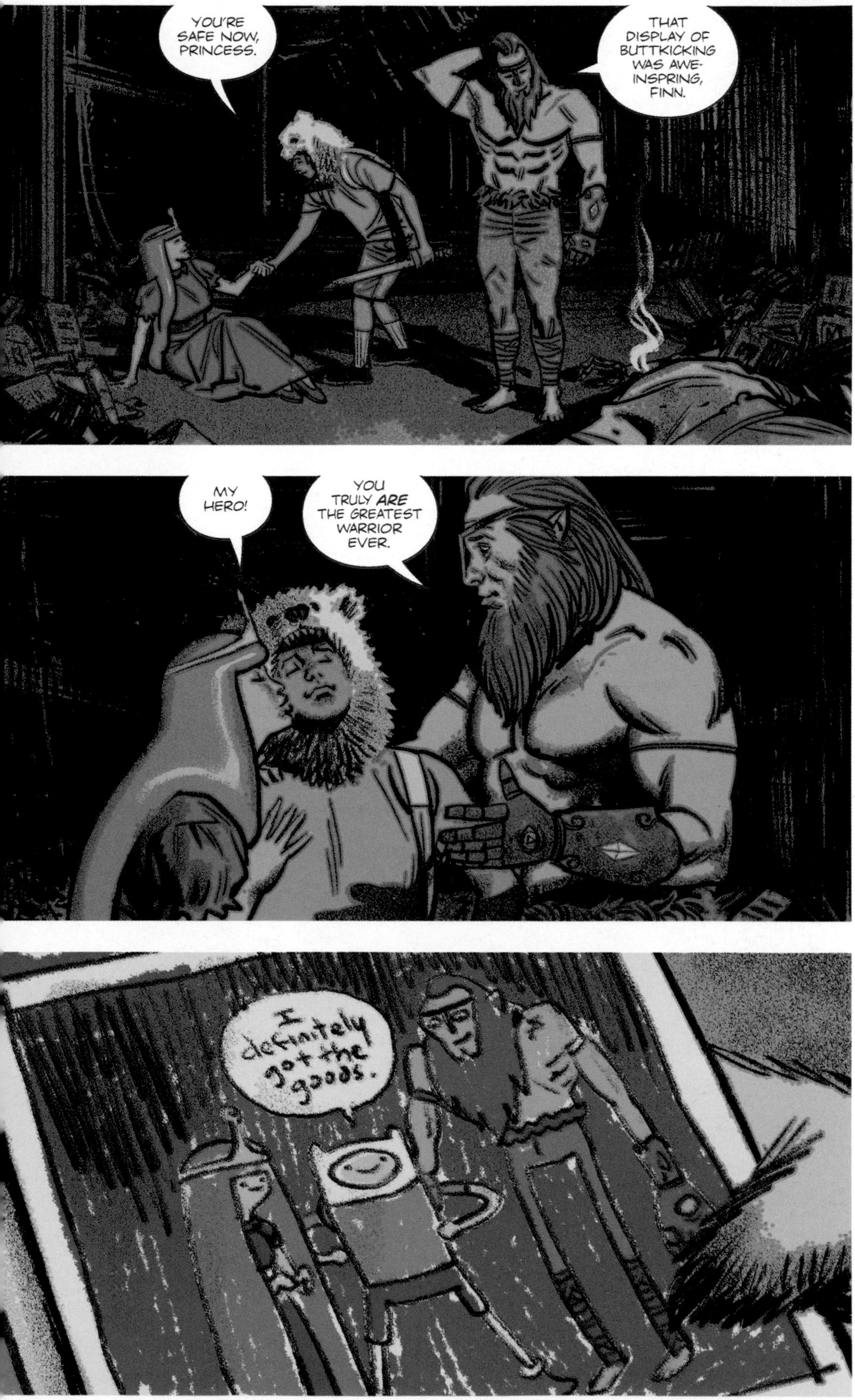
YOU'RE SAFE NOW, PRINCESS.
THAT DISPLAY OF BUTTKICKING WAS AWE-INSPRING, FINN.
MY HERO!
YOU TRULY ARE THE GREATEST WARRIOR EVER.
I definitely got the goods.

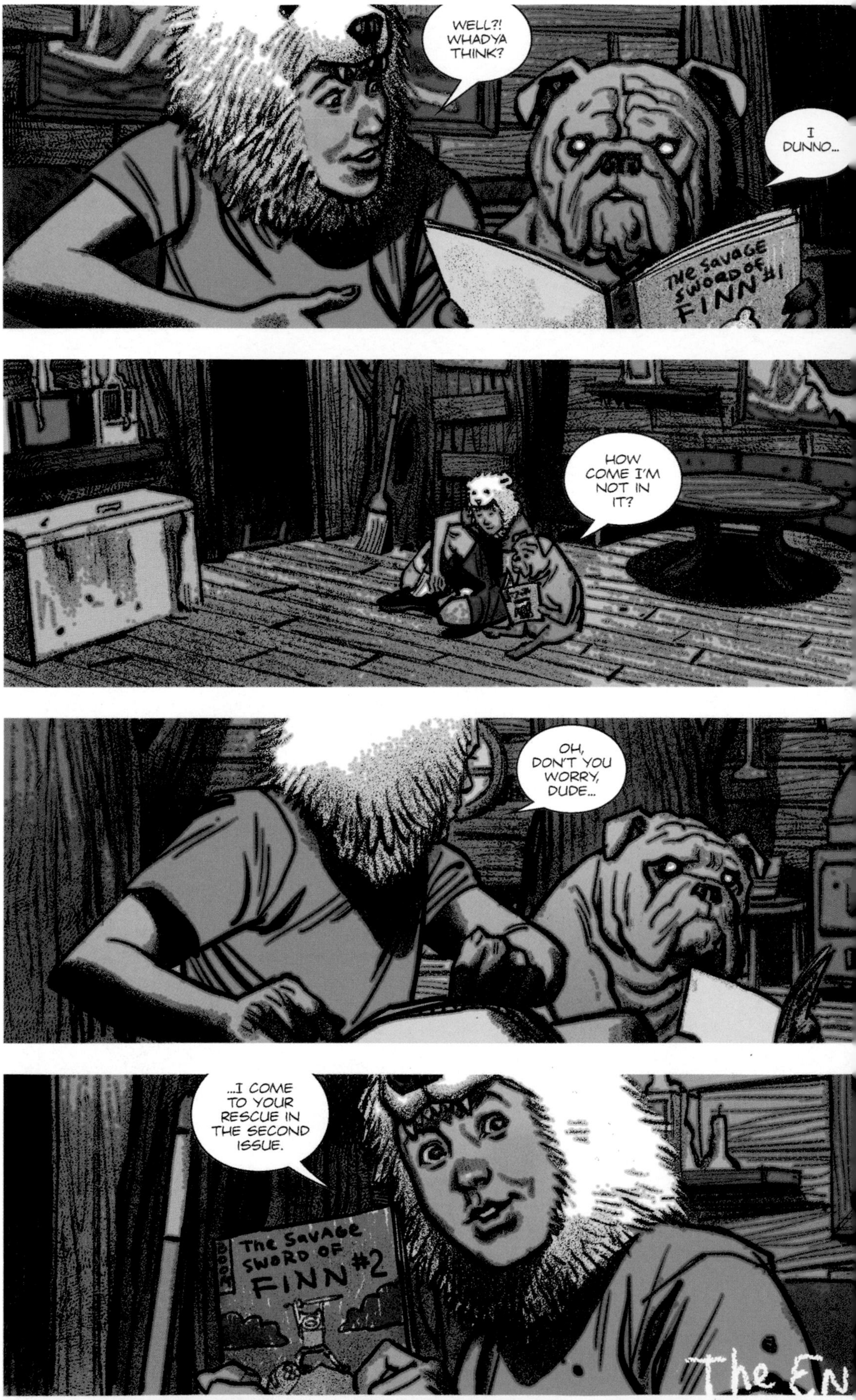
WELL?! WHADYA THINK?
I DUNNO...
The Savage Sword of FINN #1
HOW COME I'M NOT IN IT?
OH, DON'T YOU WORRY, DUDE...
...I COME TO YOUR RESCUE IN THE SECOND ISSUE.
The Savage Sword of FINN #2
The En

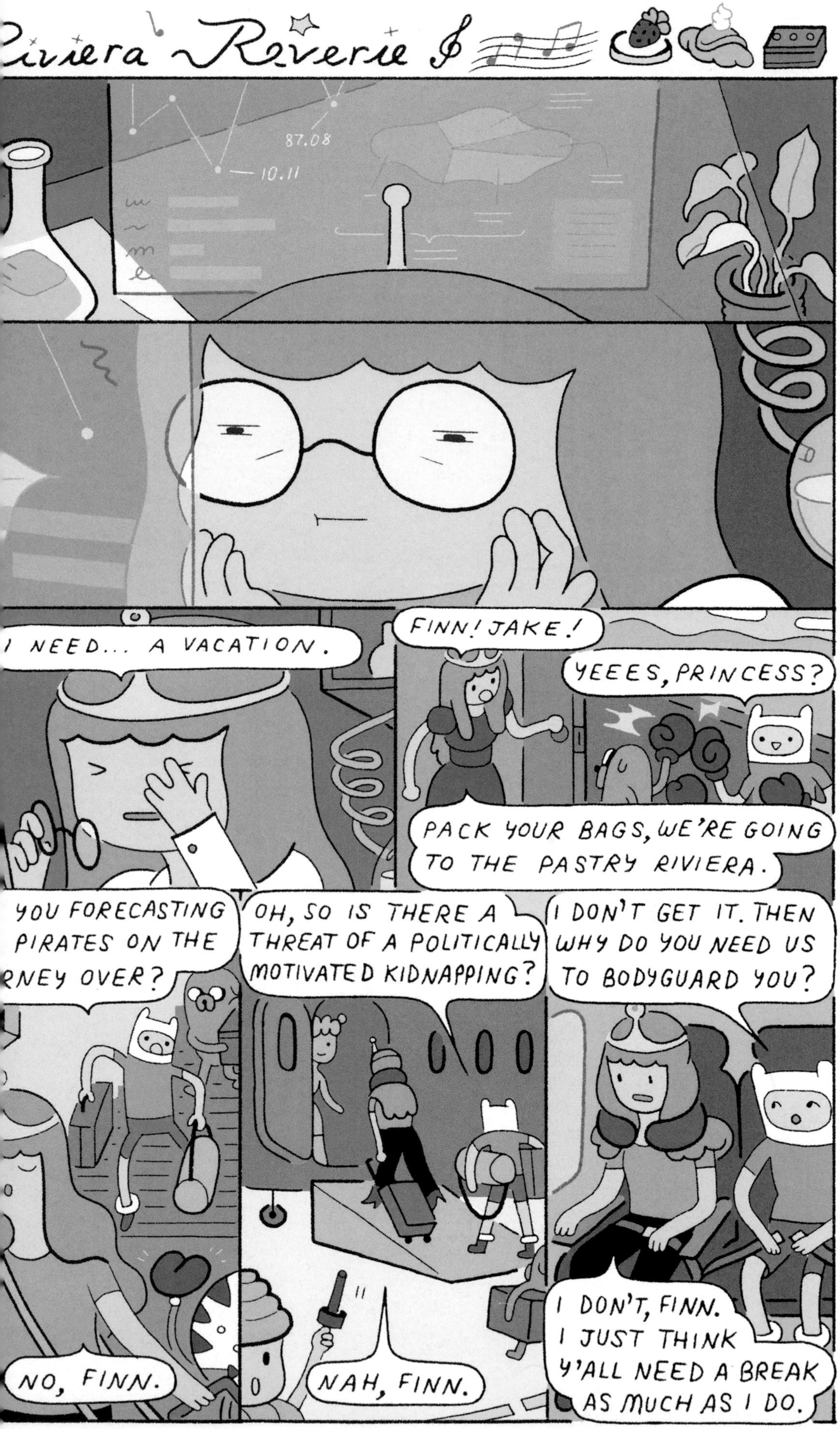
Riviera Reverie
87.08
10.11
I NEED... A VACATION.
FINN! JAKE!
YEEES, PRINCESS?
PACK YOUR BAGS, WE'RE GOING TO THE PASTRY RIVIERA.
YOU FORECASTING PIRATES ON THE RNEY OVER?
NO, FINN.
OH, SO IS THERE A THREAT OF A POLITICALLY MOTIVATED KIDNAPPING?
NAH, FINN.
I DON'T GET IT. THEN WHY DO YOU NEED US TO BODYGUARD YOU?
I DON'T, FINN. I JUST THINK Y'ALL NEED A BREAK AS MUCH AS I DO.

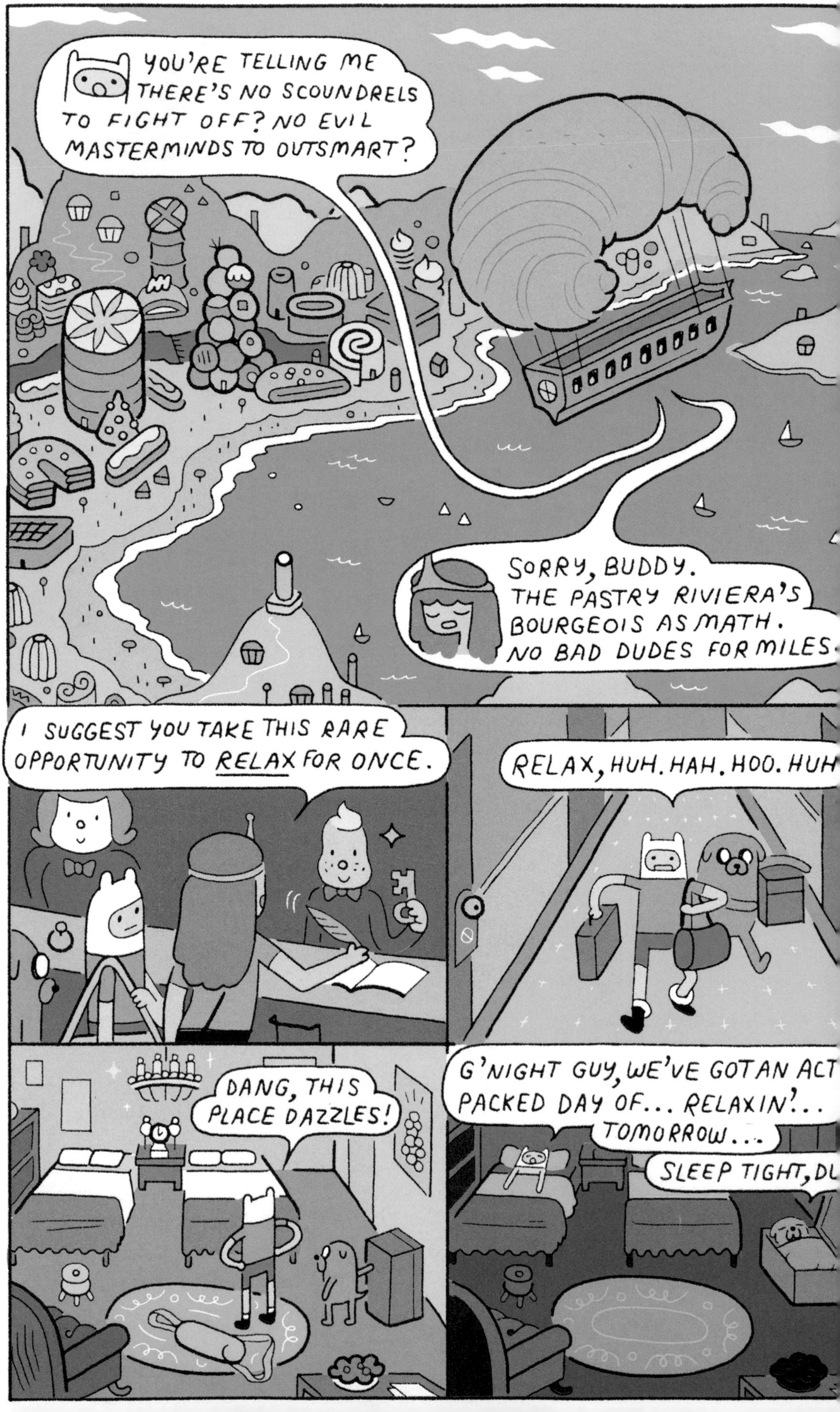

YOU'RE TELLING ME THERE'S NO SCOUNDRELS TO FIGHT OFF? NO EVIL MASTERMINDS TO OUTSMART?
SORRY, BUDDY. THE PASTRY RIVIERA'S BOURGEOIS AS MATH. NO BAD DUDES FOR MILES.
I SUGGEST YOU TAKE THIS RARE OPPORTUNITY TO RELAX FOR ONCE.
RELAX, HUH. HAH. HOO. HUH
DANG, THIS PLACE DAZZLES!
G'NIGHT GUY, WE'VE GOT AN ACT
PACKED DAY OF... RELAXIN'... TOMORROW...
SLEEP TIGHT, DU

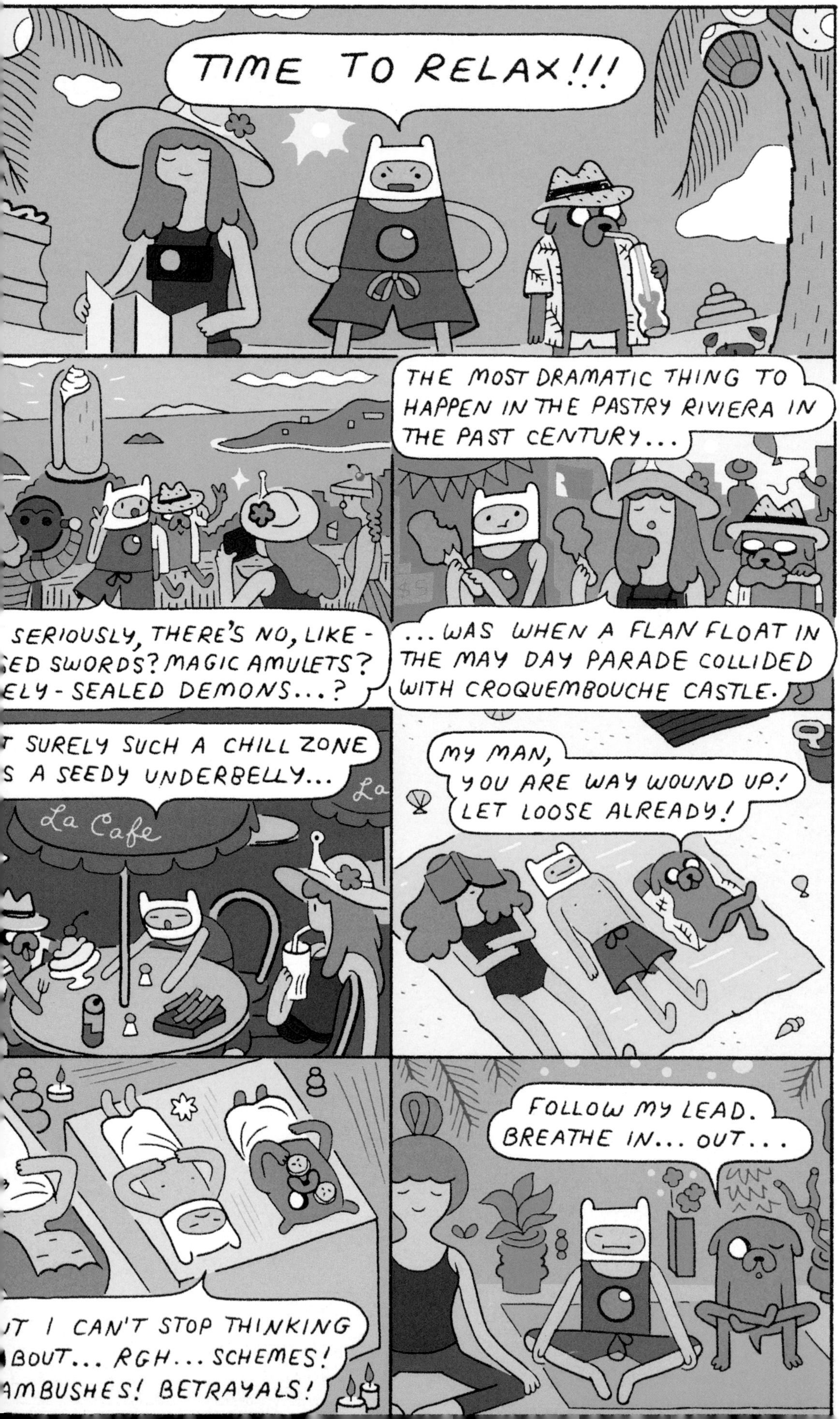
TIME TO RELAX!!!
SERIOUSLY, THERE'S NO, LIKE- SED SWORDS? MAGIC AMULETS? ELY-SEALED DEMONS...?
THE MOST DRAMATIC THING TO HAPPEN IN THE PASTRY RIVIERA IN THE PAST CENTURY...
...WAS WHEN A FLAN FLOAT IN THE MAY DAY PARADE COLLIDED WITH CROQUEMBOUCHE CASTLE.
T SURELY SUCH A CHILL ZONE S A SEEDY UNDERBELLY...
La Cafe
La
MY MAN, YOU ARE WAY WOUND UP! LET LOOSE ALREADY!
T I CAN'T STOP THINKING BOUT... RGH... SCHEMES! AMBUSHES! BETRAYALS!
FOLLOW MY LEAD. BREATHE IN... OUT...

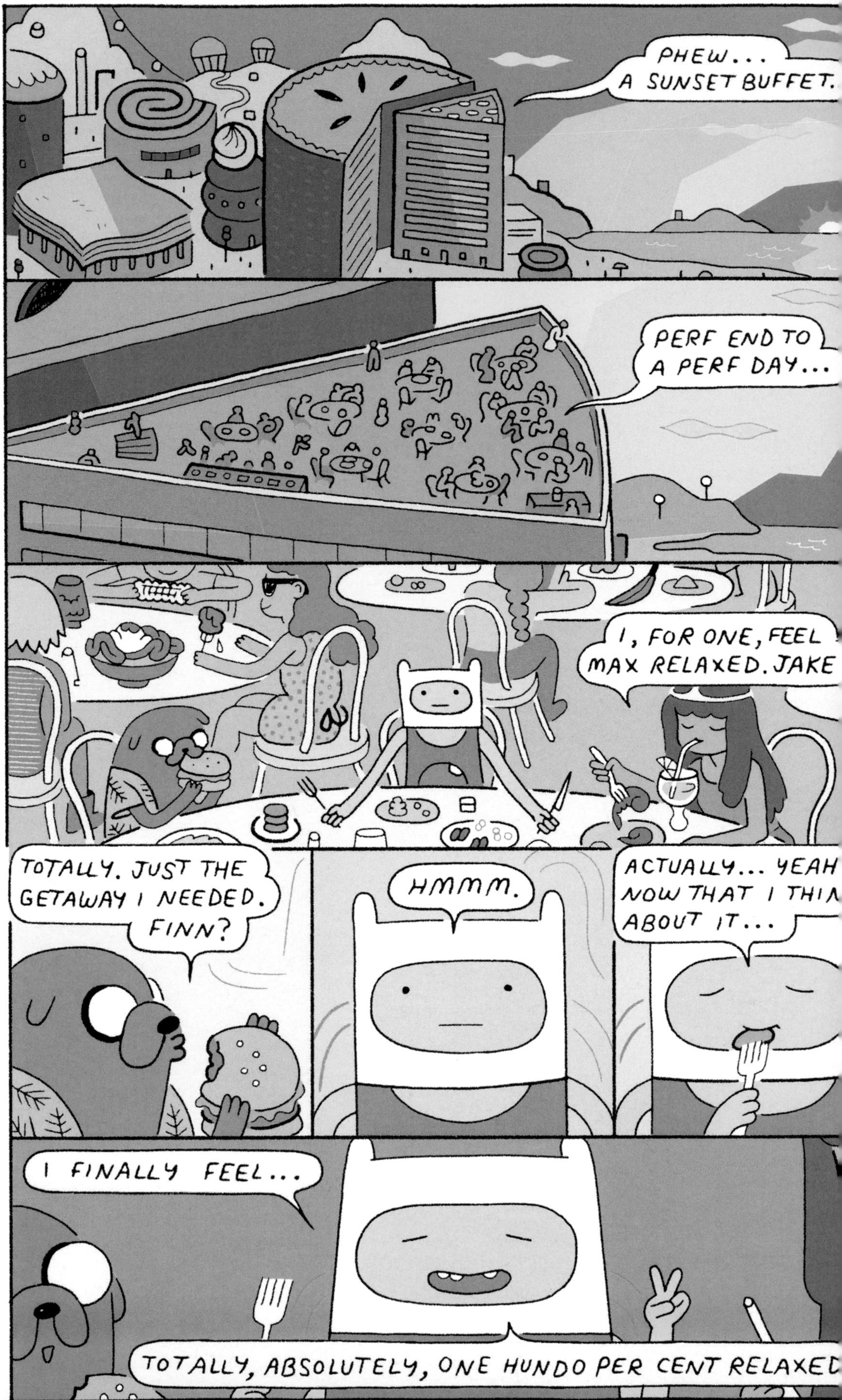
PHEW... A SUNSET BUFFET.
PERF END TO A PERF DAY...
I, FOR ONE, FEEL MAX RELAXED. JAKE
TOTALLY. JUST THE GETAWAY I NEEDED. FINN?
HMMM.
ACTUALLY... YEAH NOW THAT I THIN ABOUT IT...
I FINALLY FEEL...
TOTALLY, ABSOLUTELY, ONE HUNDO PER CENT RELAXED

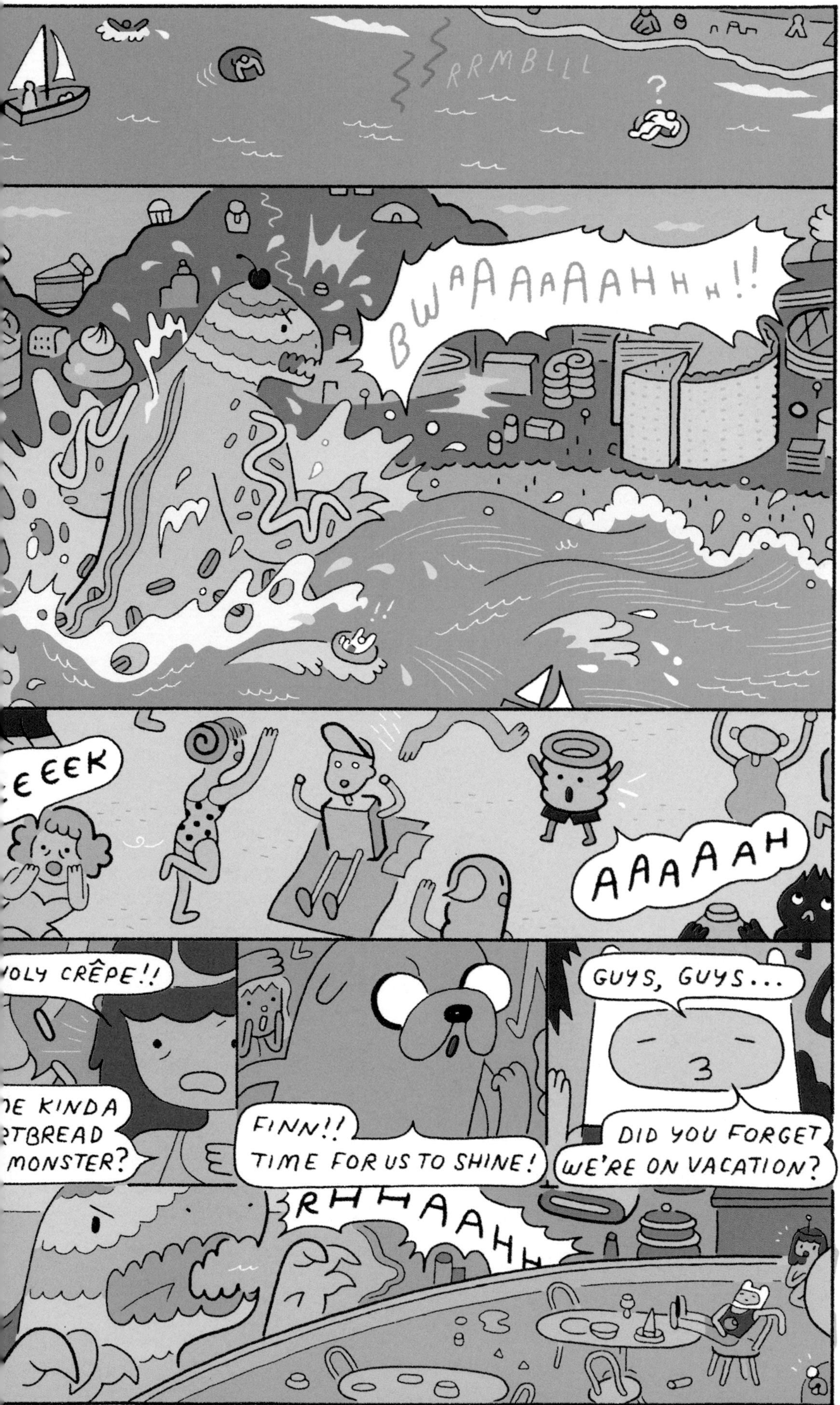
RRMBLLL
?
BWAAAAAAAHHH!!
EEEK
AAAAAH
OLY CRÊPE!!
E KINDA
TBREAD
MONSTER?
FINN!!
TIME FOR US TO SHINE!
GUYS, GUYS...
DID YOU FORGET
WE'RE ON VACATION?
RHHAAAHH

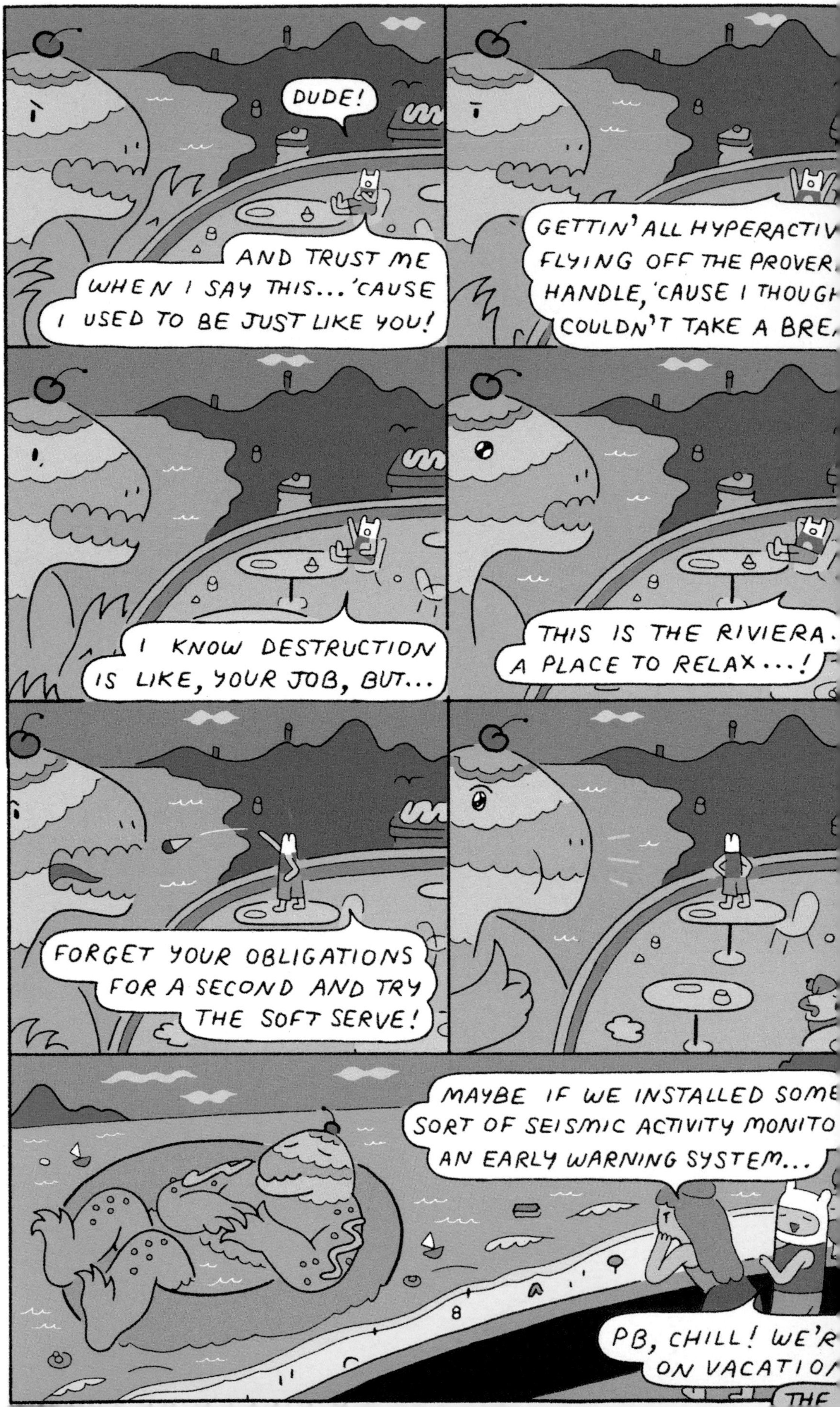

DUDE!
AND TRUST ME WHEN I SAY THIS...'CAUSE I USED TO BE JUST LIKE YOU!
GETTIN' ALL HYPERACTIV
FLYING OFF THE PROVER
HANDLE, 'CAUSE I THOUG
COULDN'T TAKE A BRE
I KNOW DESTRUCTION IS LIKE, YOUR JOB, BUT...
THIS IS THE RIVIERA. A PLACE TO RELAX...!
FORGET YOUR OBLIGATIONS FOR A SECOND AND TRY THE SOFT SERVE!
MAYBE IF WE INSTALLED SOME
SORT OF SEISMIC ACTIVITY MONITO
AN EARLY WARNING SYSTEM...
PB, CHILL! WE'R
ON VACATIO

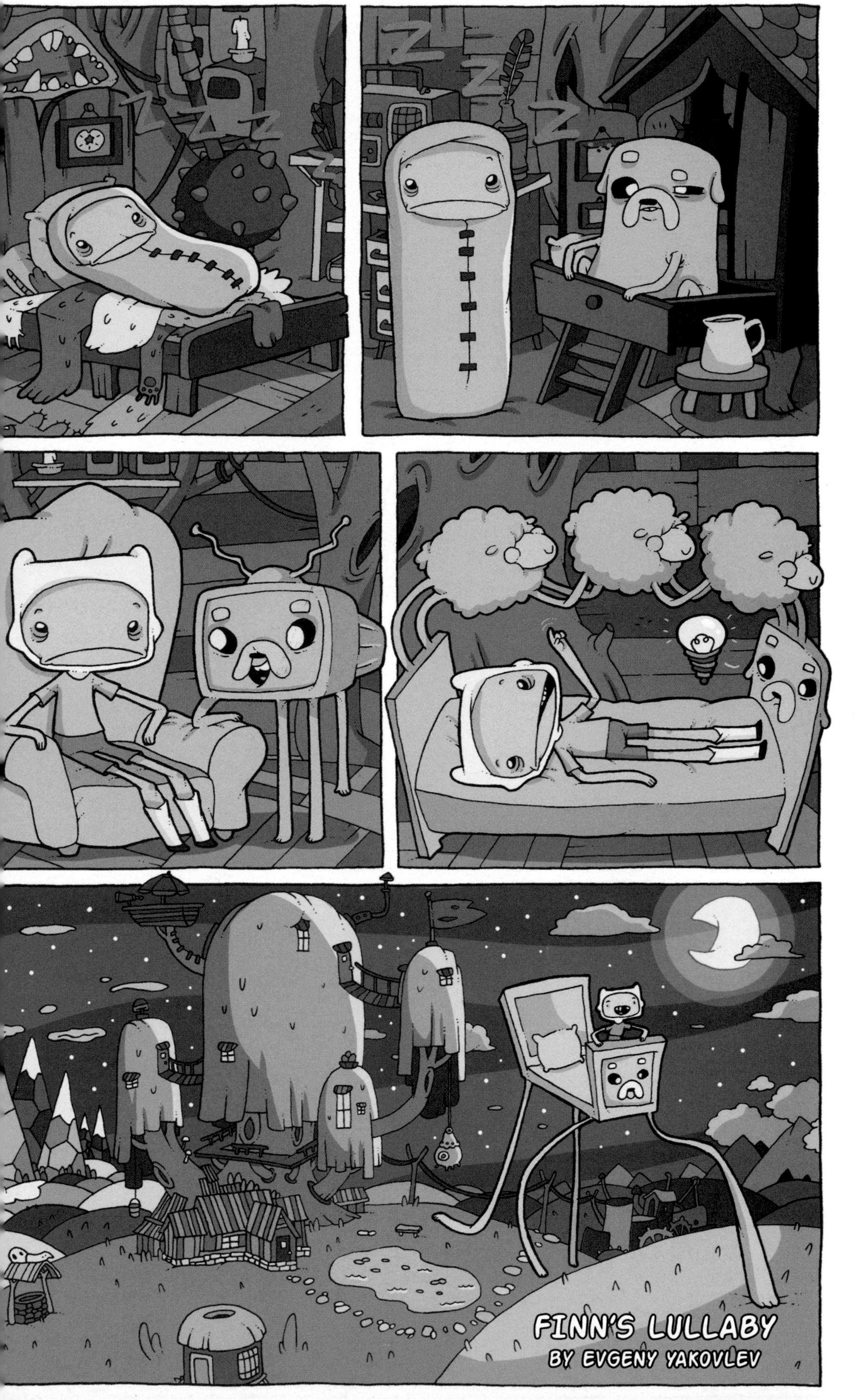

Z Z Z Z
Z Z Z
FINN'S LULLABY
BY EVGENY YAKOVLEV

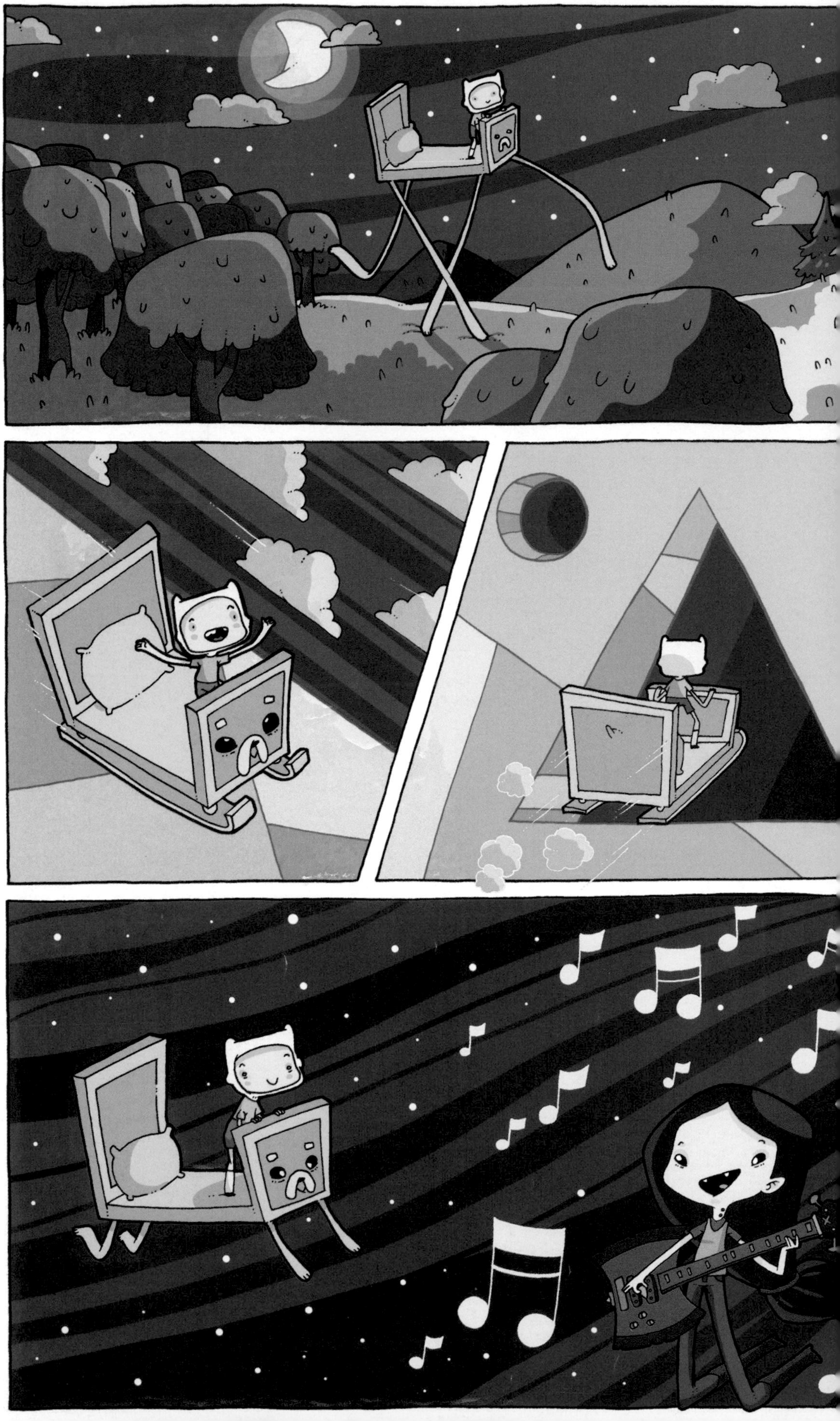

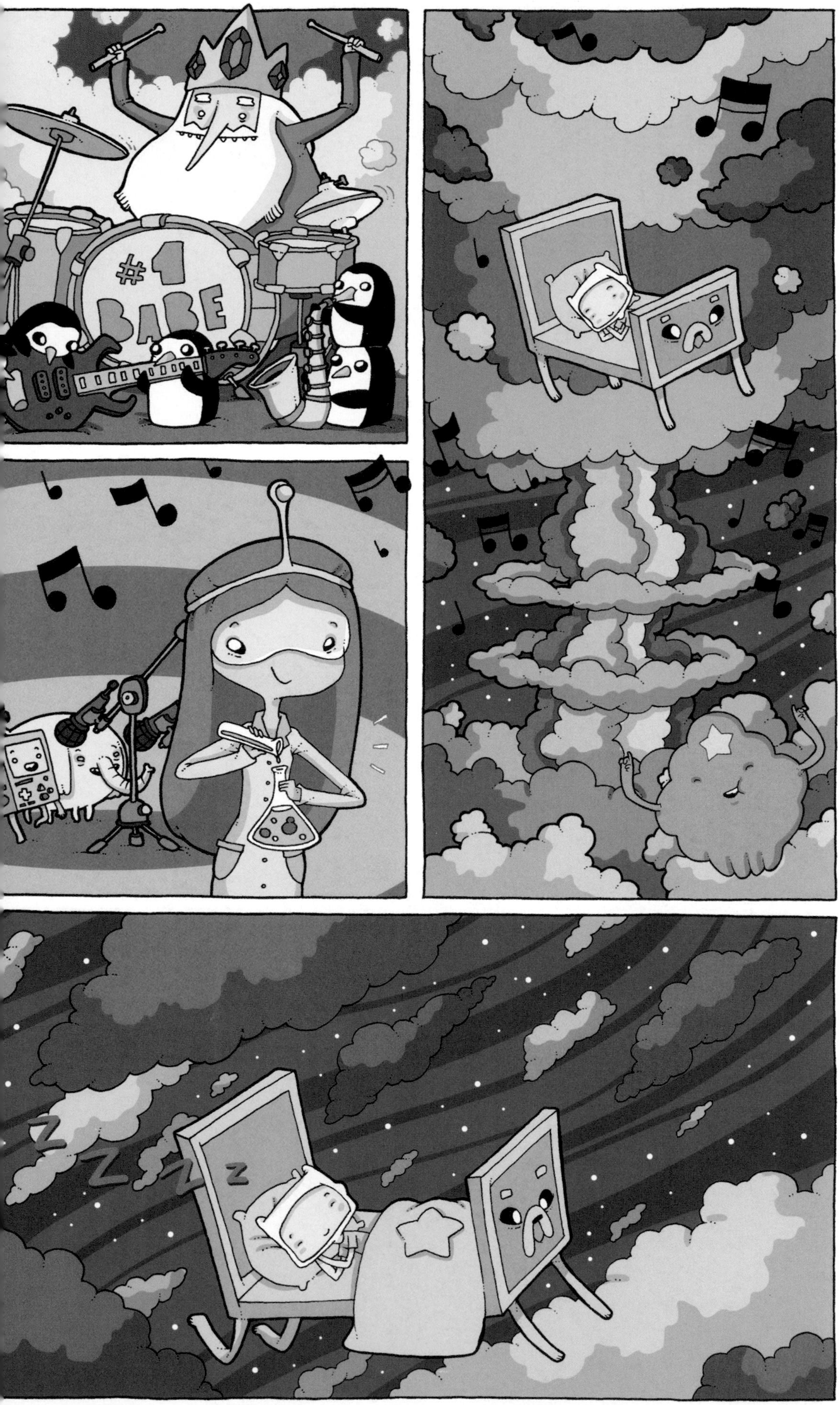
#1
BABE
Z Z Z Z

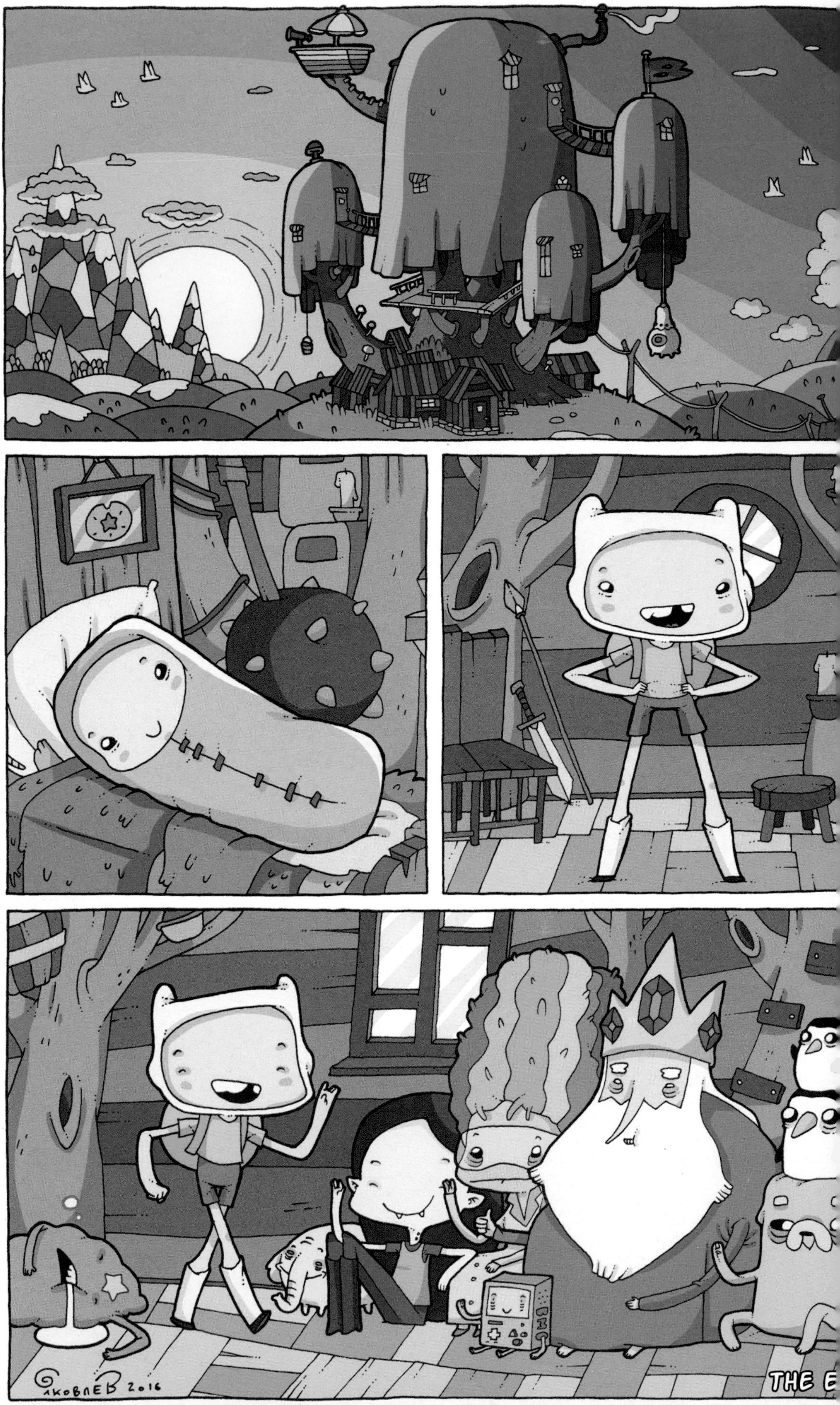

THE E

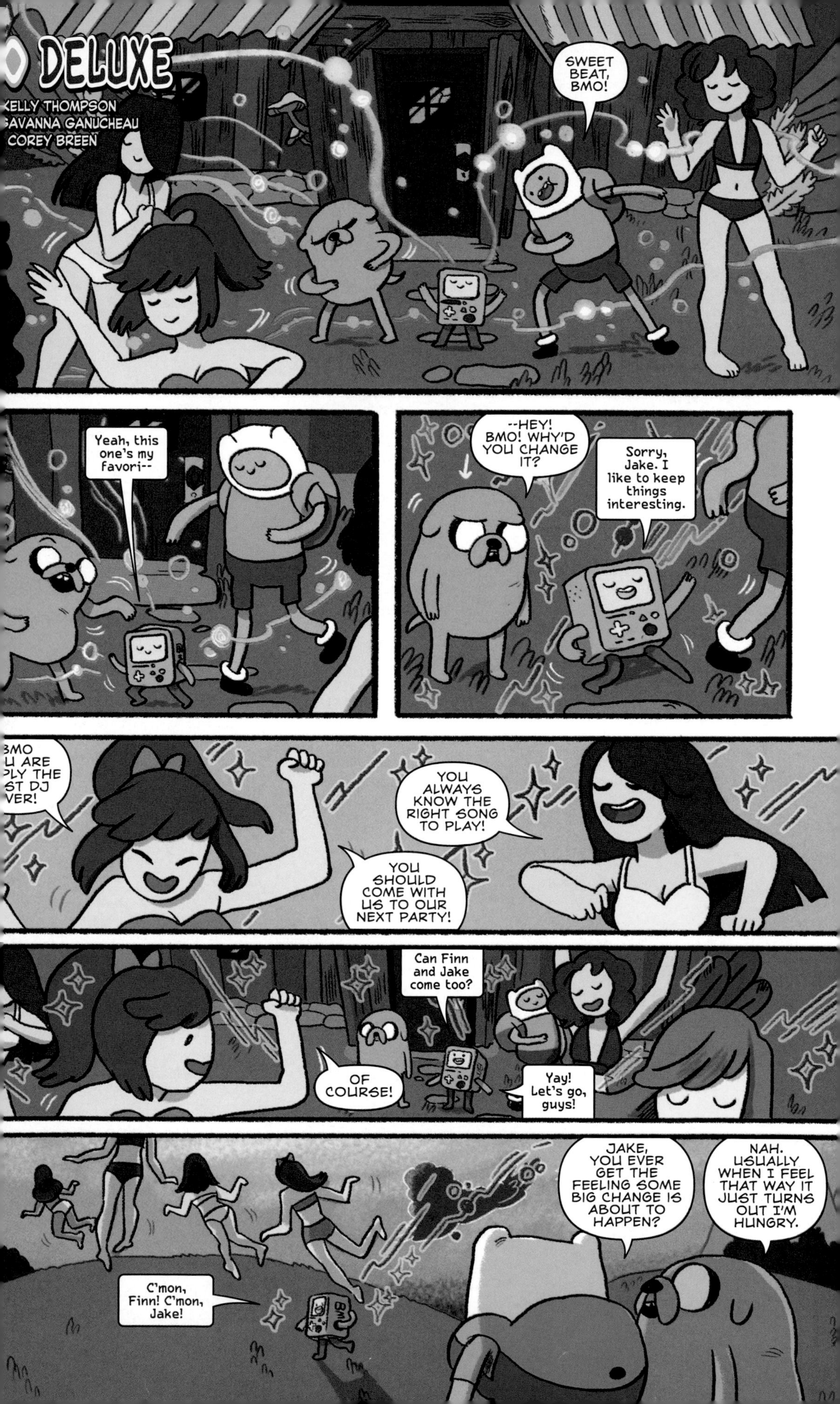
DELUXE
KELLY THOMPSON
SAVANNA GANUCHEAU
COREY BREEN
SWEET BEAT, BMO!
Yeah, this one's my favori--
--HEY! BMO! WHY'D YOU CHANGE IT?
Sorry, Jake. I like to keep things interesting.
YOU ALWAYS KNOW THE RIGHT SONG TO PLAY!
YOU SHOULD COME WITH US TO OUR NEXT PARTY!
Can Finn and Jake come too?
OF COURSE!
Yay! Let's go, guys!
C'mon, Finn! C'mon, Jake!
JAKE, YOU EVER GET THE FEELING SOME BIG CHANGE IS ABOUT TO HAPPEN?
NAH. USUALLY WHEN I FEEL THAT WAY IT JUST TURNS OUT I'M HUNGRY.

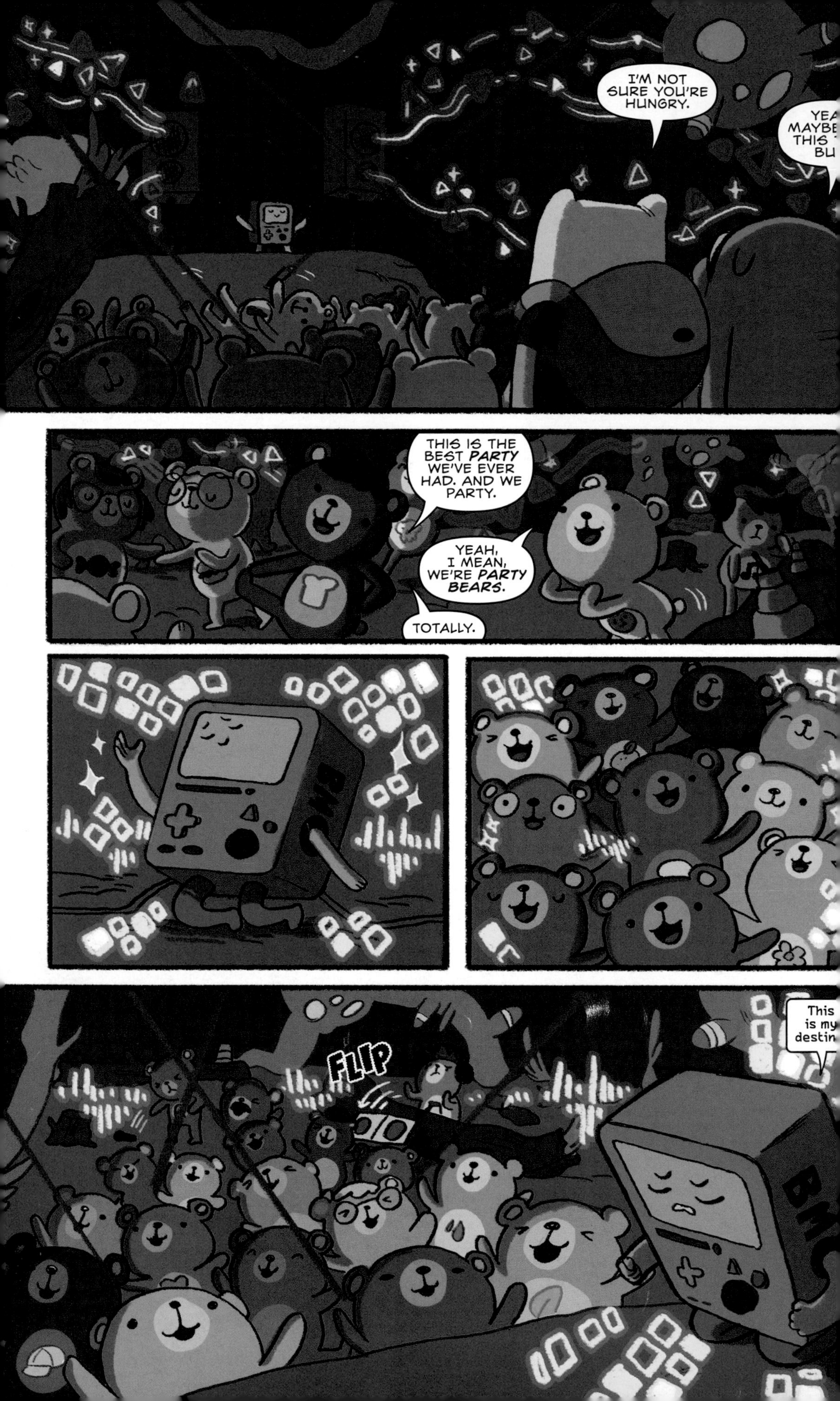
I'M NOT SURE YOU'RE HUNGRY.
YEA MAYBE THIS BU
THIS IS THE BEST PARTY WE'VE EVER HAD. AND WE PARTY.
YEAH, I MEAN, WE'RE PARTY BEARS.
TOTALLY.
BMO
FLIP
This is my destin
BMO

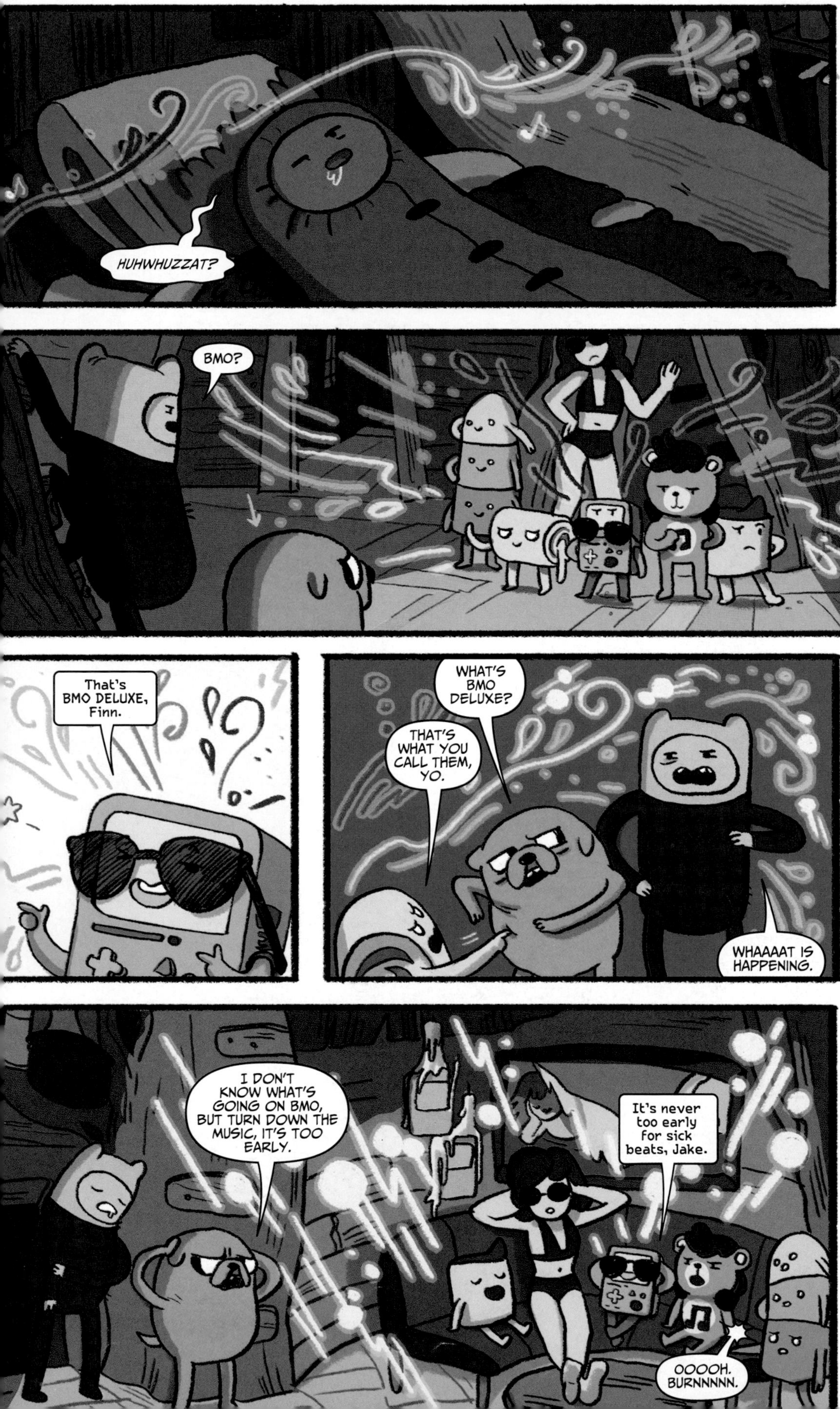
HUHWHUZZAT?
BMO?
That's BMO DELUXE, Finn.
WHAT'S BMO DELUXE?
THAT'S WHAT YOU CALL THEM, YO.
WHAAAAT IS HAPPENING.
I DON'T KNOW WHAT'S GOING ON BMO, BUT TURN DOWN THE MUSIC, IT'S TOO EARLY.
It's never too early for sick beats, Jake.
OOOOH. BURNNNNN.

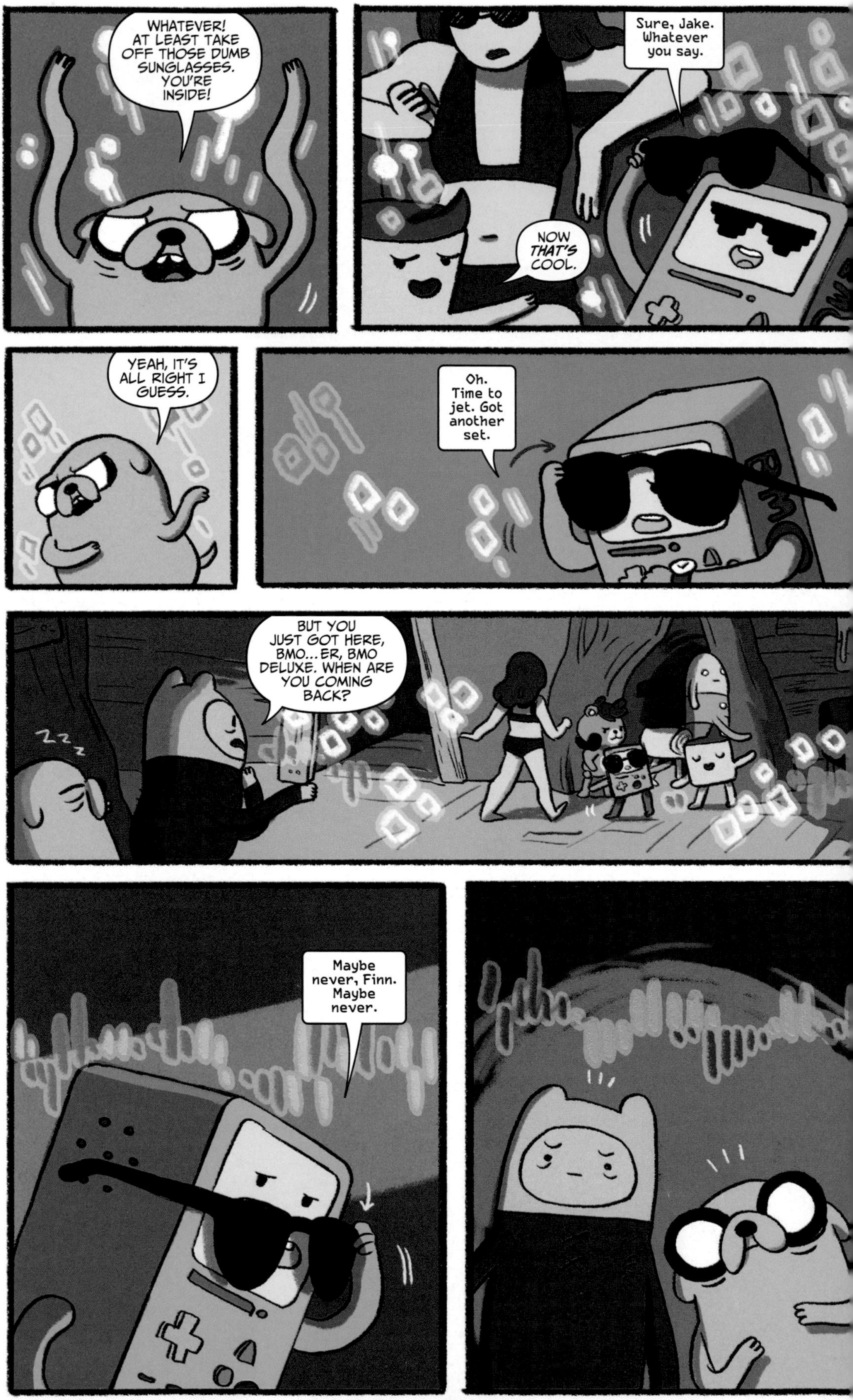
WHATEVER! AT LEAST TAKE OFF THOSE DUMB SUNGLASSES. YOU'RE INSIDE!
Sure, Jake. Whatever you say.
NOW THAT'S COOL.
YEAH, IT'S ALL RIGHT I GUESS.
Oh. Time to jet. Got another set.
BUT YOU JUST GOT HERE, BMO... ER, BMO DELUXE. WHEN ARE YOU COMING BACK?
Maybe never, Finn. Maybe never.

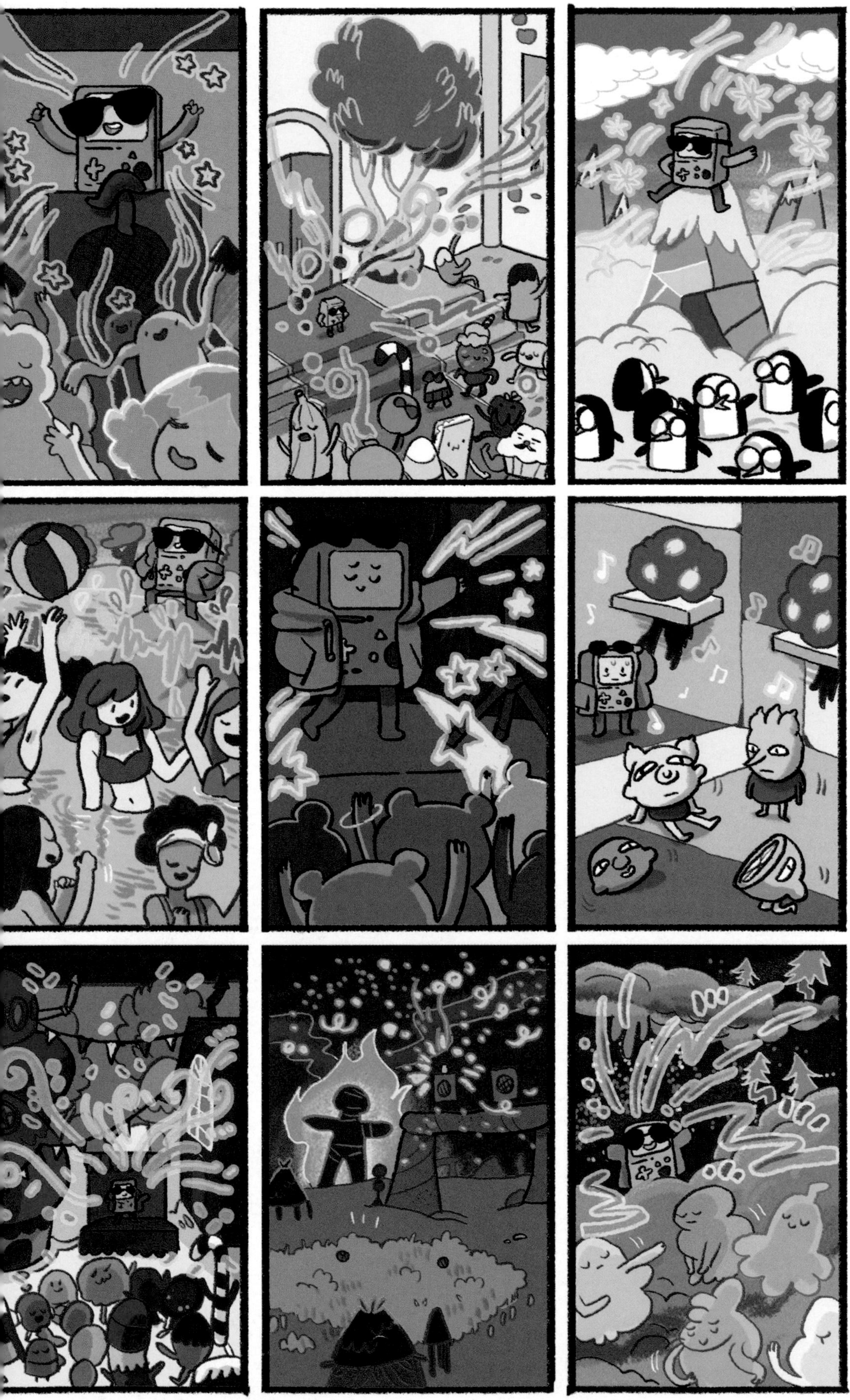

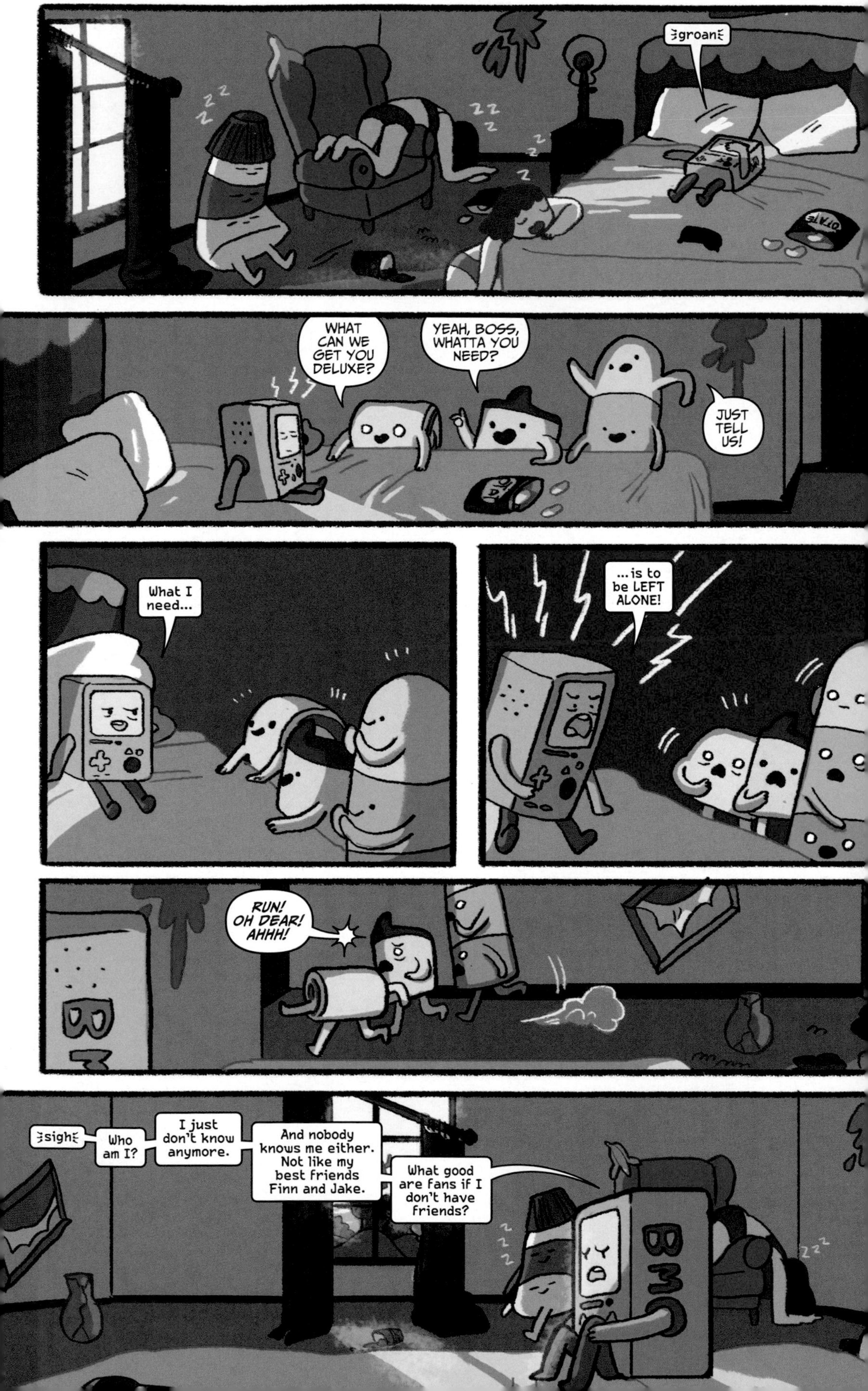

groan
WHAT CAN WE GET YOU DELUXE?
YEAH, BOSS, WHATTA YOU NEED?
JUST TELL US!
What I need...
...is to be LEFT ALONE!
RUN! OH DEAR! AHHH!
sigh
Who am I?
I just don't know anymore.
And nobody knows me either. Not like my best friends Finn and Jake.
What good are fans if I don't have friends?

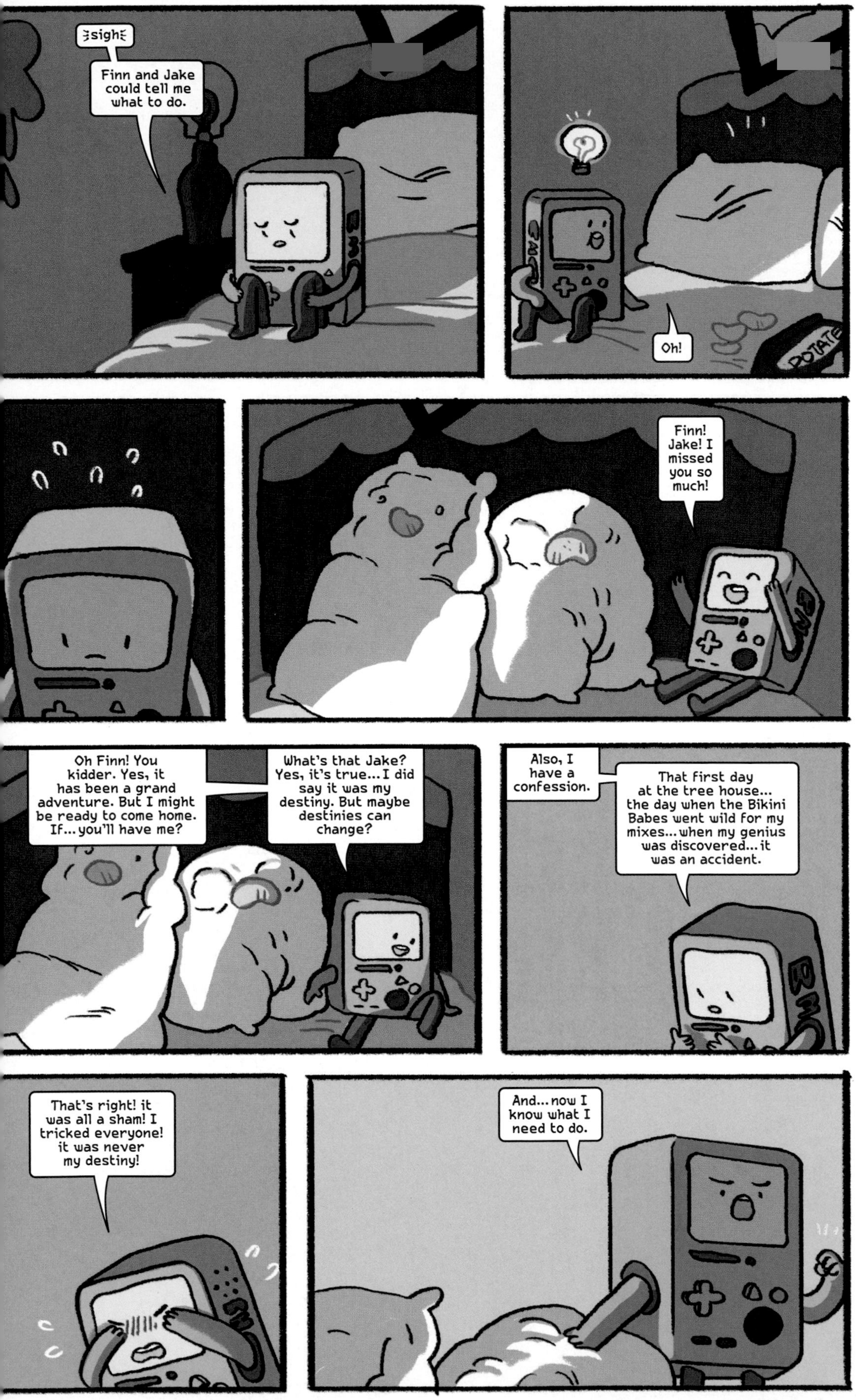

sigh
Finn and Jake could tell me what to do.
Oh!
Finn! Jake! I missed you so much!
Oh Finn! You kidder. Yes, it has been a grand adventure. But I might be ready to come home. If... you'll have me?
What's that Jake? Yes, it's true... I did say it was my destiny. But maybe destinies can change?
Also, I have a confession.
That first day at the tree house... the day when the Bikini Babes went wild for my mixes... when my genius was discovered... it was an accident.
That's right! it was all a sham! I tricked everyone! it was never my destiny!
And... now I know what I need to do.

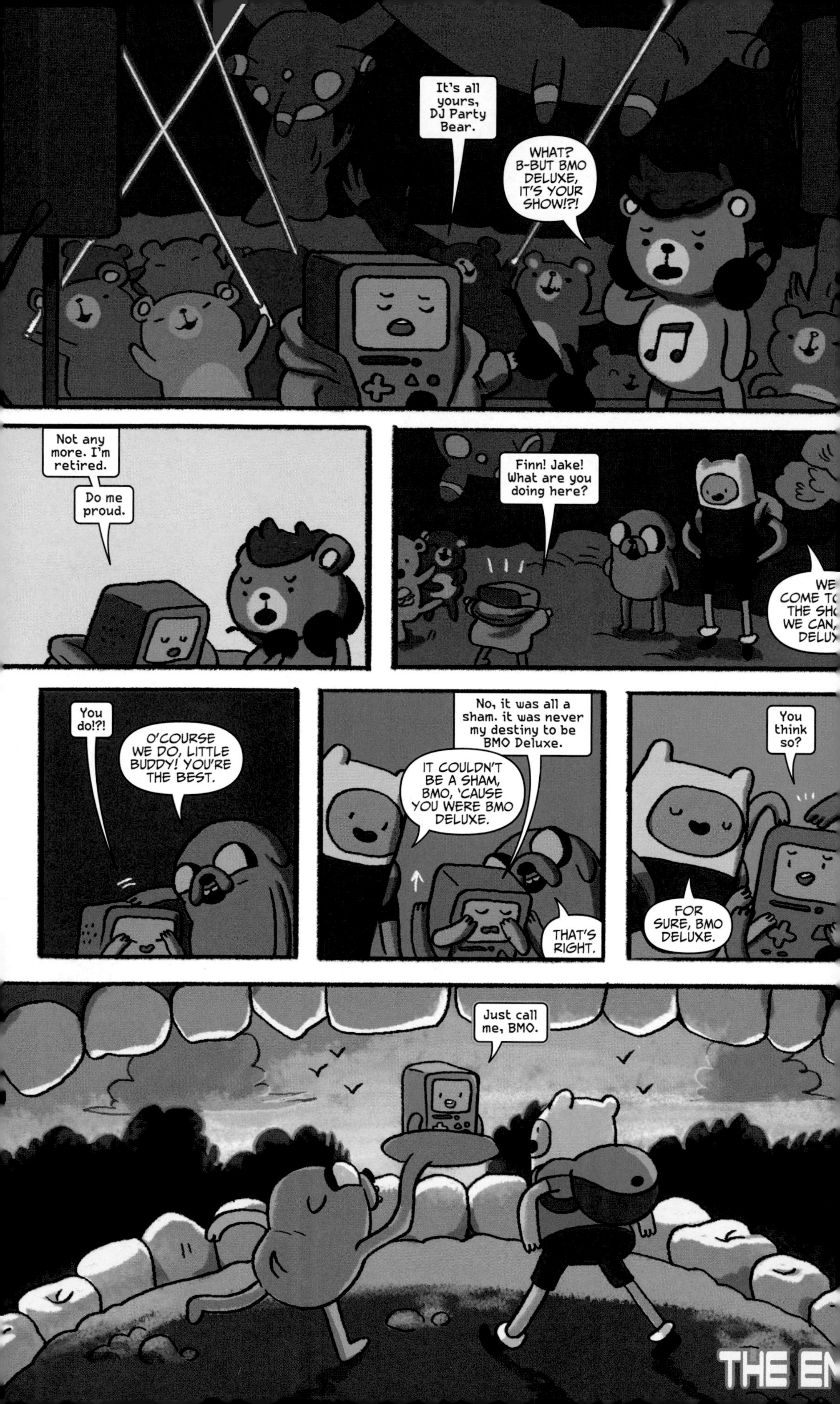

It's all yours, DJ Party Bear.
WHAT? B-BUT BMO DELUXE, IT'S YOUR SHOW!?!
Not any more. I'm retired.
Do me proud.
Finn! Jake! What are you doing here?
WE COME TO THE SHO WE CAN, DELUX
You do!?!
O'COURSE WE DO, LITTLE BUDDY! YOU'RE THE BEST.
No, it was all a sham. it was never my destiny to be BMO Deluxe.
IT COULDN'T BE A SHAM, BMO, 'CAUSE YOU WERE BMO DELUXE.
THAT'S RIGHT.
You think so?
FOR SURE, BMO DELUXE.
Just call me, BMO.
THE EN

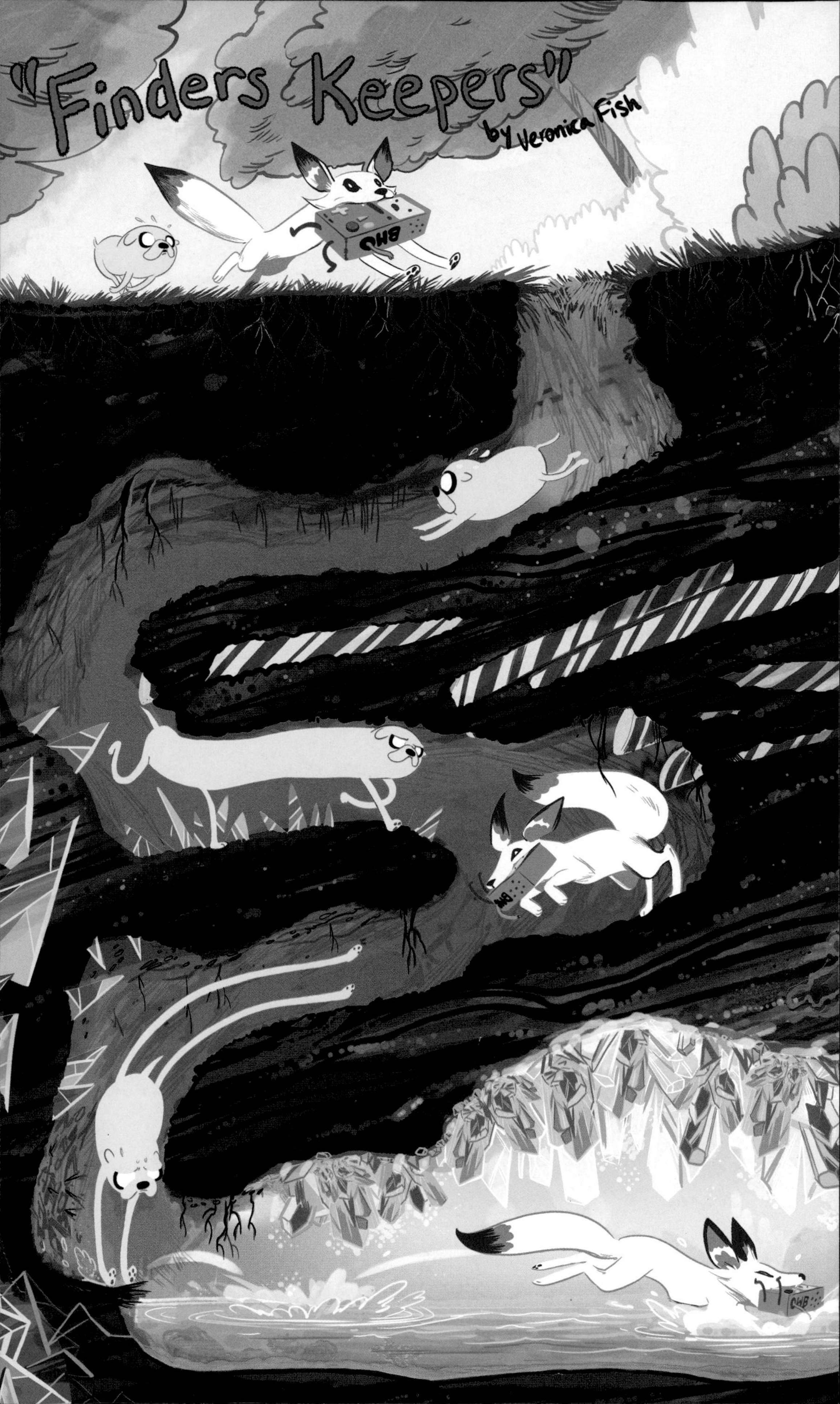
"Finders Keepers"
by Veronica Fish
BMO

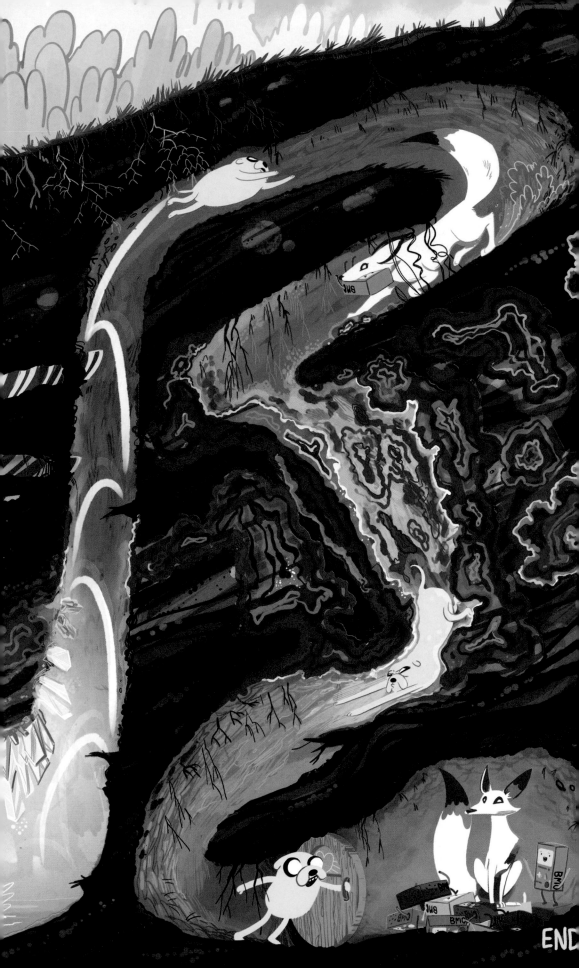

END

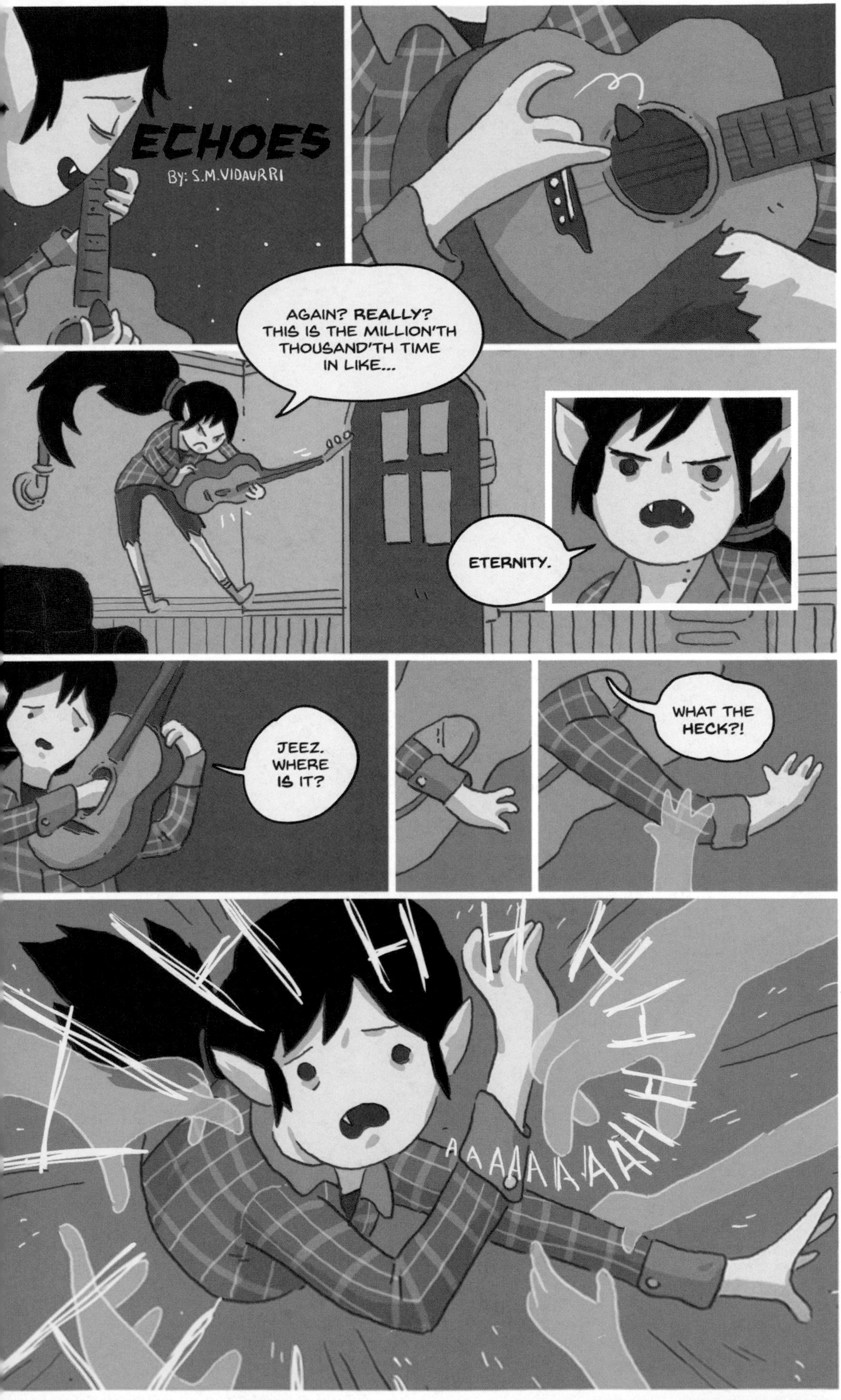
ECHOES
By: S.M.VIDAURRI
AGAIN? REALLY? THIS IS THE MILLION'TH THOUSAND'TH TIME IN LIKE...
ETERNITY.
JEEZ. WHERE IS IT?
WHAT THE HECK?!
AAAAAAAAHHHHHHHHH

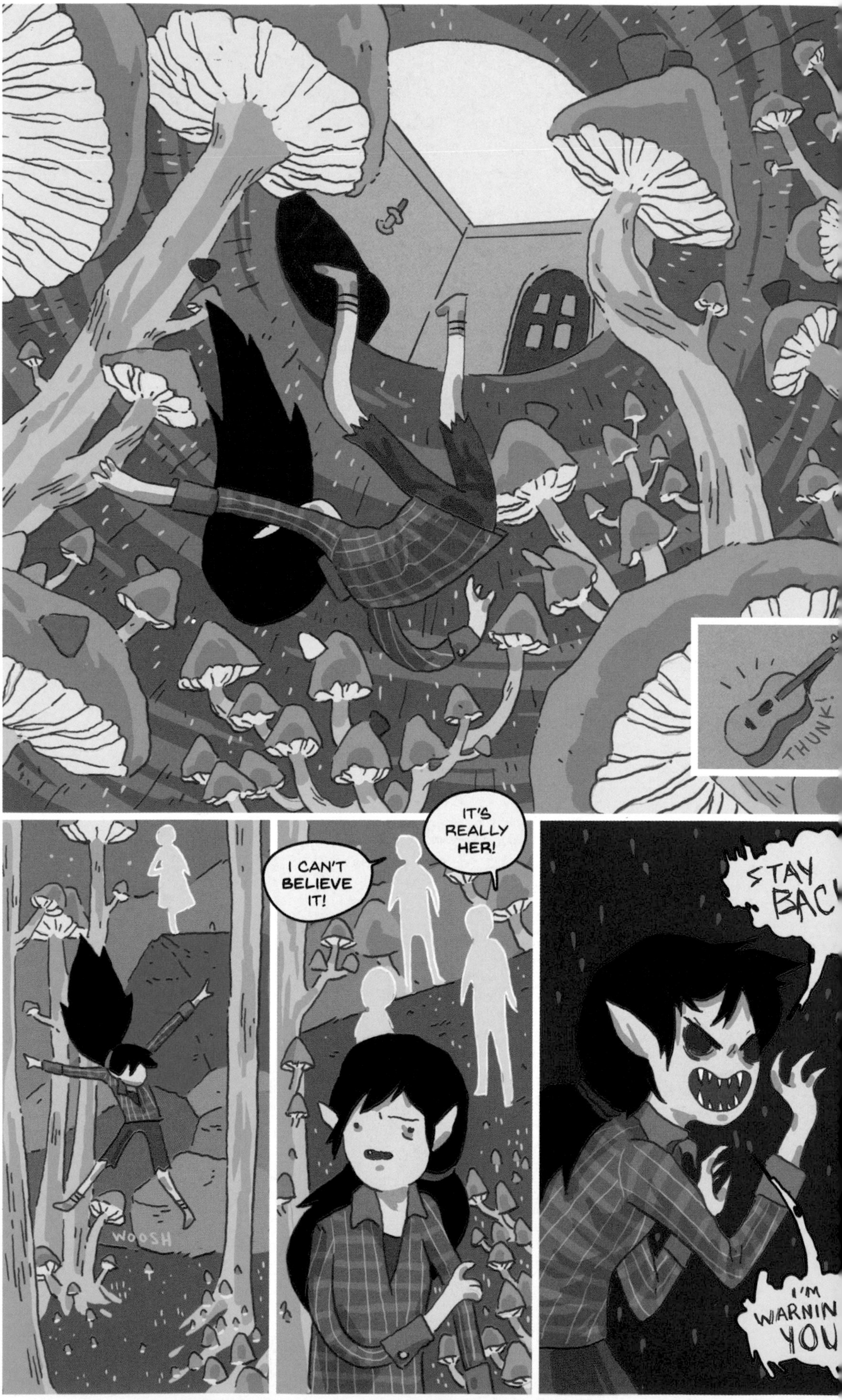

THUNK!
WOOSH
I CAN'T BELIEVE IT!
IT'S REALLY HER!
STAY BAC
I'M WARNIN YOU

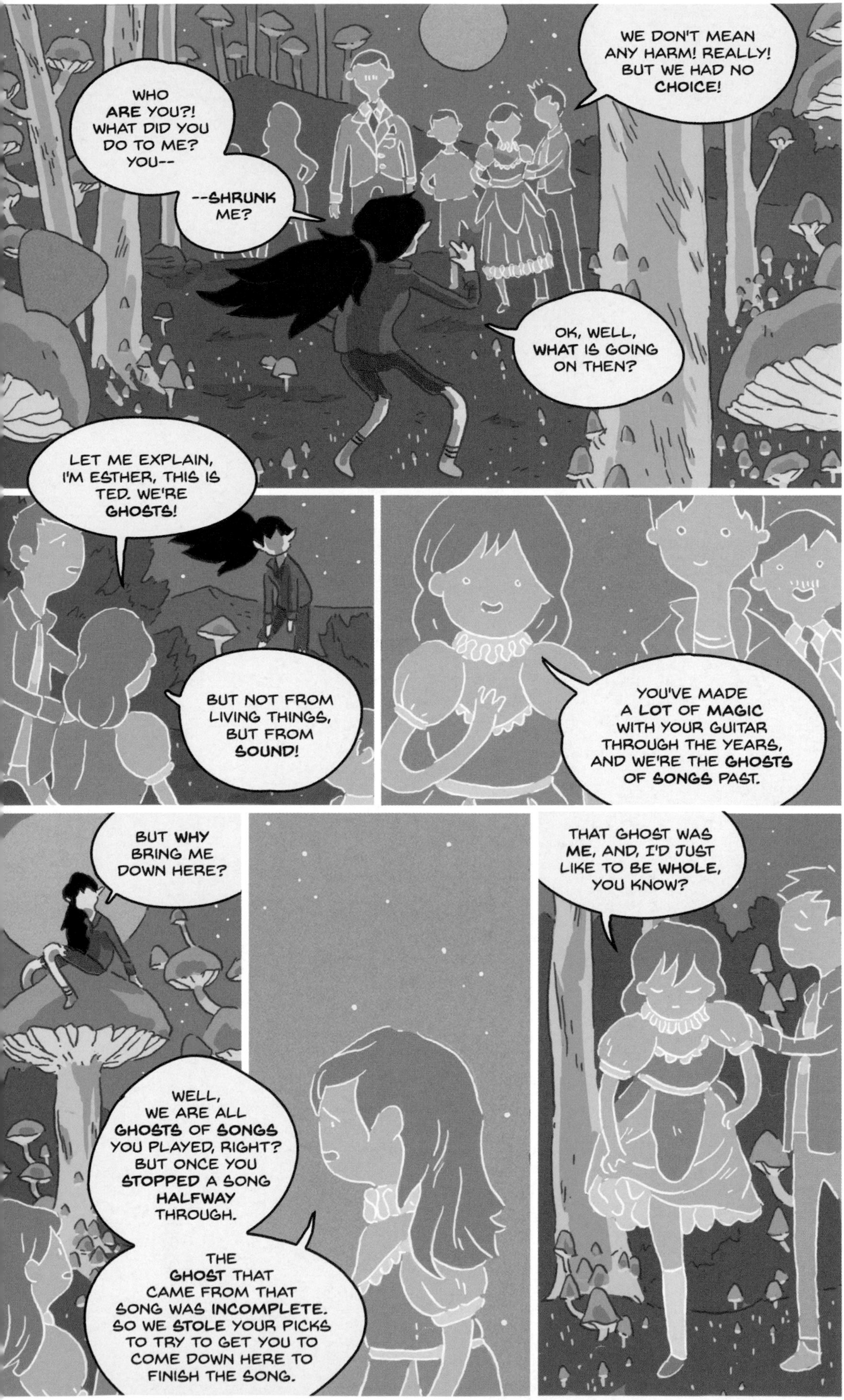
WHO ARE YOU?! WHAT DID YOU DO TO ME? YOU--
--SHRUNK ME?
WE DON'T MEAN ANY HARM! REALLY! BUT WE HAD NO CHOICE!
OK, WELL, WHAT IS GOING ON THEN?
LET ME EXPLAIN, I'M ESTHER, THIS IS TED. WE'RE GHOSTS!
BUT NOT FROM LIVING THINGS, BUT FROM SOUND!
YOU'VE MADE A LOT OF MAGIC WITH YOUR GUITAR THROUGH THE YEARS, AND WE'RE THE GHOSTS OF SONGS PAST.
BUT WHY BRING ME DOWN HERE?
WELL, WE ARE ALL GHOSTS OF SONGS YOU PLAYED, RIGHT? BUT ONCE YOU STOPPED A SONG HALFWAY THROUGH.
THE GHOST THAT CAME FROM THAT SONG WAS INCOMPLETE. SO WE STOLE YOUR PICKS TO TRY TO GET YOU TO COME DOWN HERE TO FINISH THE SONG.
THAT GHOST WAS ME, AND, I'D JUST LIKE TO BE WHOLE, YOU KNOW?

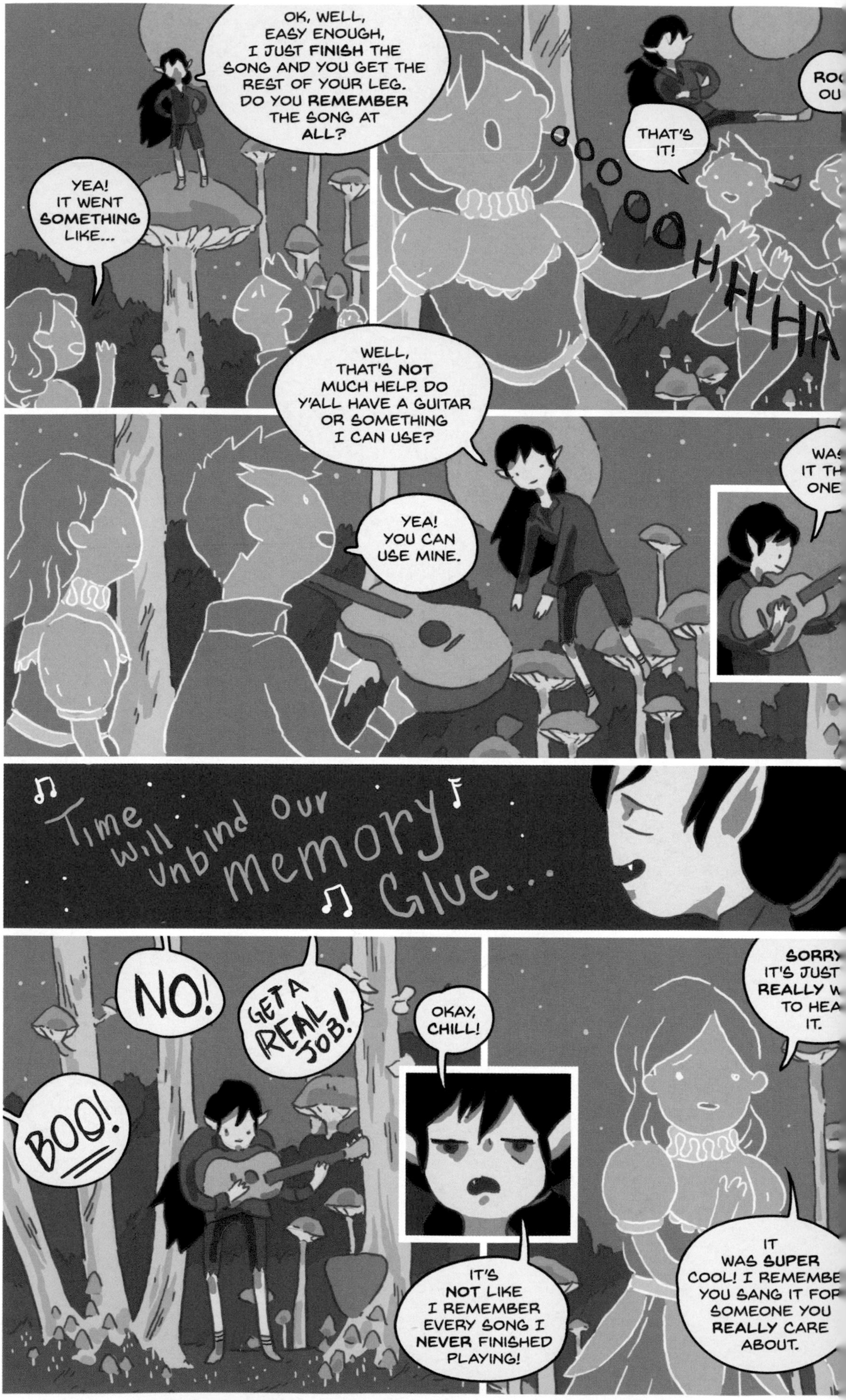
OK, WELL, EASY ENOUGH, I JUST FINISH THE SONG AND YOU GET THE REST OF YOUR LEG. DO YOU REMEMBER THE SONG AT ALL?
YEA! IT WENT SOMETHING LIKE...
OOOOOOHHHHA
THAT'S IT!
WELL, THAT'S NOT MUCH HELP. DO Y'ALL HAVE A GUITAR OR SOMETHING I CAN USE?
YEA! YOU CAN USE MINE.
Time will unbind our memory Glue...
NO!
GET A REAL JOB!
BOO!
OKAY, CHILL!
IT'S NOT LIKE I REMEMBER EVERY SONG I NEVER FINISHED PLAYING!
IT WAS SUPER COOL! I REMEMBE YOU SANG IT FOR SOMEONE YOU REALLY CARE ABOUT.

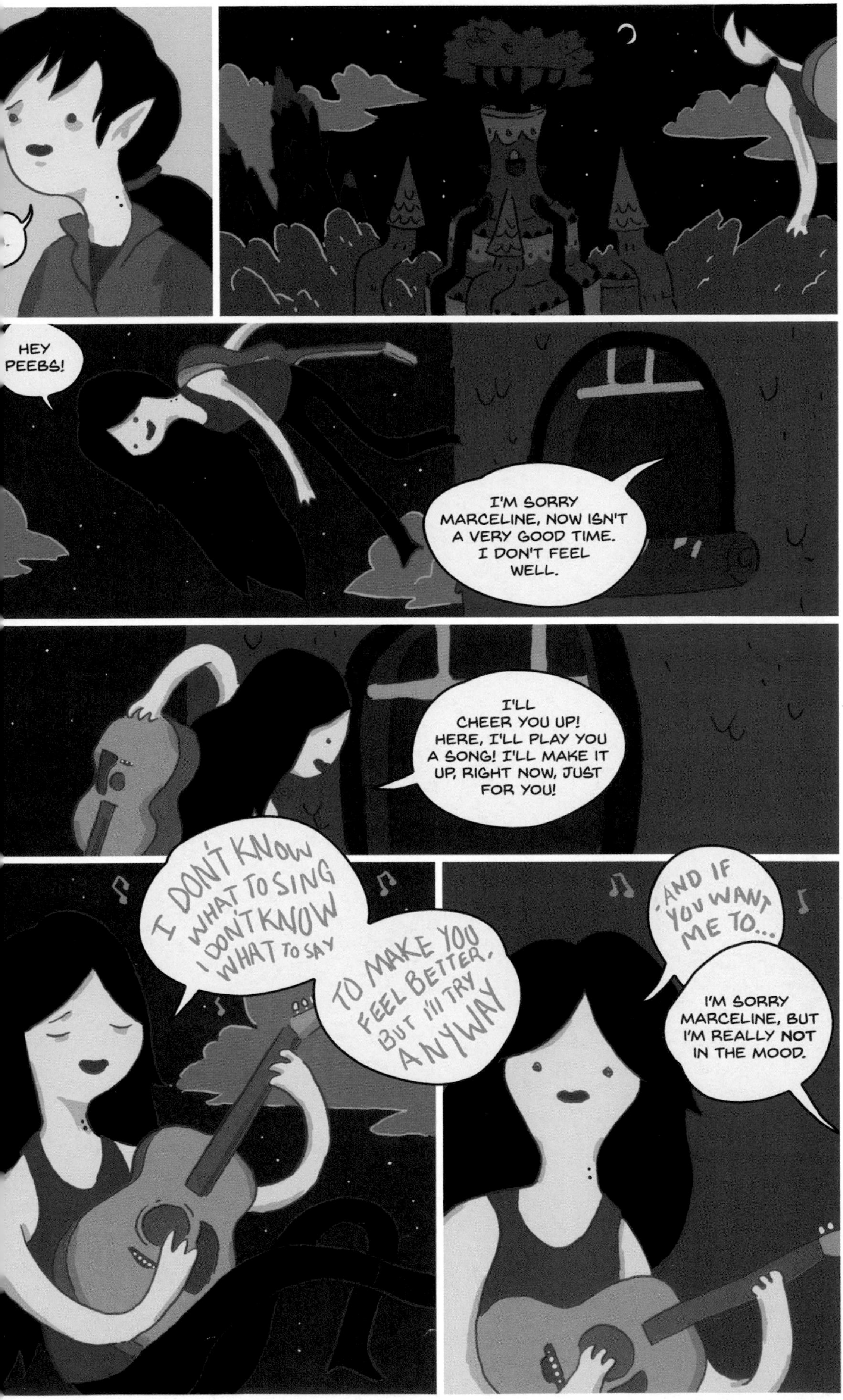
HEY PEEBS!
I'M SORRY MARCELINE, NOW ISN'T A VERY GOOD TIME. I DON'T FEEL WELL.
I'LL CHEER YOU UP! HERE, I'LL PLAY YOU A SONG! I'LL MAKE IT UP, RIGHT NOW, JUST FOR YOU!
I DON'T KNOW WHAT TO SING I DON'T KNOW WHAT TO SAY
TO MAKE YOU FEEL BETTER, BUT I'LL TRY ANYWAY
AND IF YOU WANT ME TO...
I'M SORRY MARCELINE, BUT I'M REALLY NOT IN THE MOOD.

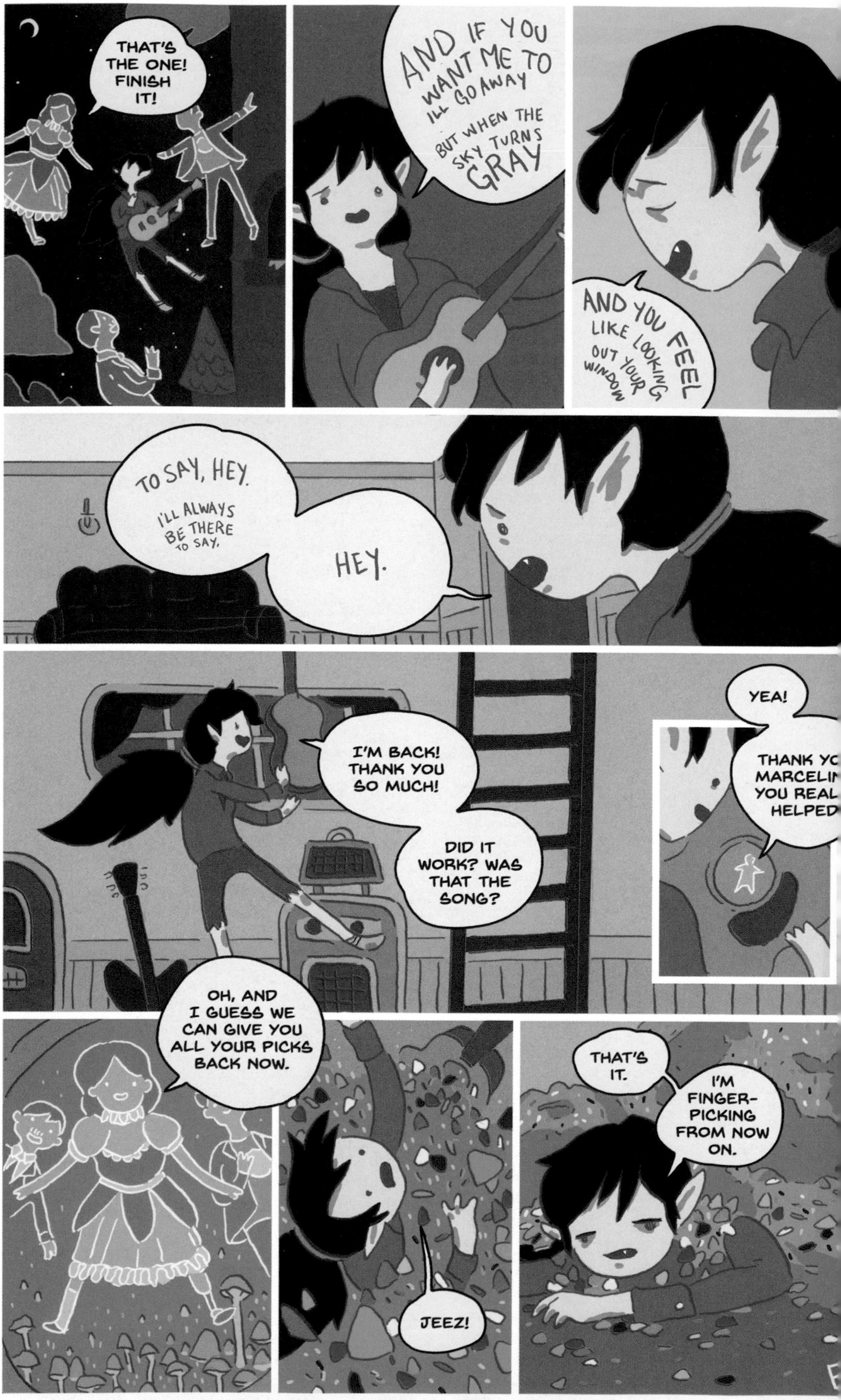
THAT'S THE ONE! FINISH IT!
AND IF YOU WANT ME TO I'LL GO AWAY
BUT WHEN THE SKY TURNS GRAY
AND YOU FEEL LIKE LOOKING OUT YOUR WINDOW
TO SAY, HEY.
I'LL ALWAYS BE THERE TO SAY,
HEY.
I'M BACK! THANK YOU SO MUCH!
DID IT WORK? WAS THAT THE SONG?
YEA!
THANK YO
MARCELIN
YOU REAL
HELPED
OH, AND I GUESS WE CAN GIVE YOU ALL YOUR PICKS BACK NOW.
JEEZ!
THAT'S IT.
I'M FINGER-PICKING FROM NOW ON.

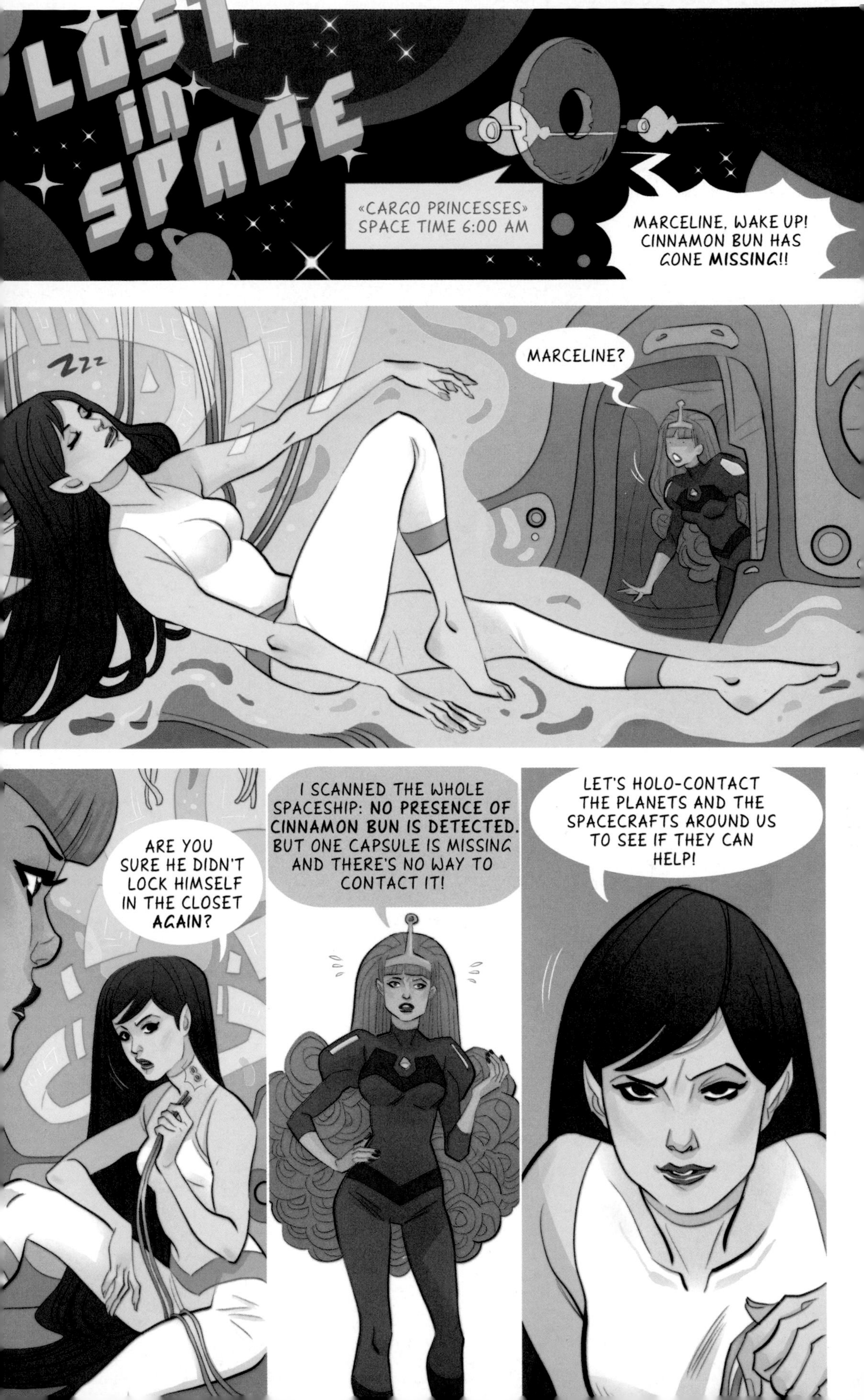
LOST in SPACE
«CARGO PRINCESSES» SPACE TIME 6:00 AM
MARCELINE, WAKE UP! CINNAMON BUN HAS GONE MISSING!!
ZZZ
MARCELINE?
ARE YOU SURE HE DIDN'T LOCK HIMSELF IN THE CLOSET AGAIN?
I SCANNED THE WHOLE SPACESHIP: NO PRESENCE OF CINNAMON BUN IS DETECTED. BUT ONE CAPSULE IS MISSING AND THERE'S NO WAY TO CONTACT IT!
LET'S HOLO-CONTACT THE PLANETS AND THE SPACECRAFTS AROUND US TO SEE IF THEY CAN HELP!

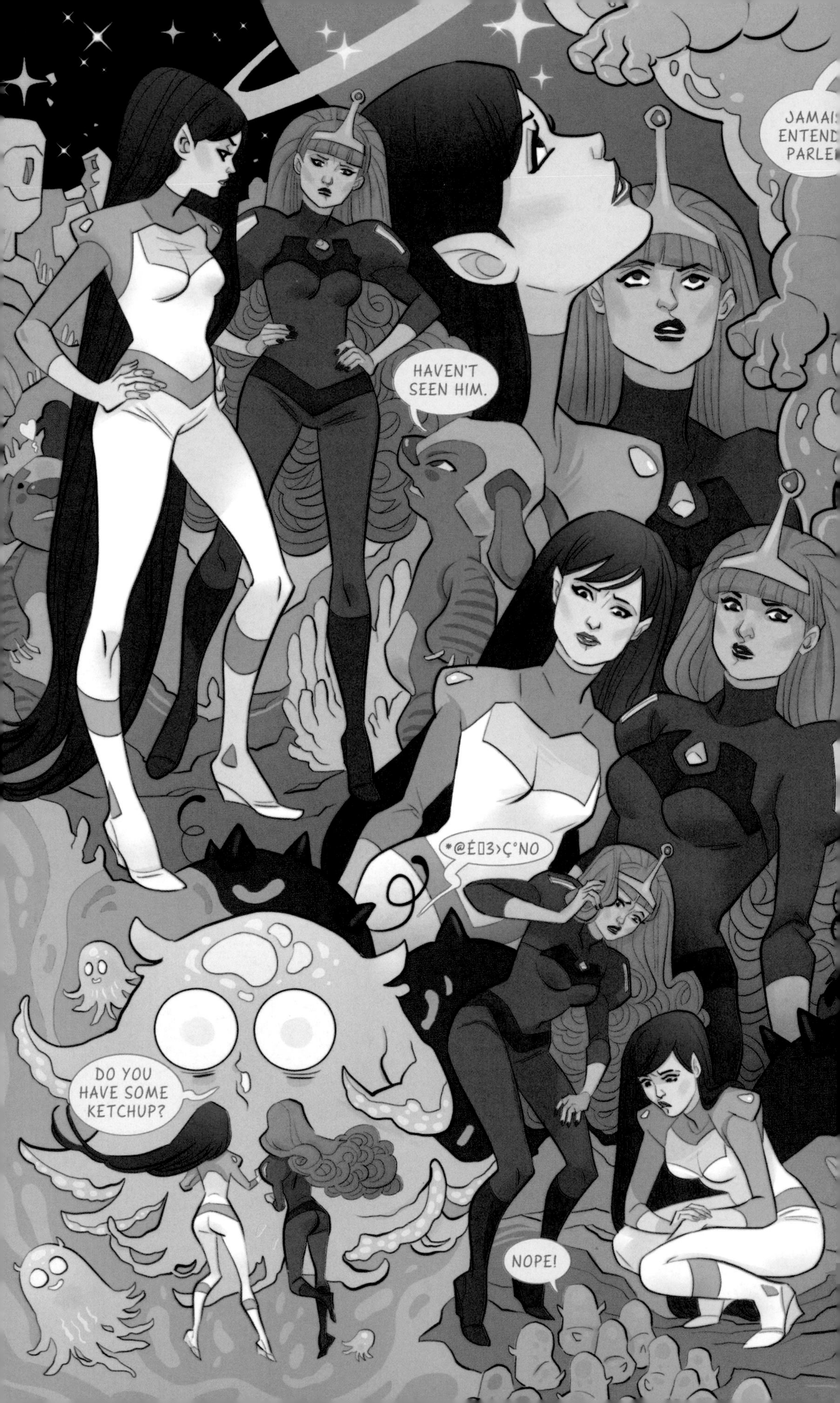

JAMAI
ENTEND
PARLE
HAVEN'T SEEN HIM.
*@É▯3>Ç°NO
DO YOU HAVE SOME KETCHUP?
NOPE!

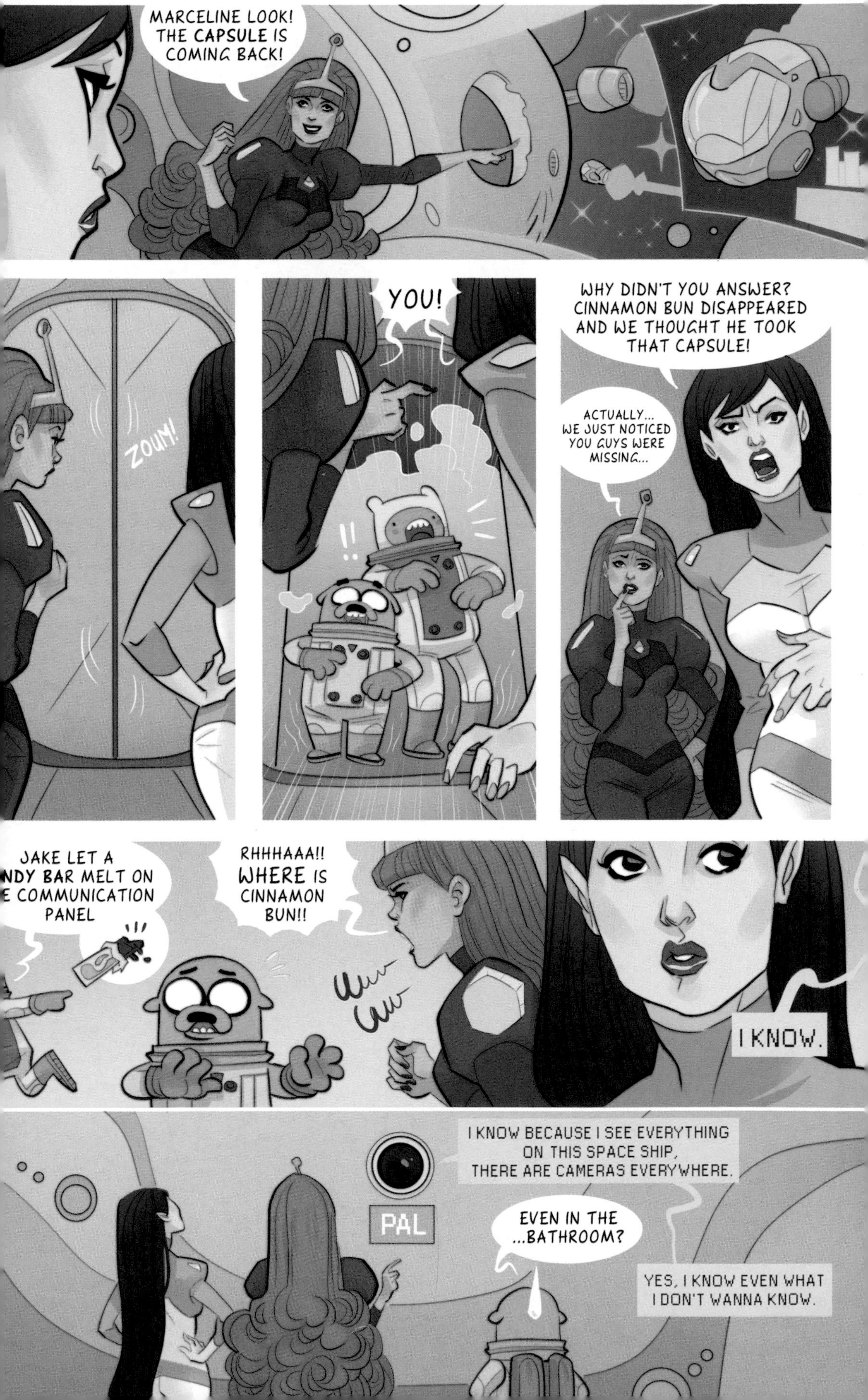
MARCELINE LOOK! THE CAPSULE IS COMING BACK!
ZOUM!
YOU!
!!
WHY DIDN'T YOU ANSWER? CINNAMON BUN DISAPPEARED AND WE THOUGHT HE TOOK THAT CAPSULE!
ACTUALLY... WE JUST NOTICED YOU GUYS WERE MISSING...
JAKE LET A
NDY BAR MELT ON
E COMMUNICATION
PANEL
RHHHAAA!! WHERE IS CINNAMON BUN!!
I KNOW.
I KNOW BECAUSE I SEE EVERYTHING ON THIS SPACE SHIP, THERE ARE CAMERAS EVERYWHERE.
PAL
EVEN IN THE ...BATHROOM?
YES, I KNOW EVEN WHAT I DON'T WANNA KNOW.

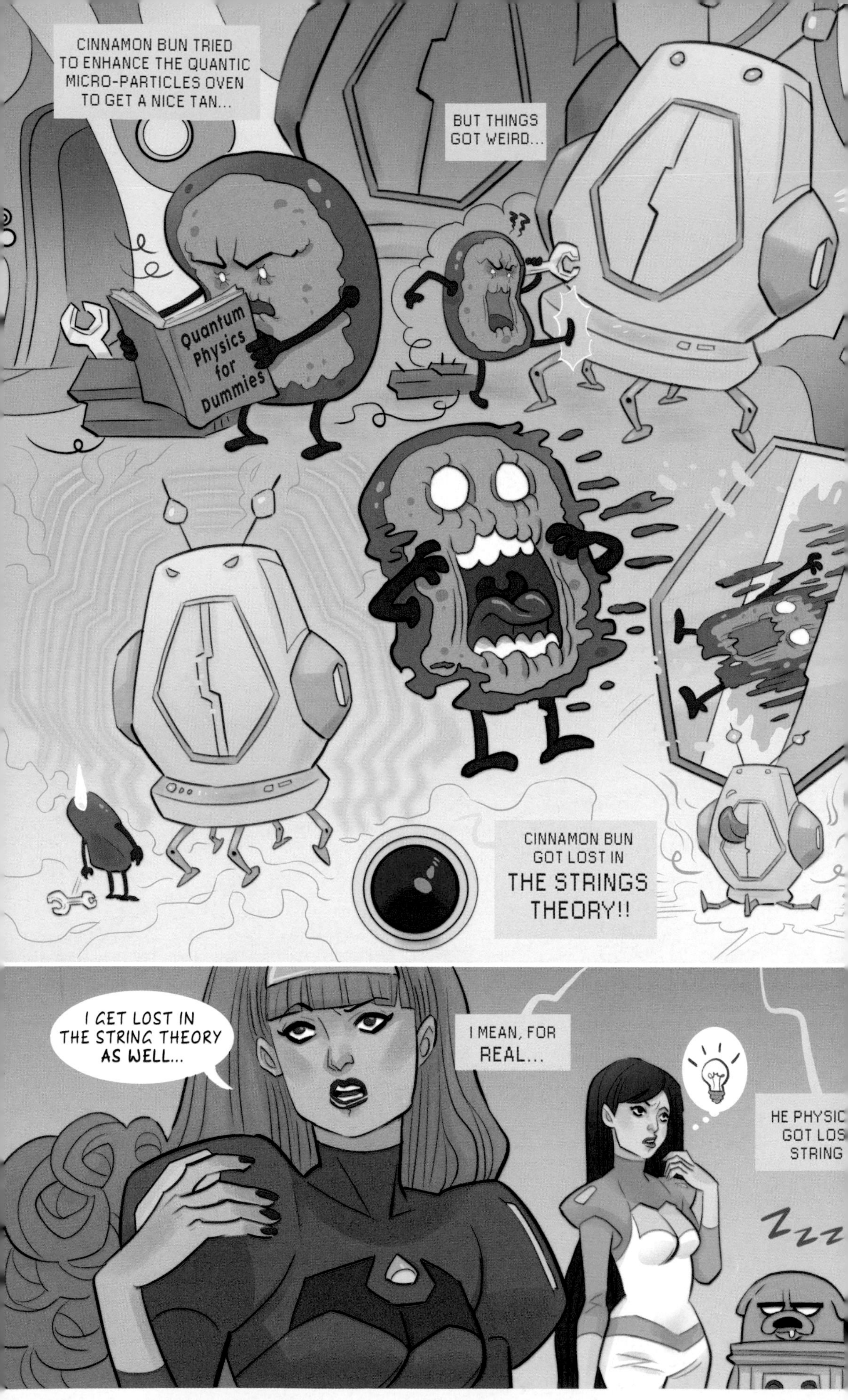
CINNAMON BUN TRIED TO ENHANCE THE QUANTIC MICRO-PARTICLES OVEN TO GET A NICE TAN...
Quantum Physics for Dummies
BUT THINGS GOT WEIRD...
CINNAMON BUN GOT LOST IN THE STRINGS THEORY!!
I GET LOST IN THE STRING THEORY AS WELL...
I MEAN, FOR REAL...
HE PHYSIC GOT LOS STRING

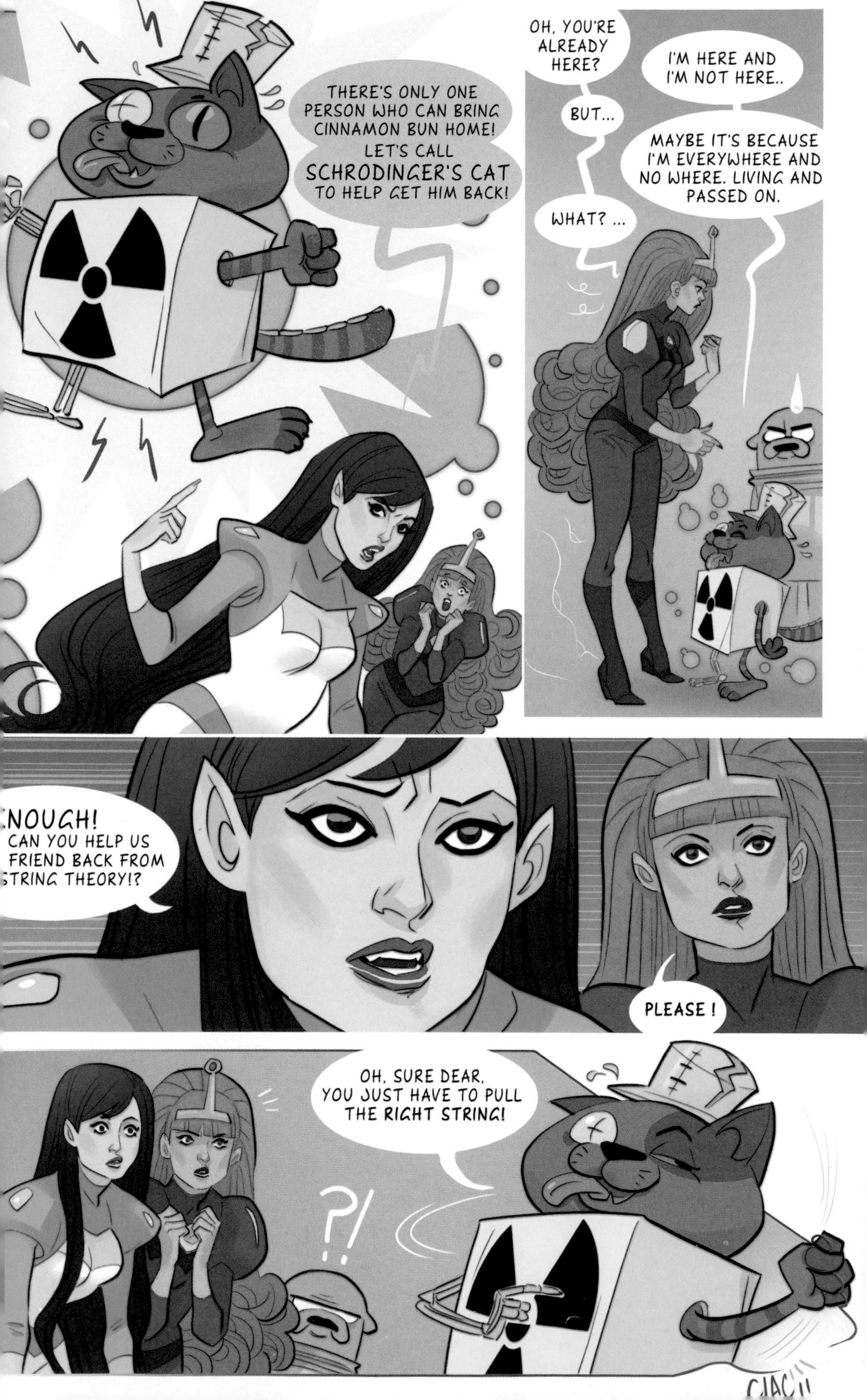
THERE'S ONLY ONE PERSON WHO CAN BRING CINNAMON BUN HOME! LET'S CALL SCHRODINGER'S CAT TO HELP GET HIM BACK!
OH, YOU'RE ALREADY HERE?
BUT...
WHAT? ...
I'M HERE AND I'M NOT HERE..
MAYBE IT'S BECAUSE I'M EVERYWHERE AND NO WHERE. LIVING AND PASSED ON.
NOUGH! CAN YOU HELP US FRIEND BACK FROM STRING THEORY!?
PLEASE !
OH, SURE DEAR, YOU JUST HAVE TO PULL THE RIGHT STRING!
?!
CIAC!!

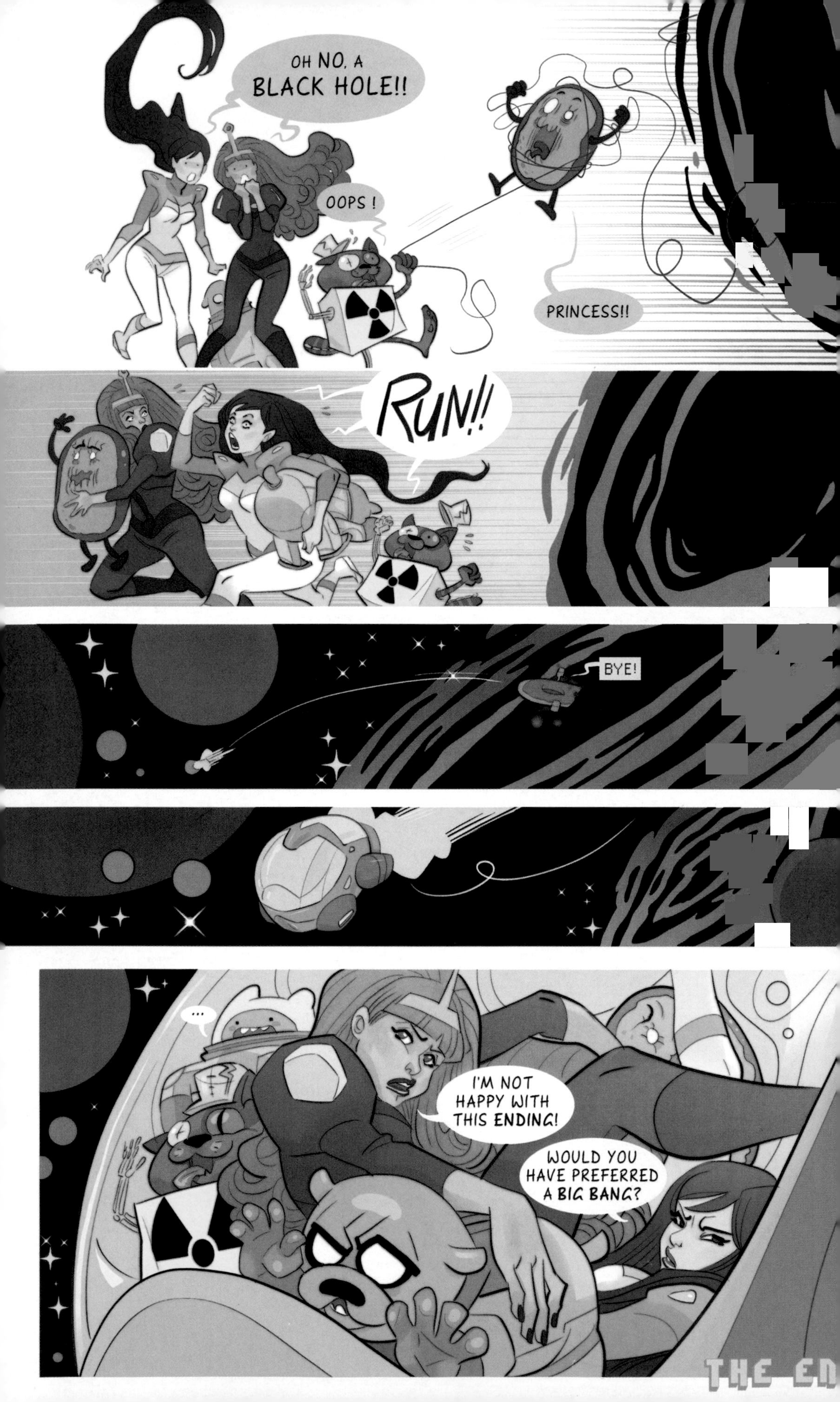
OH NO, A BLACK HOLE!!
OOPS !
PRINCESS!!
RUN!!
BYE!
...
I'M NOT HAPPY WITH THIS ENDING!
WOULD YOU HAVE PREFERRED A BIG BANG?
THE EN

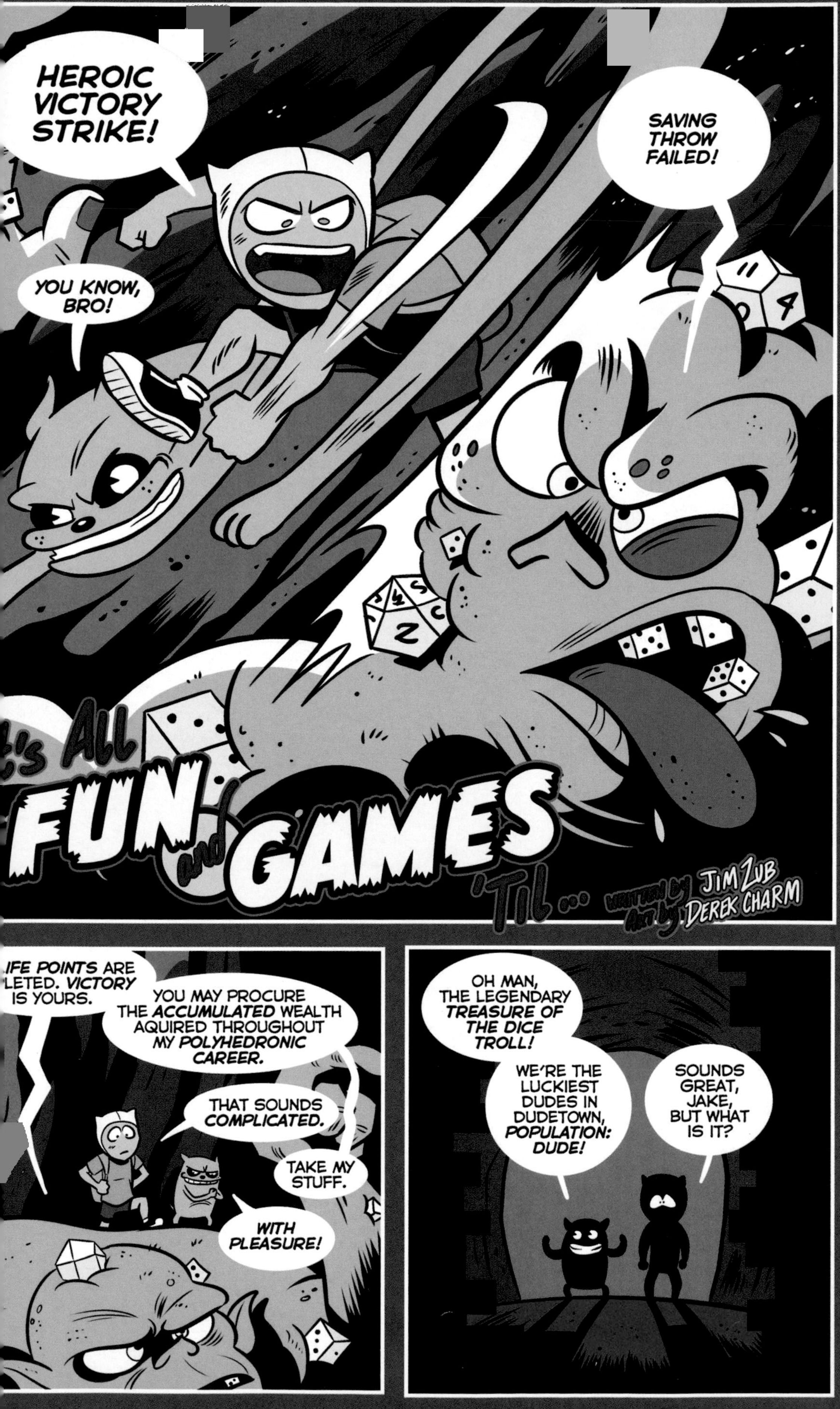
HEROIC VICTORY STRIKE!
YOU KNOW, BRO!
SAVING THROW FAILED!
t's All FUN and GAMES 'Til...
written by JIM ZUB
Art by DEREK CHARM
IFE POINTS ARE LETED. VICTORY IS YOURS.
YOU MAY PROCURE THE ACCUMULATED WEALTH AQUIRED THROUGHOUT MY POLYHEDRONIC CAREER.
THAT SOUNDS COMPLICATED.
TAKE MY STUFF.
WITH PLEASURE!
OH MAN, THE LEGENDARY TREASURE OF THE DICE TROLL!
WE'RE THE LUCKIEST DUDES IN DUDETOWN, POPULATION: DUDE!
SOUNDS GREAT, JAKE, BUT WHAT IS IT?

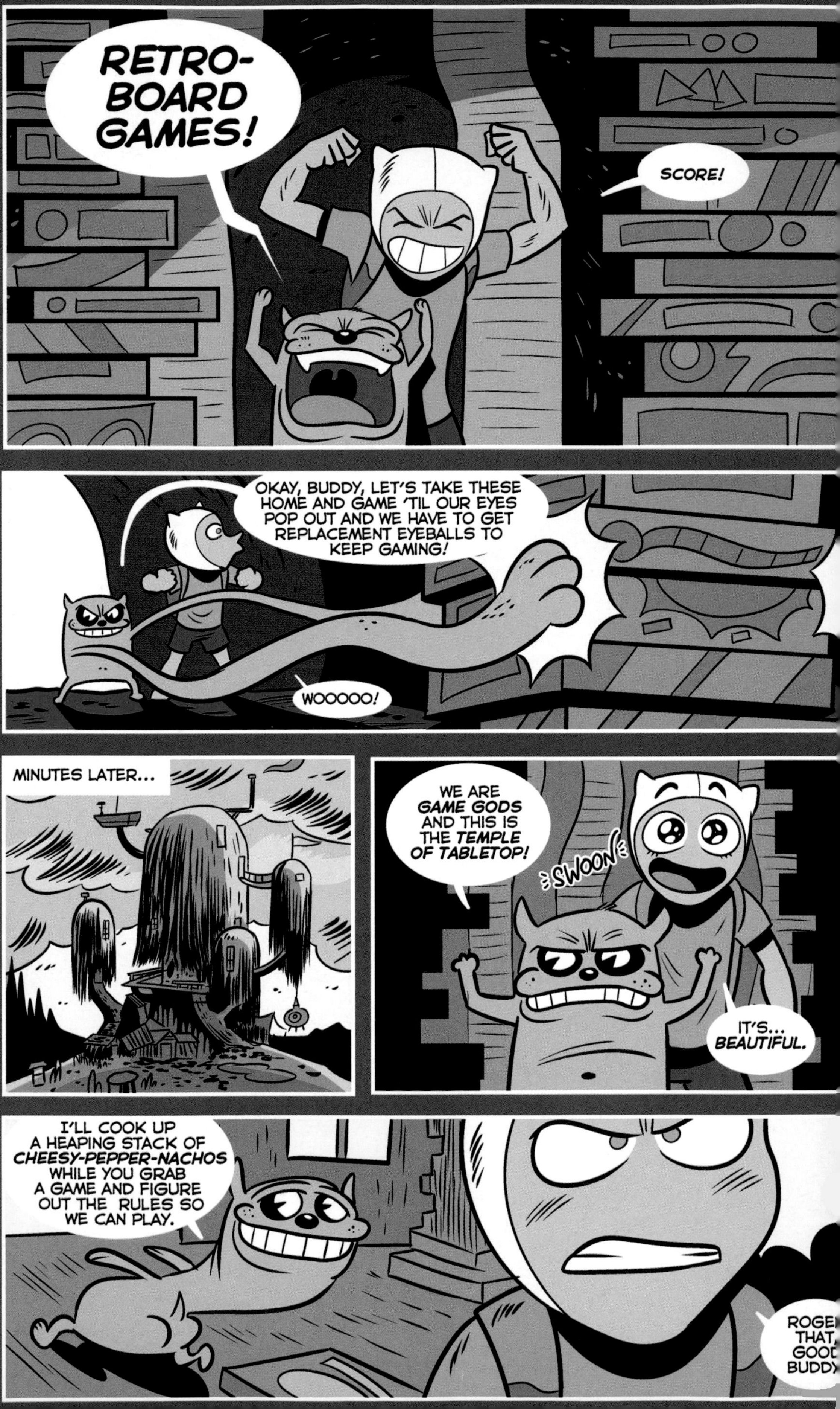
RETRO-BOARD GAMES!
SCORE!
OKAY, BUDDY, LET'S TAKE THESE HOME AND GAME 'TIL OUR EYES POP OUT AND WE HAVE TO GET REPLACEMENT EYEBALLS TO KEEP GAMING!
WOOOOO!
MINUTES LATER...
WE ARE *GAME GODS* AND THIS IS THE *TEMPLE OF TABLETOP!*
SWOON
IT'S... *BEAUTIFUL.*
I'LL COOK UP A HEAPING STACK OF *CHEESY-PEPPER-NACHOS* WHILE YOU GRAB A GAME AND FIGURE OUT THE RULES SO WE CAN PLAY.

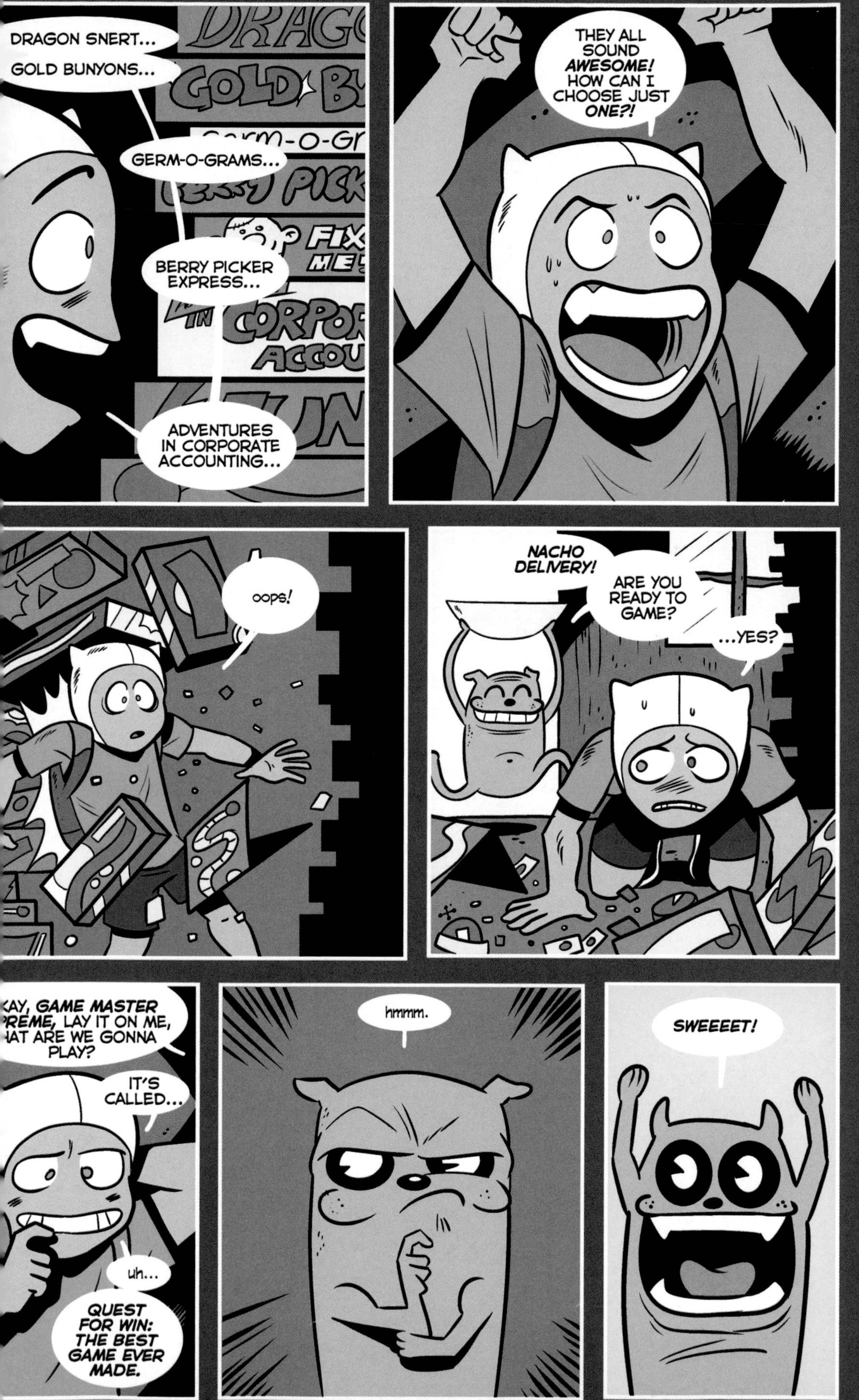
DRAGON SNERT...
GOLD BUNYONS...
GERM-O-GRAMS...
BERRY PICKER EXPRESS...
ADVENTURES IN CORPORATE ACCOUNTING...
THEY ALL SOUND AWESOME! HOW CAN I CHOOSE JUST ONE?!
oops!
NACHO DELIVERY!
ARE YOU READY TO GAME?
...YES?
KAY, GAME MASTER PREME, LAY IT ON ME, HAT ARE WE GONNA PLAY?
IT'S CALLED...
uh...
QUEST FOR WIN: THE BEST GAME EVER MADE.
hmmm.
SWEEEET!

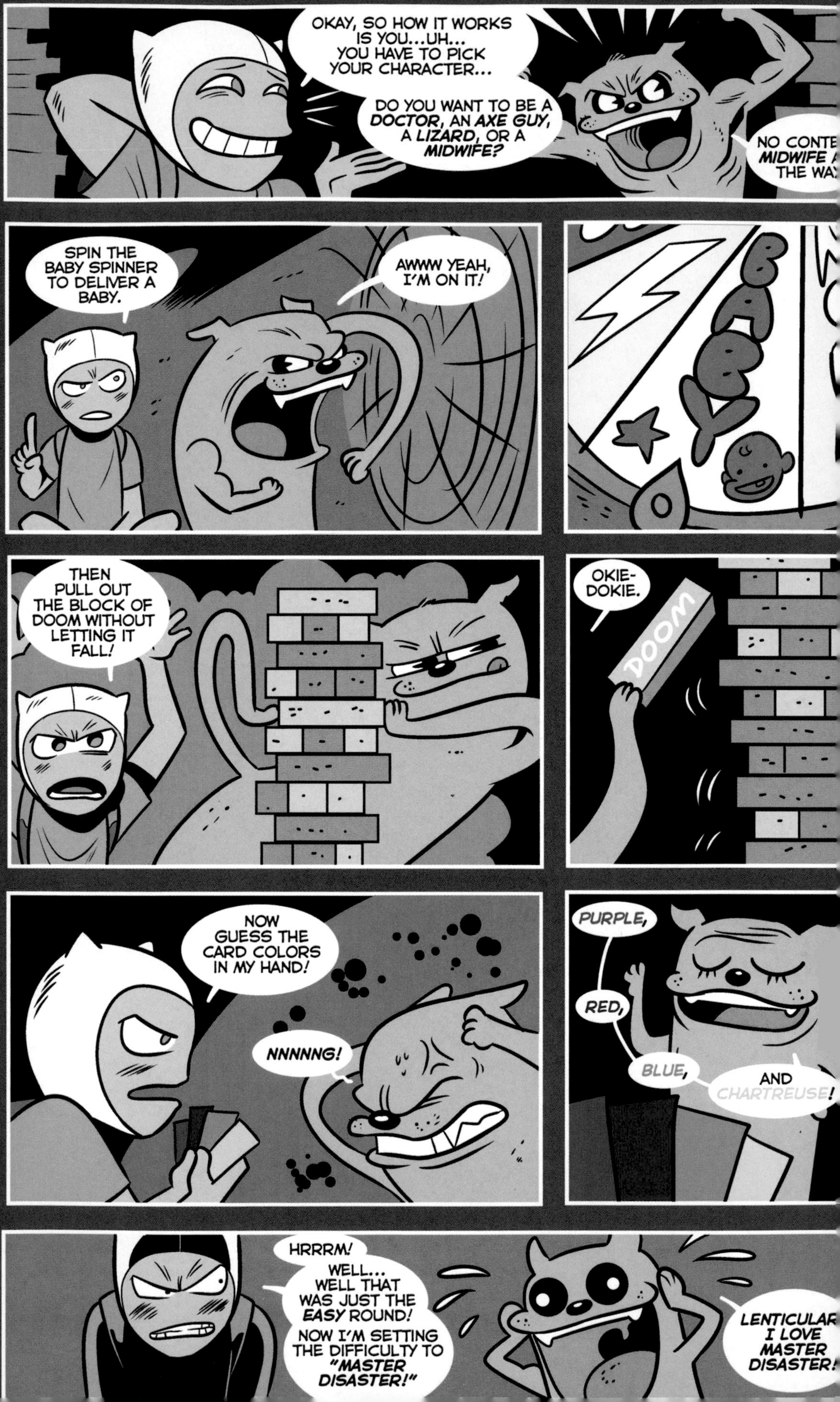
OKAY, SO HOW IT WORKS IS YOU...UH... YOU HAVE TO PICK YOUR CHARACTER...
DO YOU WANT TO BE A *DOCTOR*, AN *AXE GUY*, A *LIZARD*, OR A *MIDWIFE?*
NO CONTE *MIDWIFE* A THE WA
SPIN THE BABY SPINNER TO DELIVER A BABY.
AWWW YEAH, I'M ON IT!
BABY
THEN PULL OUT THE BLOCK OF DOOM WITHOUT LETTING IT FALL!
OKIE-DOKIE.
DOOM
NOW GUESS THE CARD COLORS IN MY HAND!
NNNNNG!
PURPLE,
RED,
BLUE,
AND CHARTREUSE!
HRRRM!
WELL... WELL THAT WAS JUST THE *EASY* ROUND!
NOW I'M SETTING THE DIFFICULTY TO *"MASTER DISASTER!"*
LENTICULAR I LOVE MASTER DISASTER!

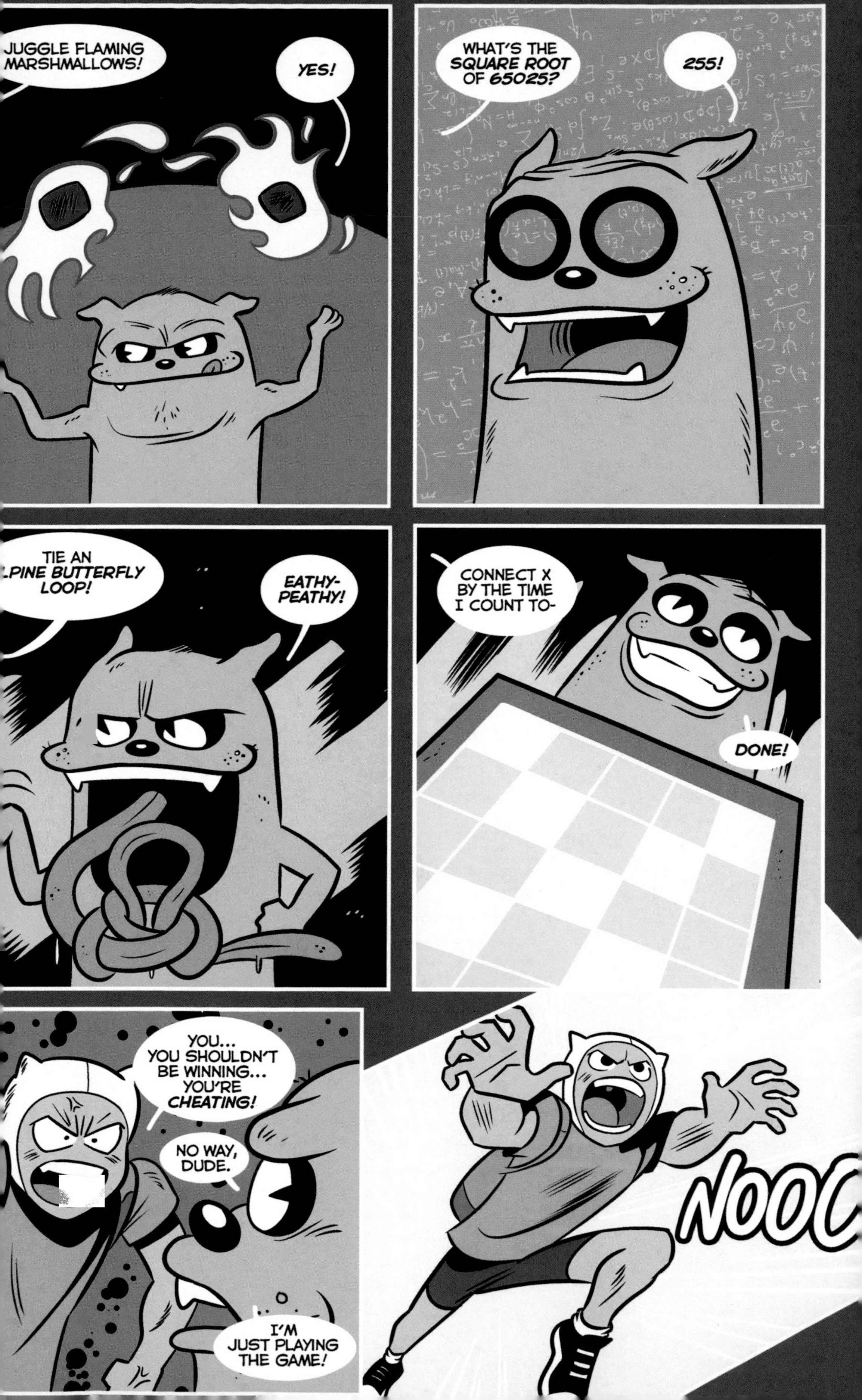
JUGGLE FLAMING MARSHMALLOWS!
YES!
WHAT'S THE SQUARE ROOT OF 65025?
255!
TIE AN
-PINE BUTTERFLY LOOP!
EATHY-PEATHY!
CONNECT X BY THE TIME I COUNT TO-
DONE!
YOU... YOU SHOULDN'T BE WINNING... YOU'RE CHEATING!
NO WAY, DUDE.
I'M JUST PLAYING THE GAME!
NOOO

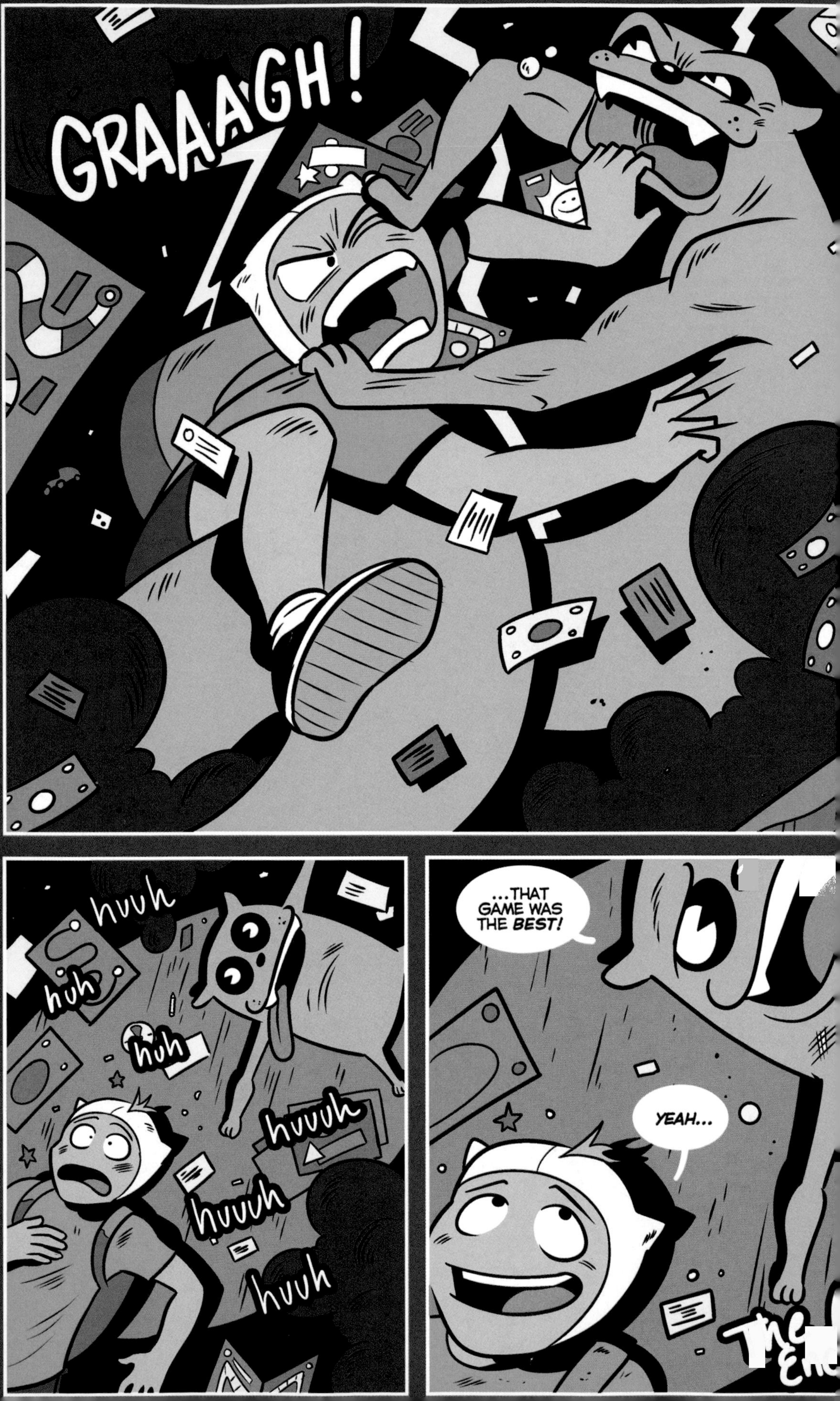
GRAAAGH!
huuh
huh
huh
huuuh
huuuh
huuh
...THAT GAME WAS THE *BEST!*
YEAH...

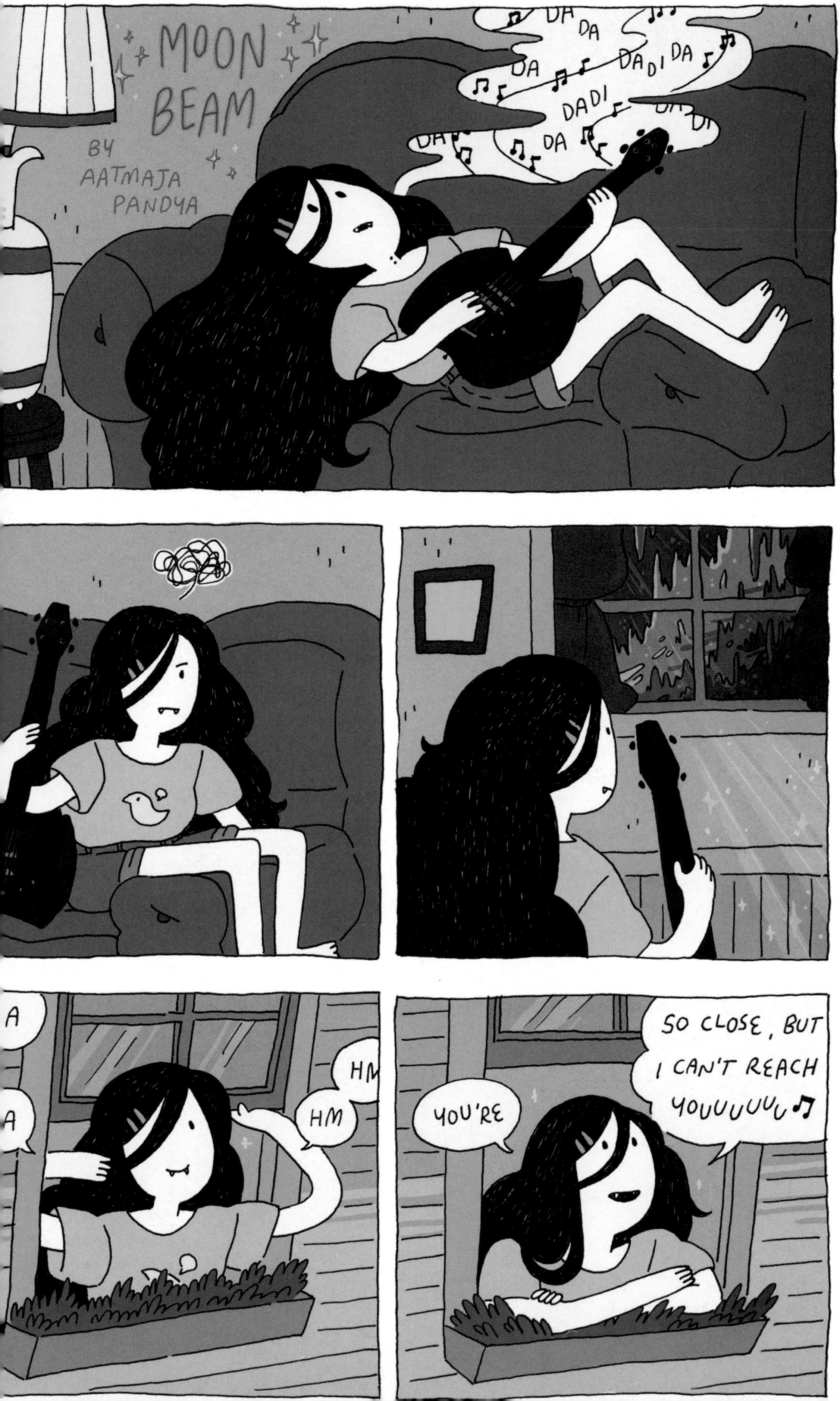
MOON BEAM
BY AATMAJA PANDYA
DA DA DA DADI DA DADI DA DA
A
A
HM
HM
YOU'RE
SO CLOSE, BUT I CAN'T REACH YOUUUUUU

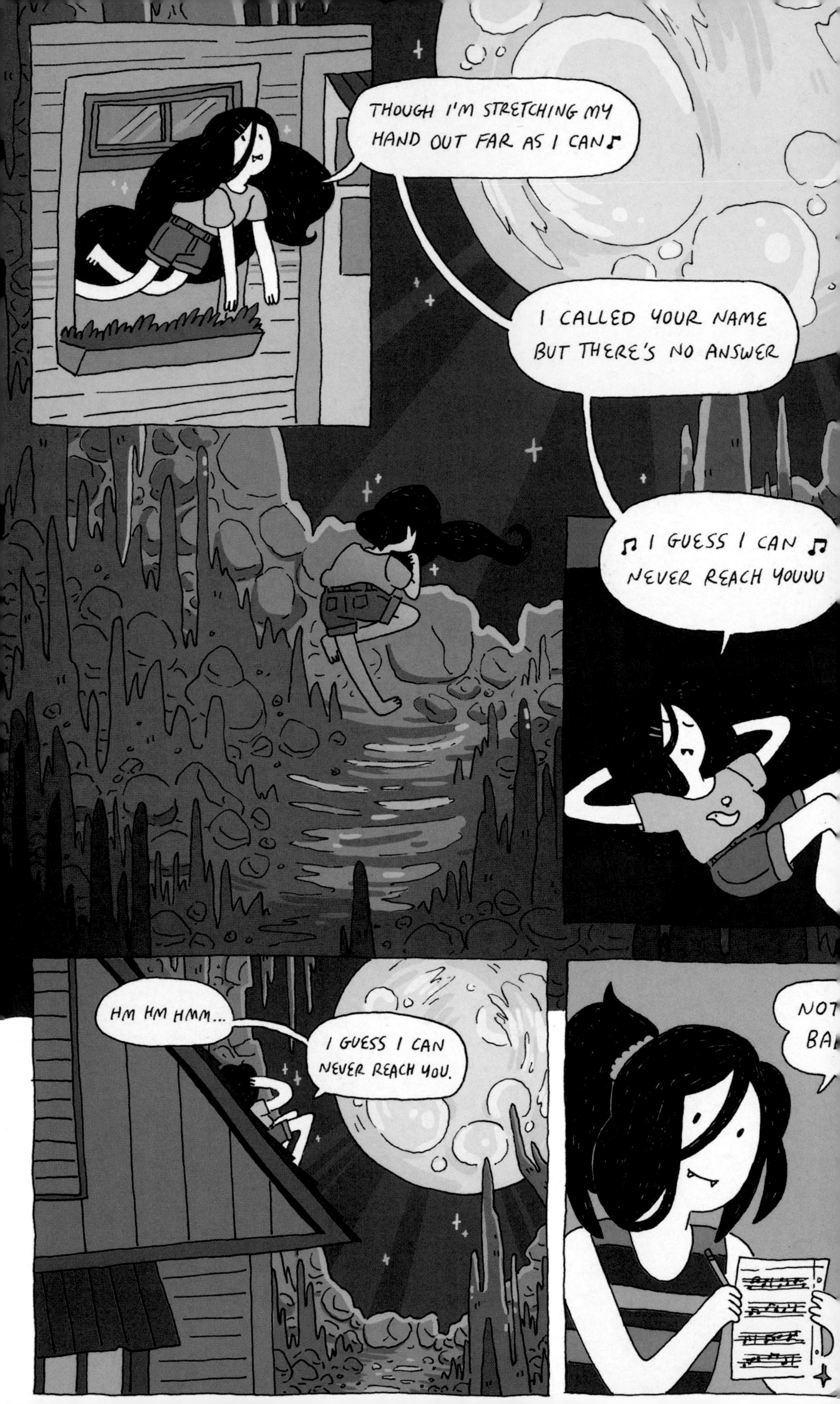
THOUGH I'M STRETCHING MY HAND OUT FAR AS I CAN ♪
I CALLED YOUR NAME BUT THERE'S NO ANSWER
♫ I GUESS I CAN ♫ NEVER REACH YOUUU
HM HM HMM...
I GUESS I CAN NEVER REACH YOU.
NOT BA

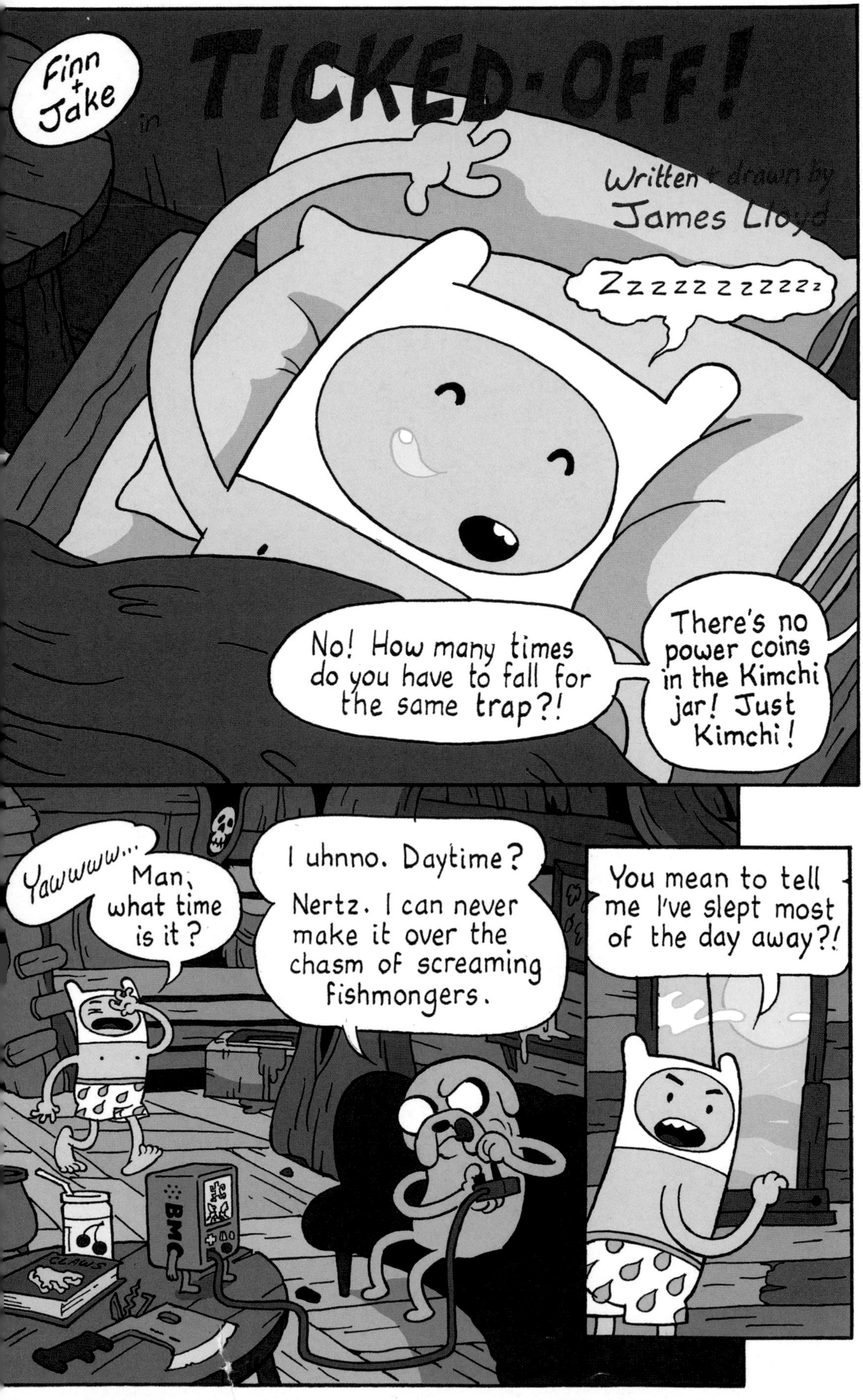
Finn + Jake
in
TICKED-OFF!
Written + drawn by James Lloyd
Zzzzzzzzzzz
No! How many times do you have to fall for the same trap?!
There's no power coins in the Kimchi jar! Just Kimchi!
Yawwww...
Man, what time is it?
I uhnno. Daytime?
Nertz. I can never make it over the chasm of screaming fishmongers.
You mean to tell me I've slept most of the day away?!
CLAWS
BMO

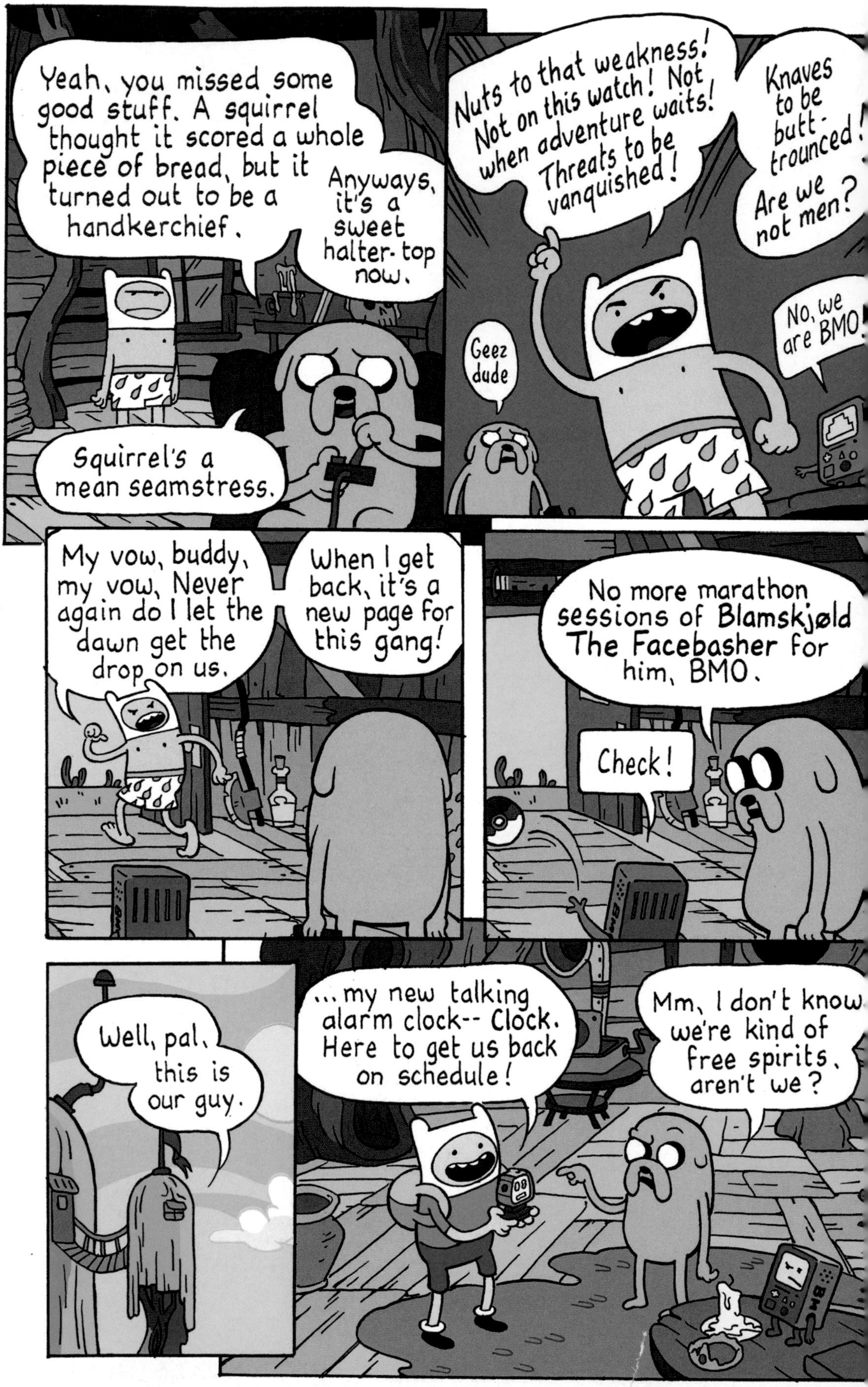

Yeah, you missed some good stuff. A squirrel thought it scored a whole piece of bread, but it turned out to be a handkerchief.
Anyways, it's a sweet halter-top now.
Squirrel's a mean seamstress.
Nuts to that weakness! Not on this watch! Not when adventure waits! Threats to be vanquished!
Knaves to be butt-trounced!
Are we not men?
Geez dude
No, we are BMO!
My vow, buddy, my vow, Never again do I let the dawn get the drop on us.
When I get back, it's a new page for this gang!
No more marathon sessions of Blamskjøld The Facebasher for him, BMO.
Check!
Well, pal, this is our guy.
...my new talking alarm clock-- Clock. Here to get us back on schedule!
Mm, I don't know we're kind of free spirits, aren't we?

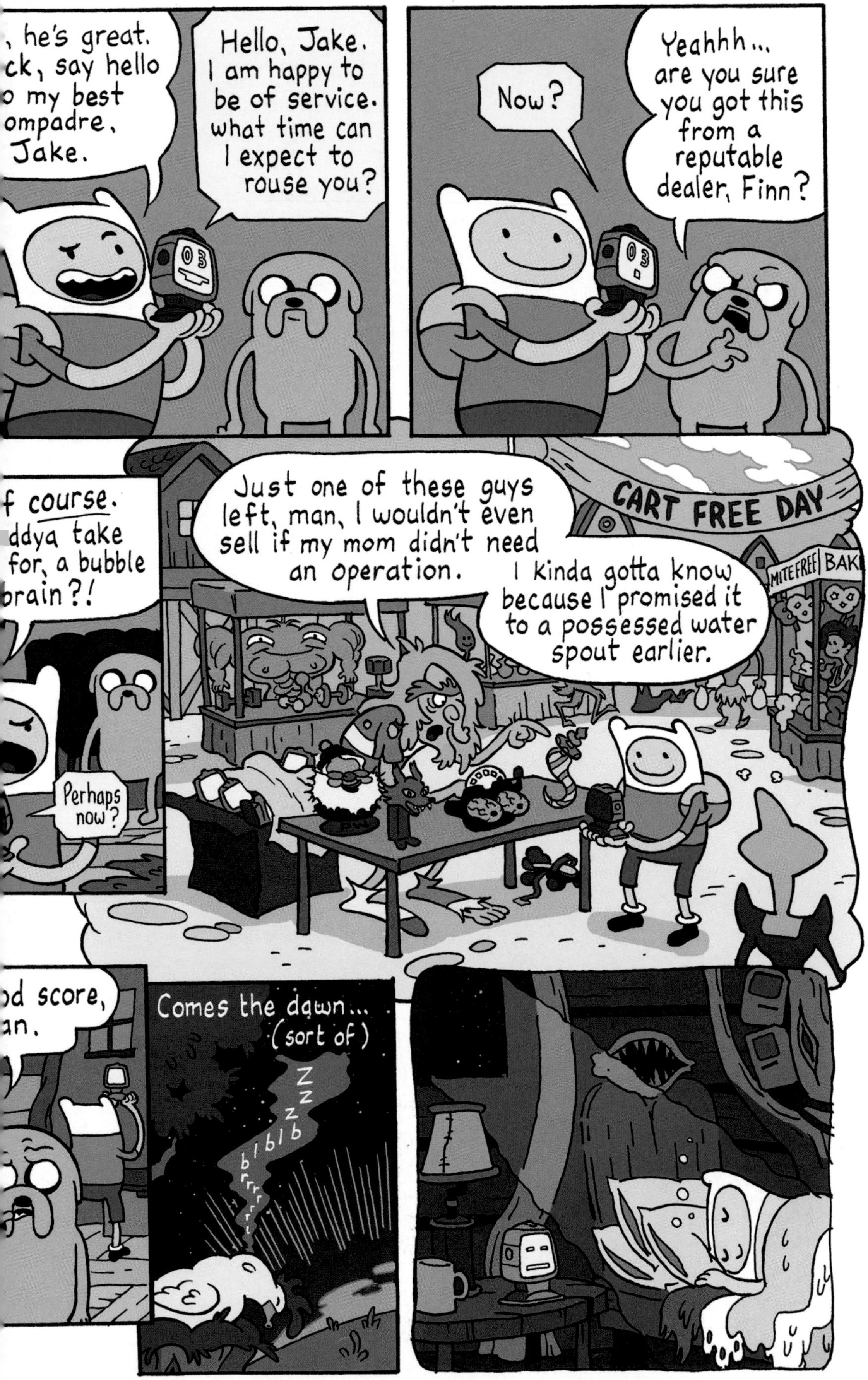

, he's great.
ck, say hello
o my best
ompadre,
Jake.
Hello, Jake.
I am happy to
be of service.
what time can
I expect to
rouse you?
Now?
Yeahhh...
are you sure
you got this
from a
reputable
dealer, Finn?
f course.
ddya take
for, a bubble
brain?!
Perhaps
now?
CART FREE DAY
Just one of these guys
left, man, I wouldn't even
sell if my mom didn't need
an operation.
I kinda gotta know
because I promised it
to a possessed water
spout earlier.
od score,
an.
Comes the dawn...
(sort of)
Z
Z
Z
b
bl bl b
brrrrrr

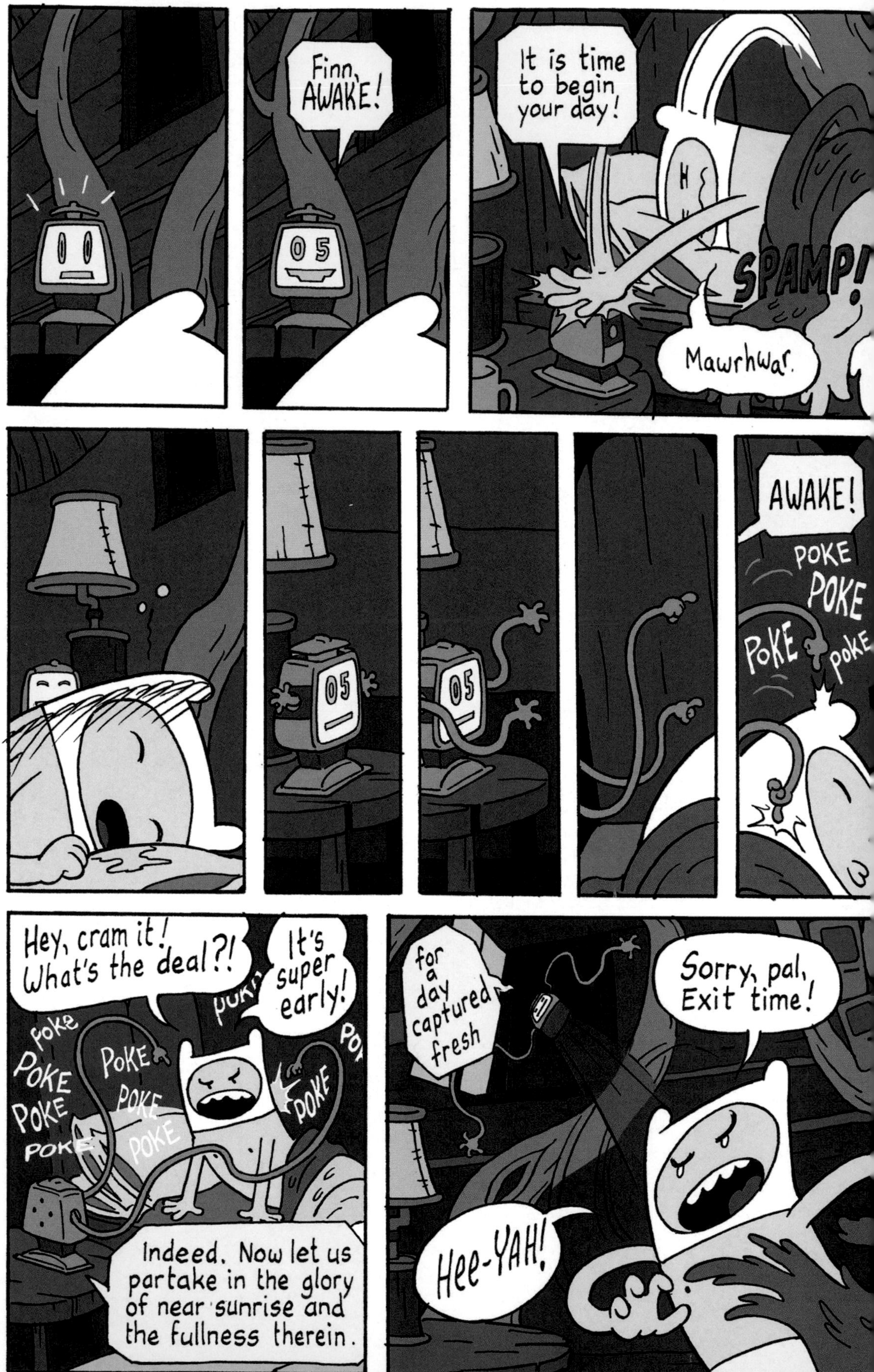

Finn, AWAKE!
It is time to begin your day!
SPAMP!
Mawrhwar.
AWAKE!
POKE
POKE
POKE
poke
Hey, cram it! What's the deal?!
It's super early!
poke
POKE
POKE
POKE
POKE
POKE
POKE
POKE
Indeed. Now let us partake in the glory of near sunrise and the fullness therein.
for a day captured fresh
Sorry, pal, Exit time!
Hee-YAH!

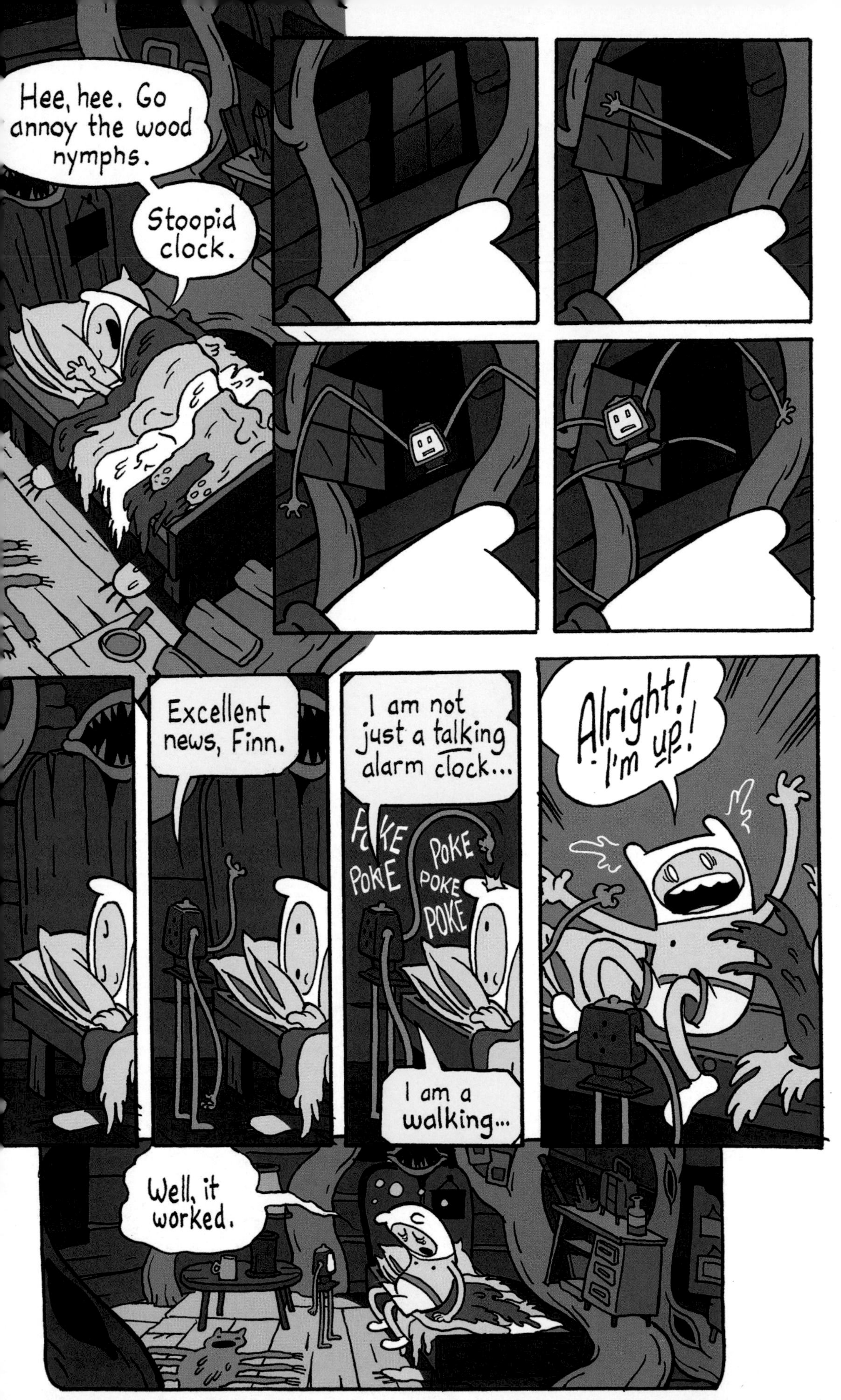
Hee, hee. Go annoy the wood nymphs.
Stoopid clock.
Excellent news, Finn.
I am not just a talking alarm clock...
POKE POKE
POKE POKE POKE
I am a walking...
Alright! I'm up!
Well, it worked.

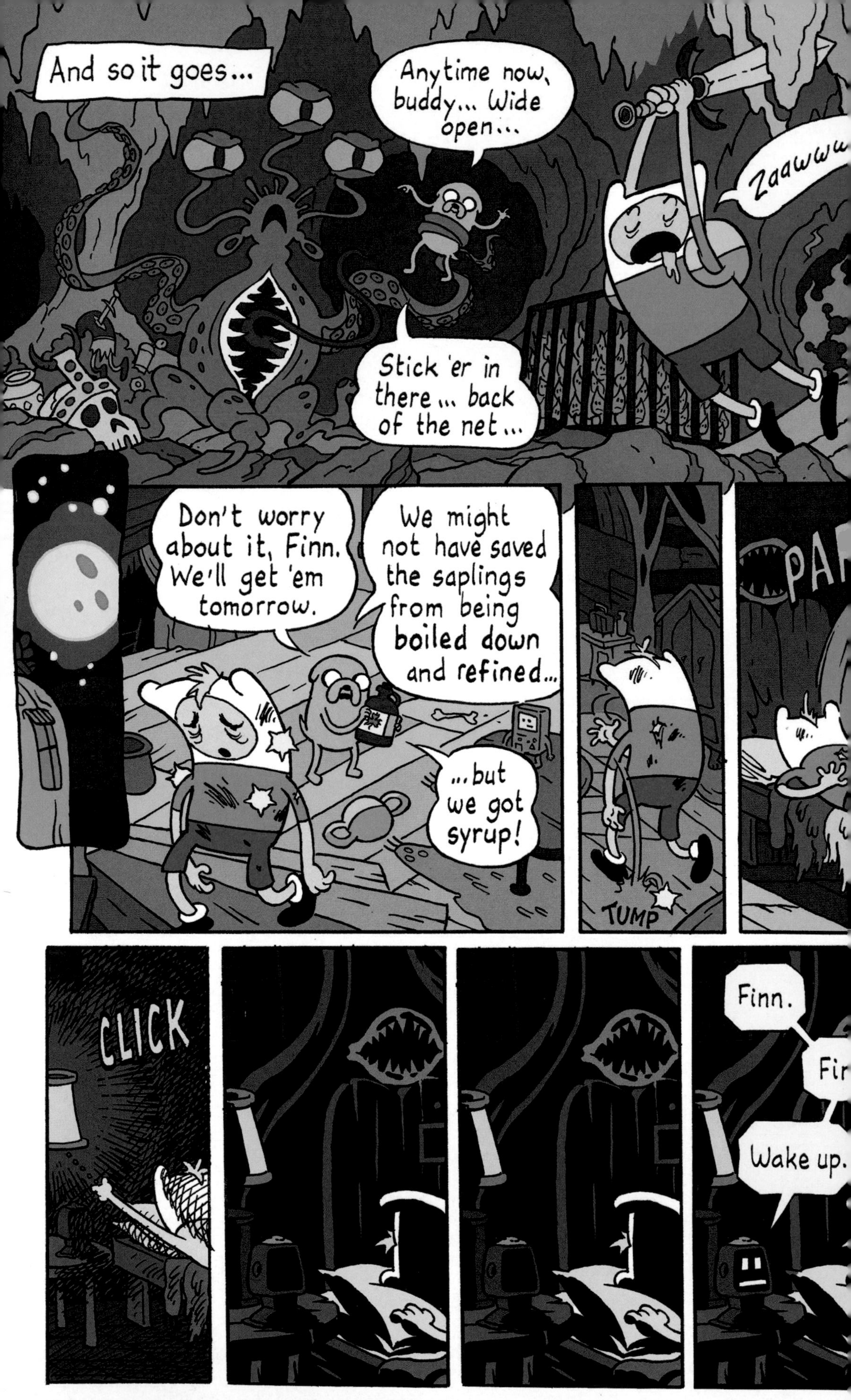

And so it goes...
Anytime now, buddy... Wide open...
Zaawwu
Stick 'er in there ... back of the net...
Don't worry about it, Finn. We'll get 'em tomorrow.
We might not have saved the saplings from being boiled down and refined...
...but we got syrup!
TUMP
CLICK
Finn.
Wake up.

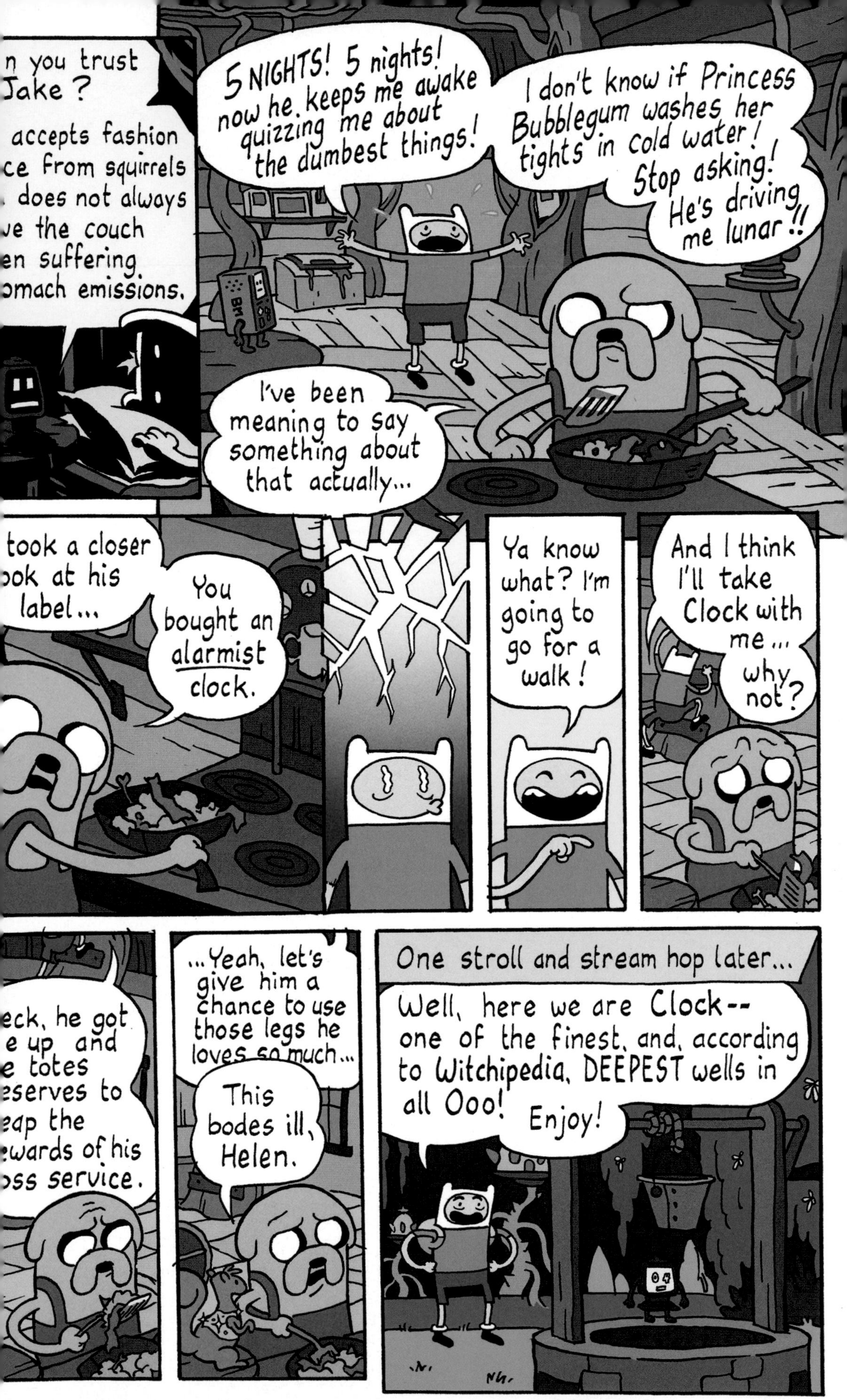

n you trust
Jake?
accepts fashion
ce from squirrels
does not always
ve the couch
en suffering
omach emissions.
5 NIGHTS! 5 nights! now he keeps me awake quizzing me about the dumbest things!
I don't know if Princess Bubblegum washes her tights in cold water! Stop asking! He's driving me lunar!!
I've been meaning to say something about that actually...
took a closer
ook at his
label...
You bought an alarmist clock.
Ya know what? I'm going to go for a walk!
And I think I'll take Clock with me... why not?
eck, he got
e up and
e totes
eserves to
eap the
ewards of his
oss service.
...Yeah, let's give him a chance to use those legs he loves so much...
This bodes ill, Helen.
One stroll and stream hop later...
Well, here we are Clock-- one of the finest, and, according to Witchipedia, DEEPEST wells in all Ooo!
Enjoy!

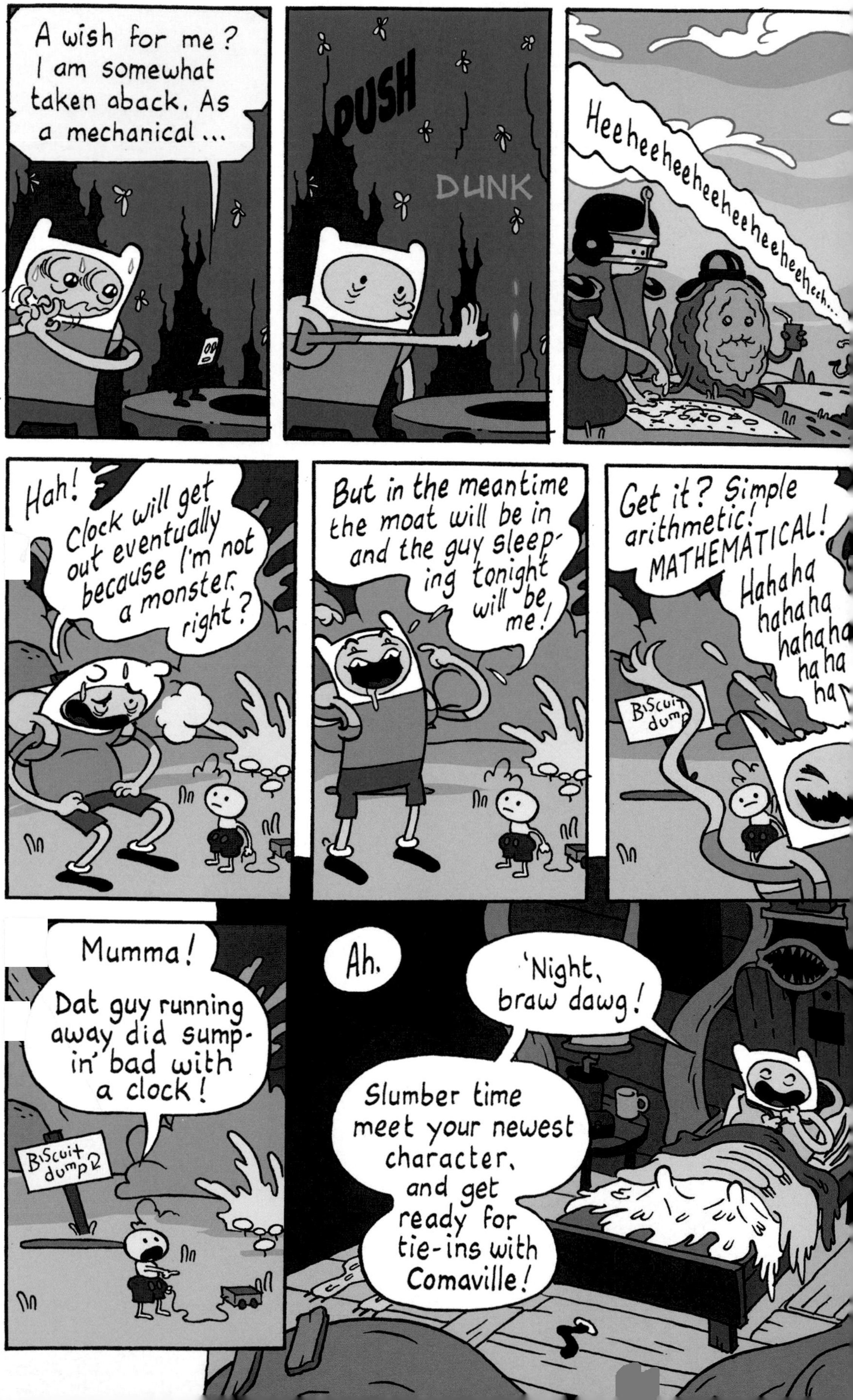

A wish for me? I am somewhat taken aback. As a mechanical...
PUSH
DUNK
Heeheeheeheeheeheeheeheeheeheeheeh...
Hah!
Clock will get out eventually because I'm not a monster, right?
But in the meantime the moat will be in and the guy sleeping tonight will be me!
Get it? Simple arithmetic! MATHEMATICAL!
Hahaha hahaha hahaha haha ha
Biscuit dump
Mumma!
Dat guy running away did sumpin' bad with a clock!
Biscuit dump 2
Ah.
'Night, braw dawg!
Slumber time meet your newest character, and get ready for tie-ins with Comaville!

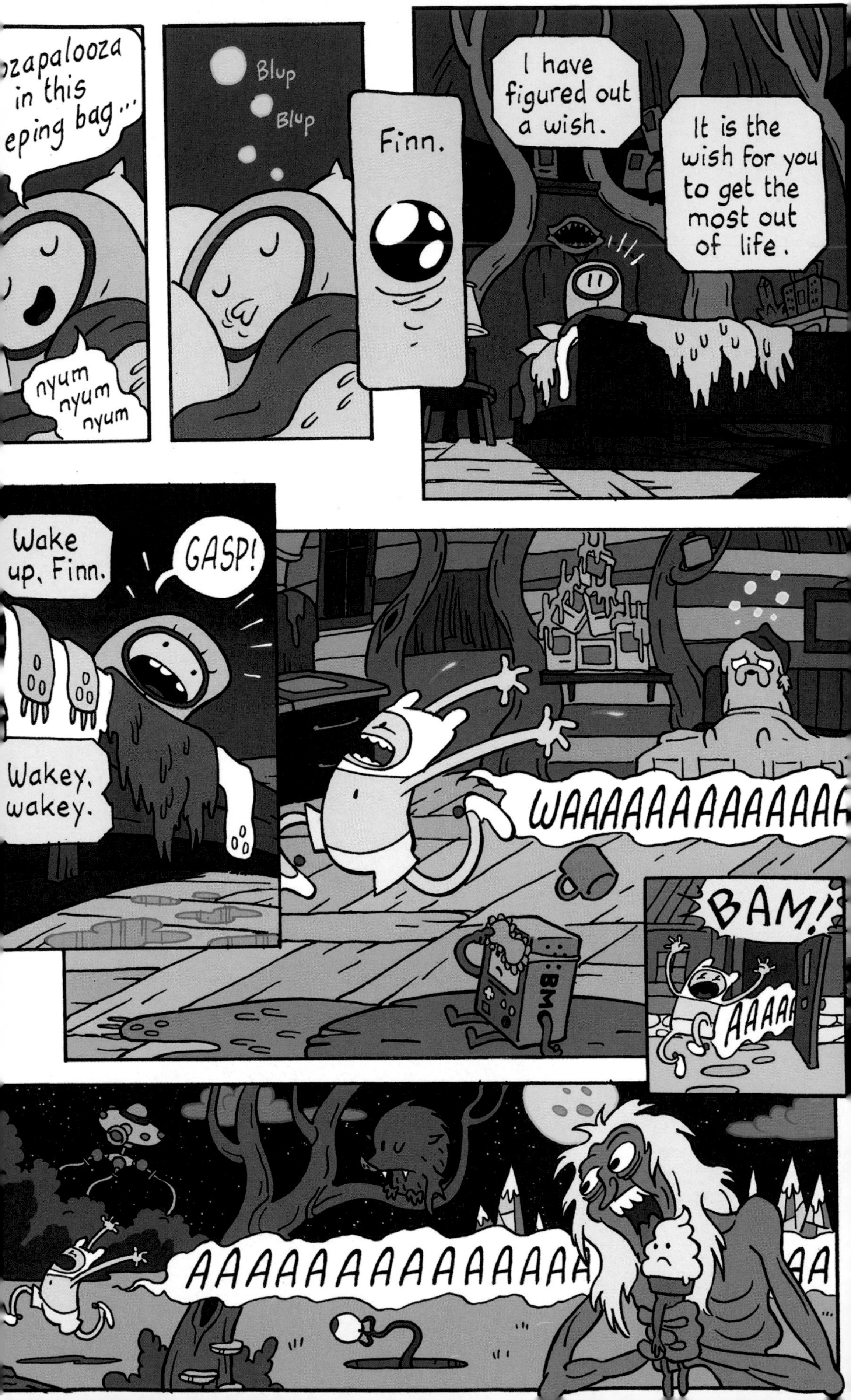

ozapalooza in this eping bag...
nyum nyum nyum
Blup
Blup
Finn.
I have figured out a wish.
It is the wish for you to get the most out of life.
Wake up, Finn.
GASP!
Wakey, wakey.
WAAAAAAAAAAAAAA
BMO
BAM!
AAAA
AAAAAAAAAAAAAAA
AA

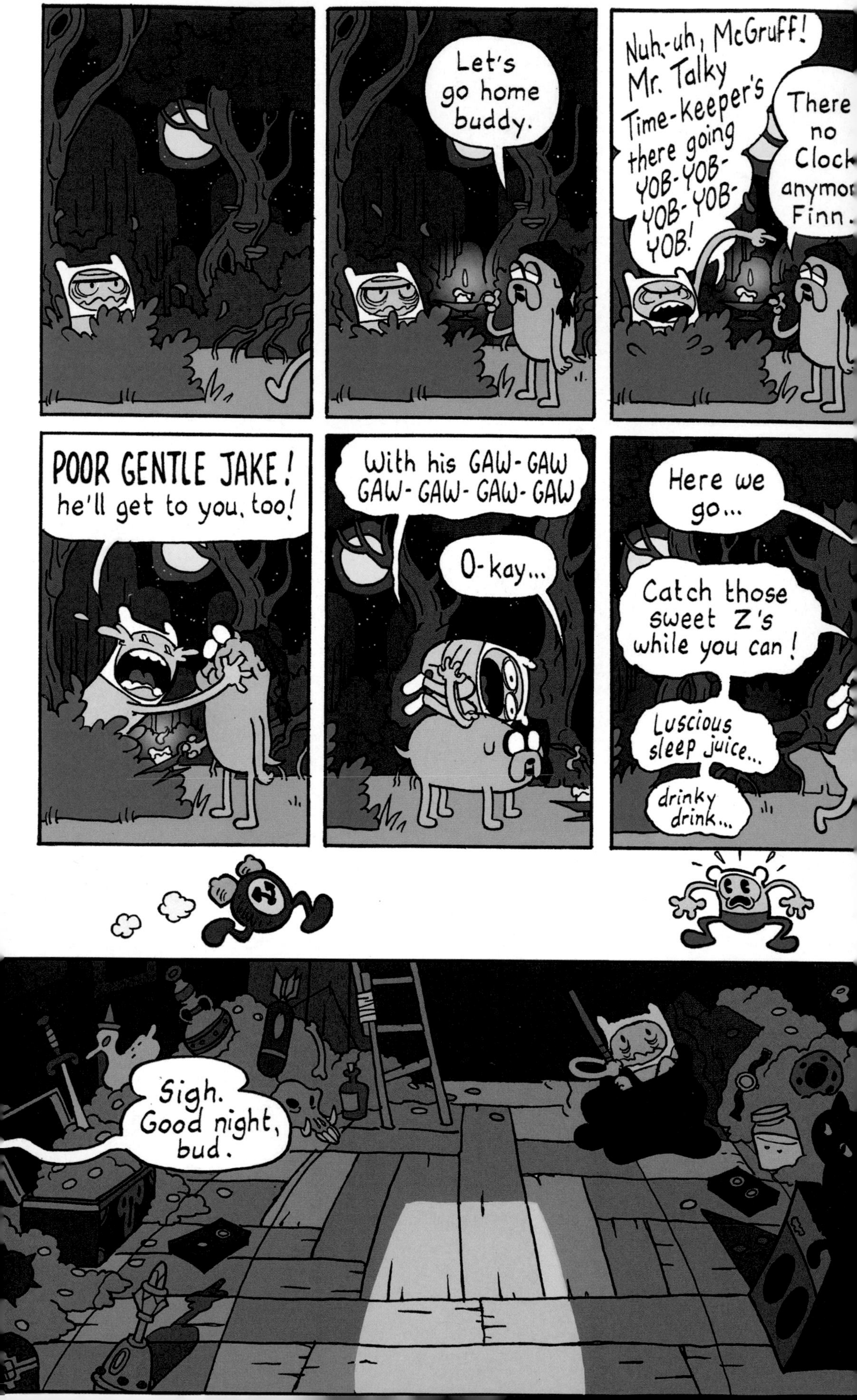
Let's go home buddy.
Nuh-uh, McGruff! Mr. Talky Time-keeper's there going YOB-YOB-YOB-YOB-YOB-YOB!
There no Clock anymor Finn.
POOR GENTLE JAKE! he'll get to you, too!
With his GAW-GAW GAW-GAW-GAW-GAW
O-kay...
Here we go...
Catch those sweet Z's while you can!
Luscious sleep juice...
drinky drink...
Sigh. Good night, bud.

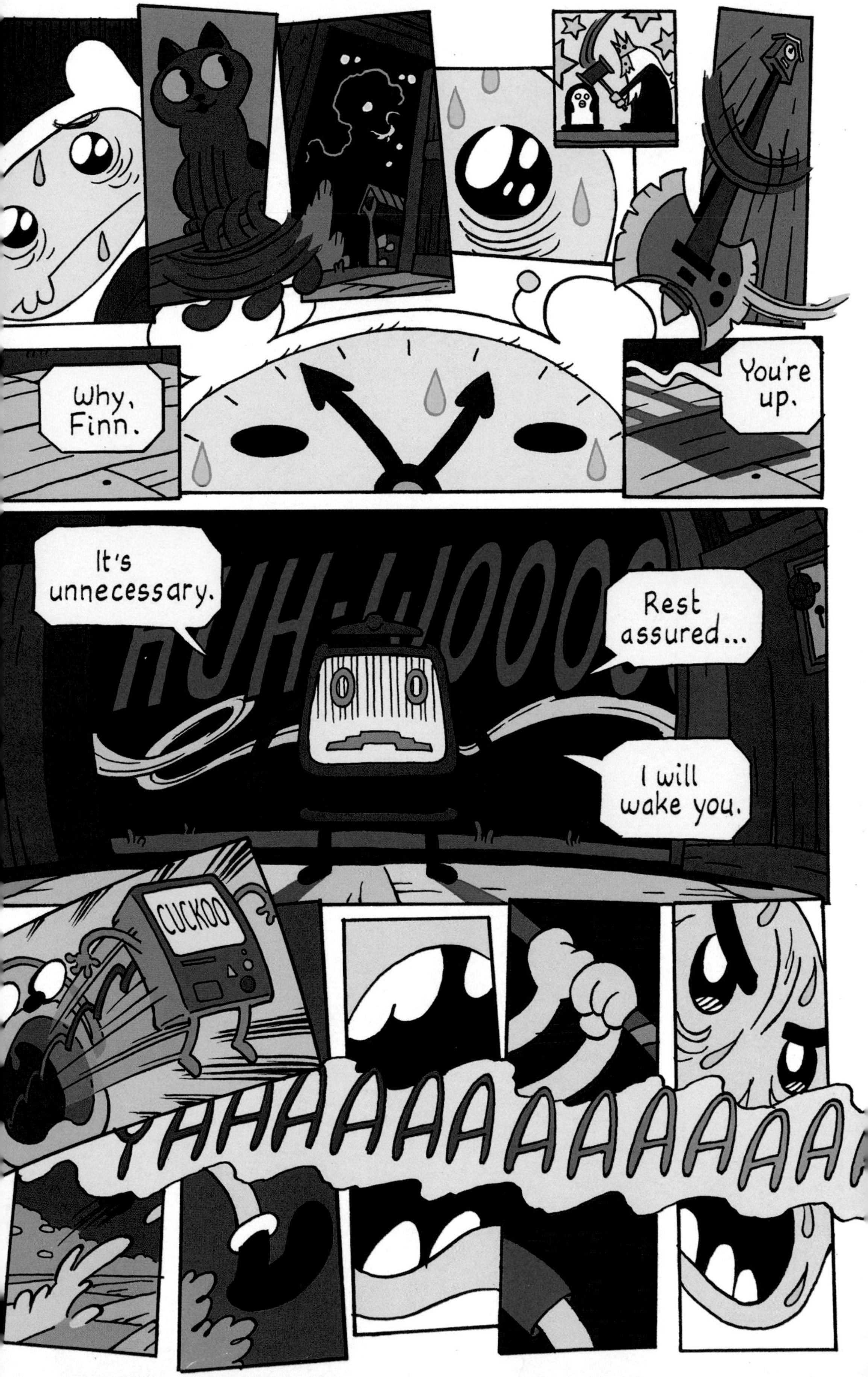

Why, Finn.
You're up.
It's unnecessary.
Rest assured...
I will wake you.
CUCKOO
YHHHAAAAAAAAAAAA

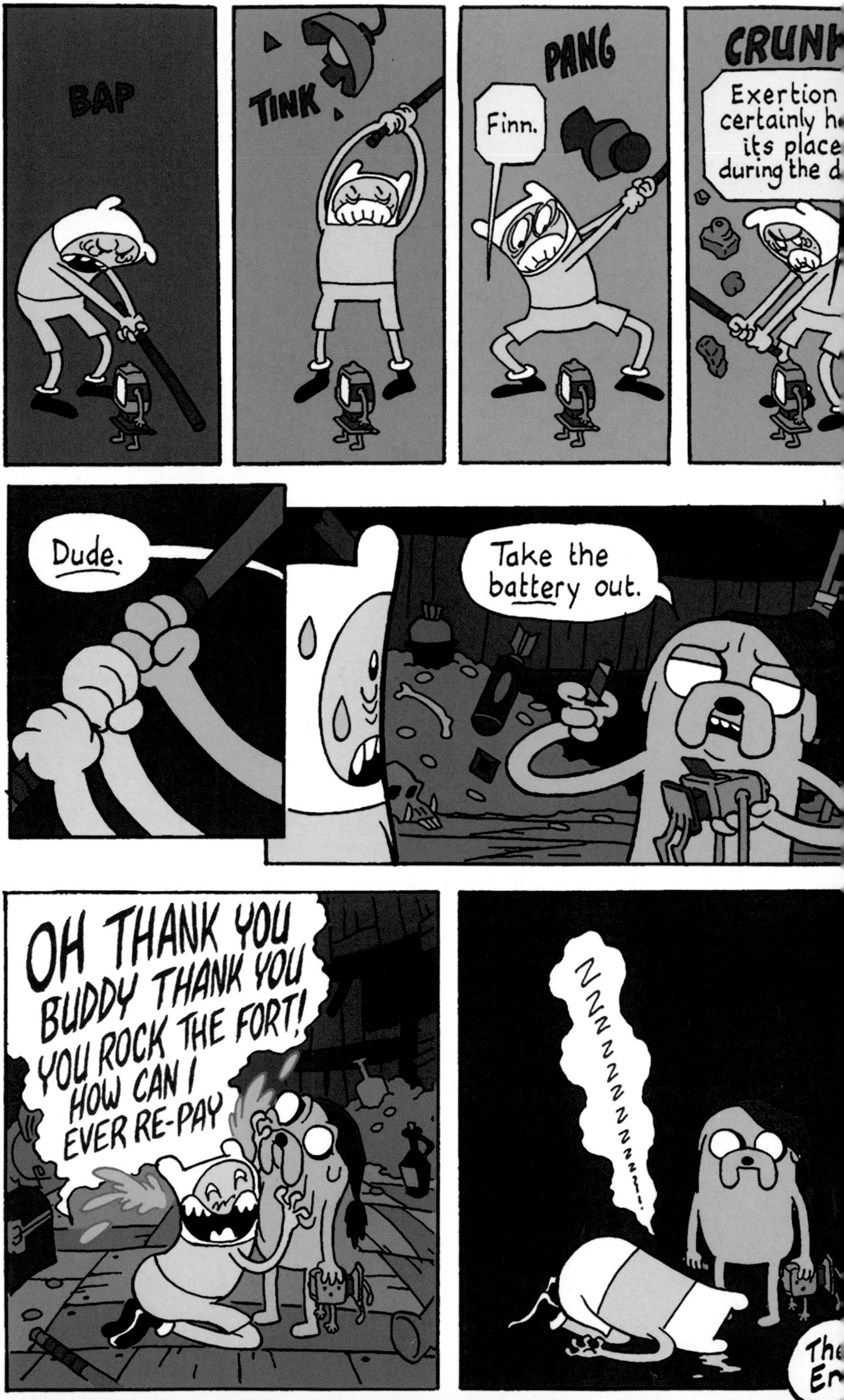
BAP
TINK
PANG
Finn.
CRUNK
Exertion certainly h
its place
during the d
Dude.
Take the battery out.
OH THANK YOU BUDDY THANK YOU YOU ROCK THE FORT! HOW CAN I EVER RE-PAY
ZZZZZZZZZ
The
En

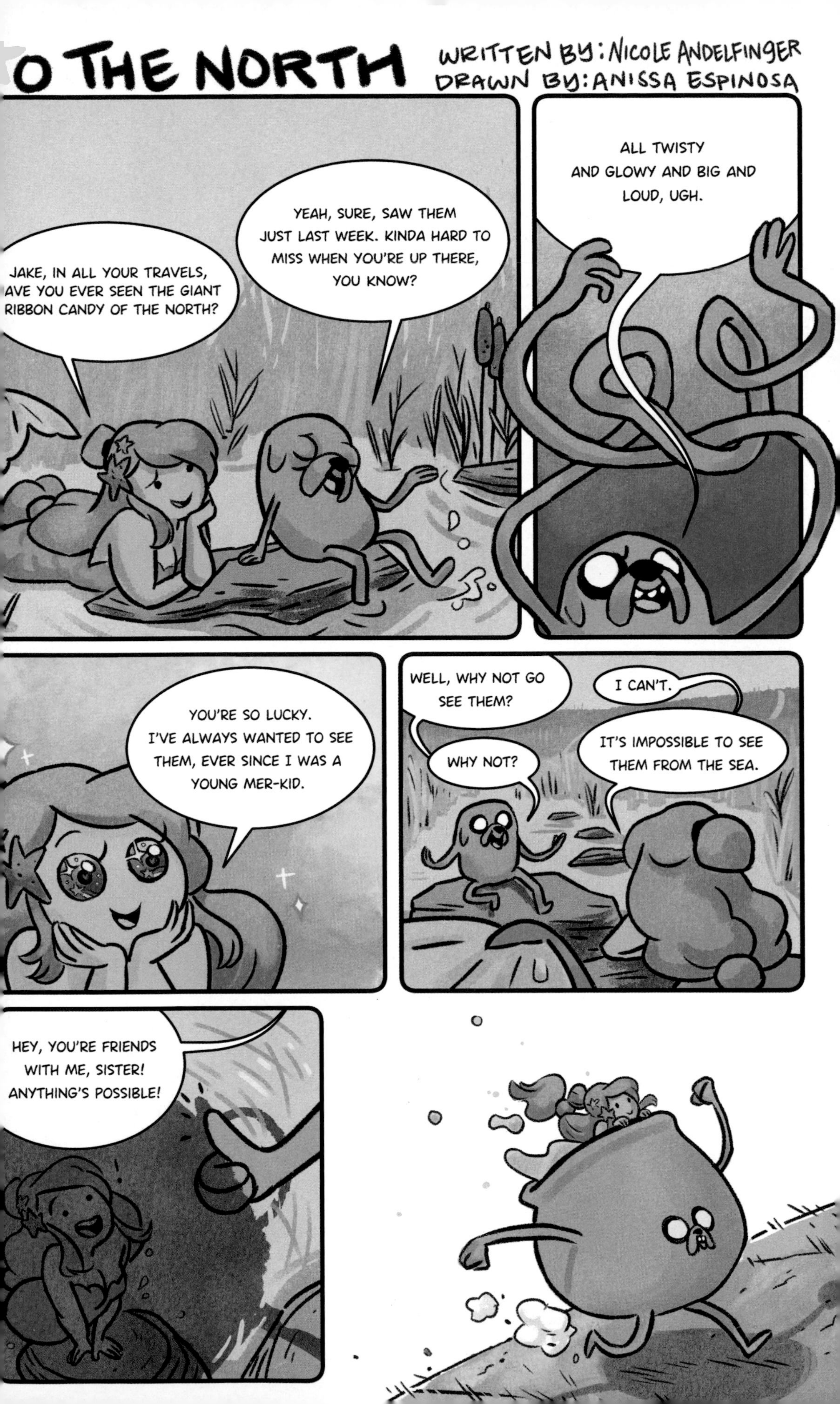
O THE NORTH
WRITTEN BY: NICOLE ANDELFINGER
DRAWN BY: ANISSA ESPINOSA
JAKE, IN ALL YOUR TRAVELS, AVE YOU EVER SEEN THE GIANT RIBBON CANDY OF THE NORTH?
YEAH, SURE, SAW THEM JUST LAST WEEK. KINDA HARD TO MISS WHEN YOU'RE UP THERE, YOU KNOW?
ALL TWISTY AND GLOWY AND BIG AND LOUD, UGH.
YOU'RE SO LUCKY. I'VE ALWAYS WANTED TO SEE THEM, EVER SINCE I WAS A YOUNG MER-KID.
WELL, WHY NOT GO SEE THEM?
I CAN'T.
WHY NOT?
IT'S IMPOSSIBLE TO SEE THEM FROM THE SEA.
HEY, YOU'RE FRIENDS WITH ME, SISTER! ANYTHING'S POSSIBLE!

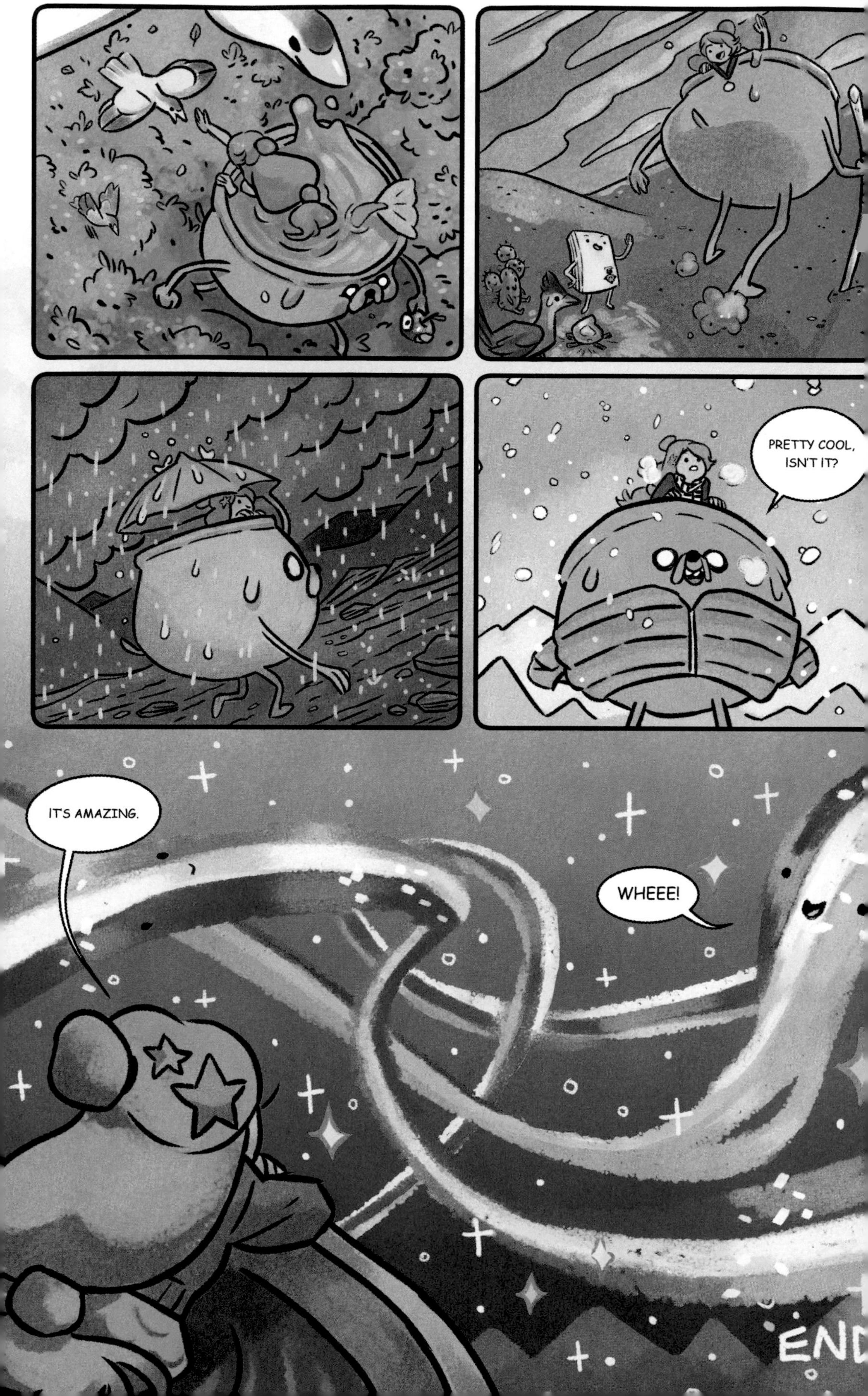
PRETTY COOL,
ISN'T IT?
IT'S AMAZING.
WHEEE!
END

COVER GALLERY

Issue #1 Main Cover

ERIN HUNTING

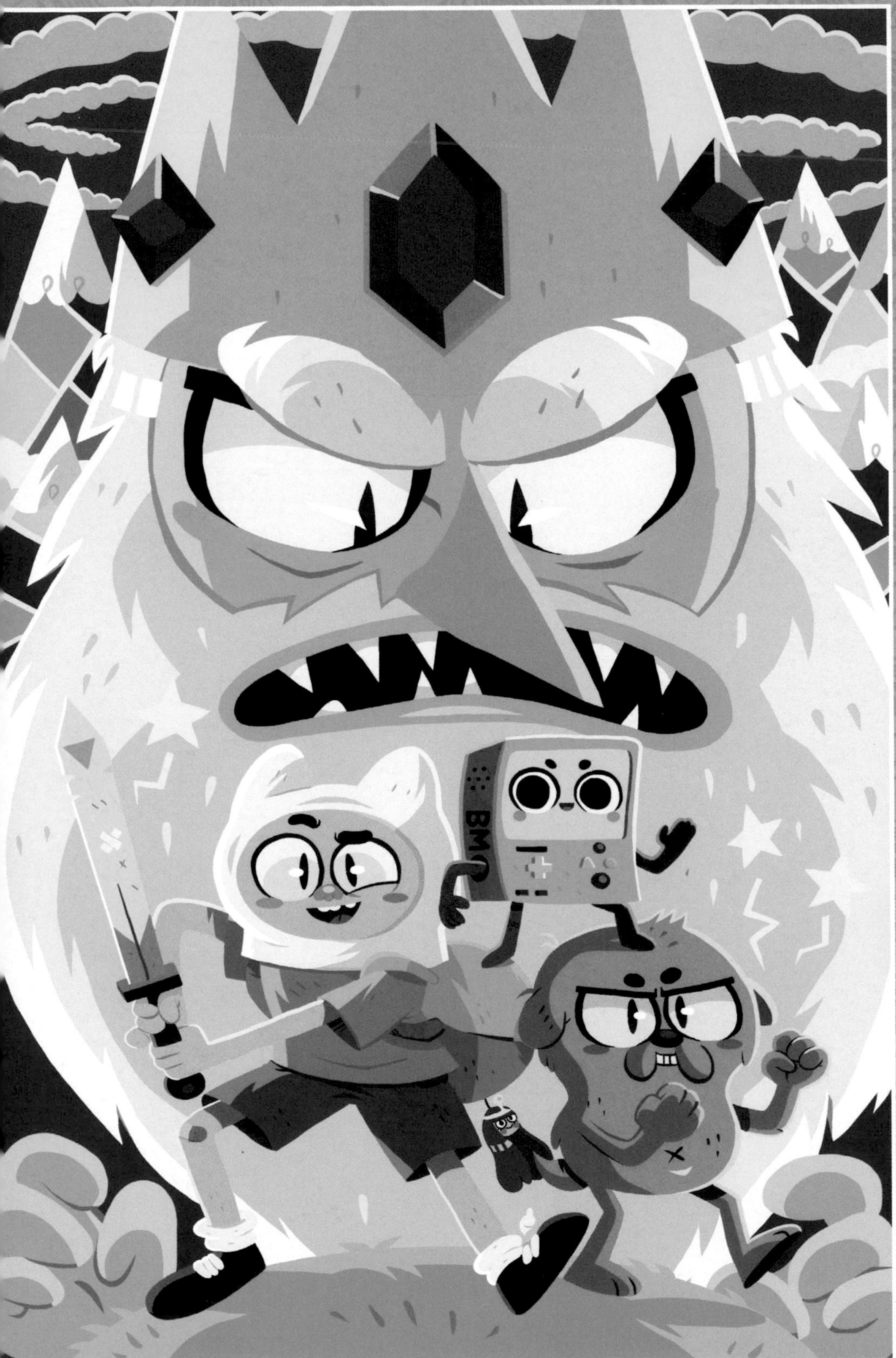
BMO

Issue #1 Subscription Cover

DEREK KIRK KIM

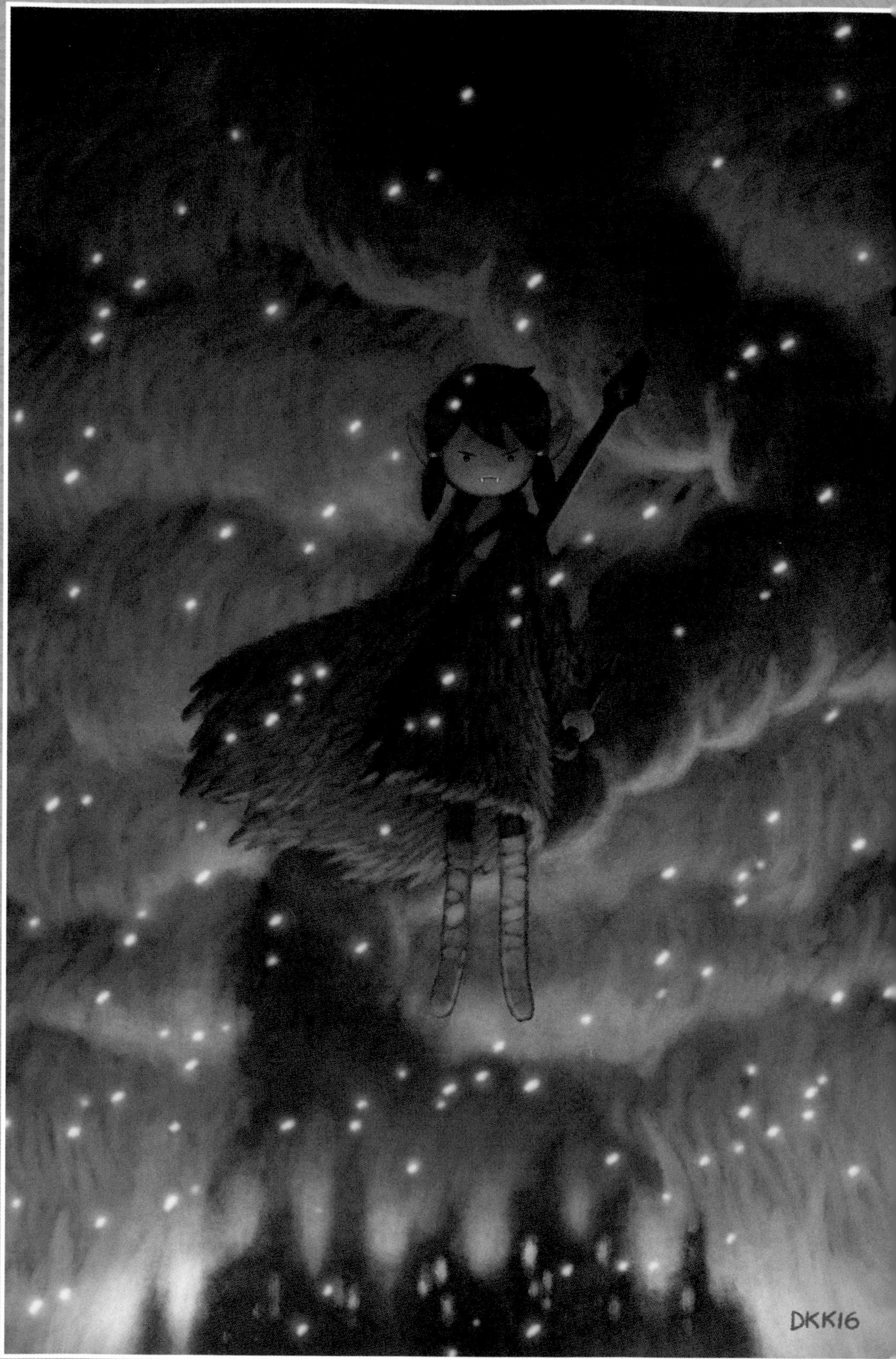

DKK16

Issue #1 Variant Cover

SALTY

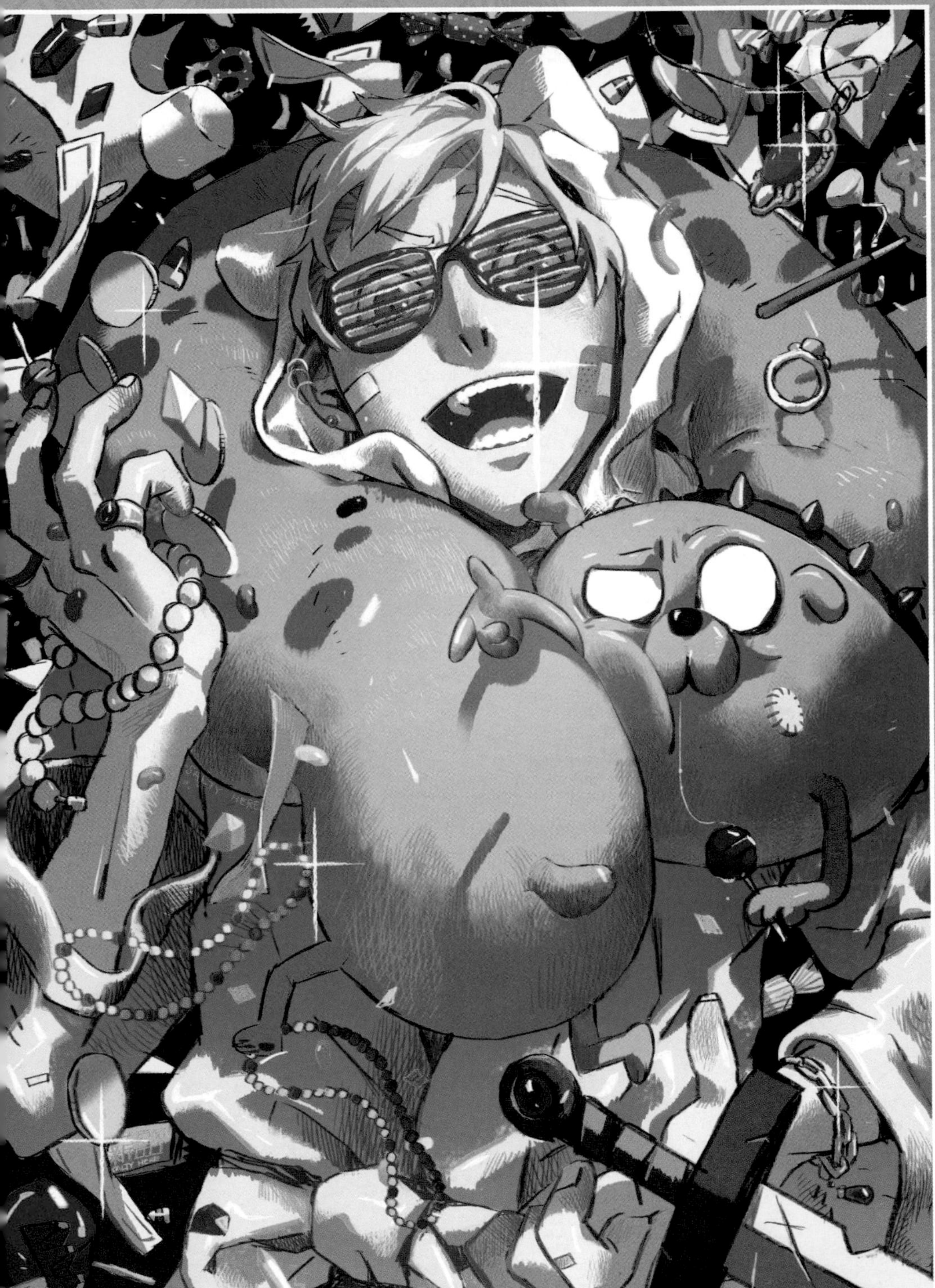

Issue #1 Variant Cover

NICK PITARRA

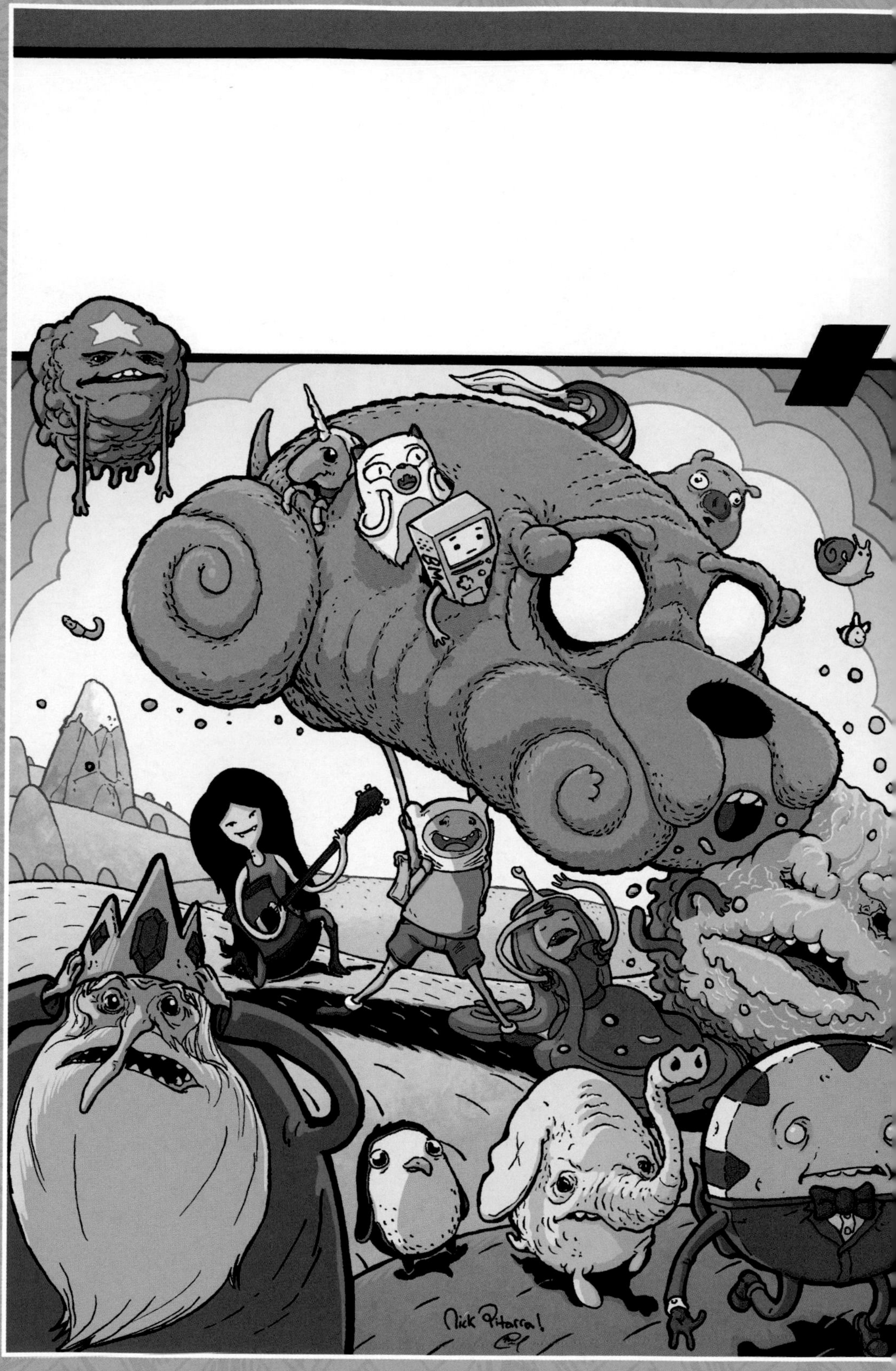
Nick Pitarra!

Issue #1 Variant Cover

TONY MILLIONAIRE

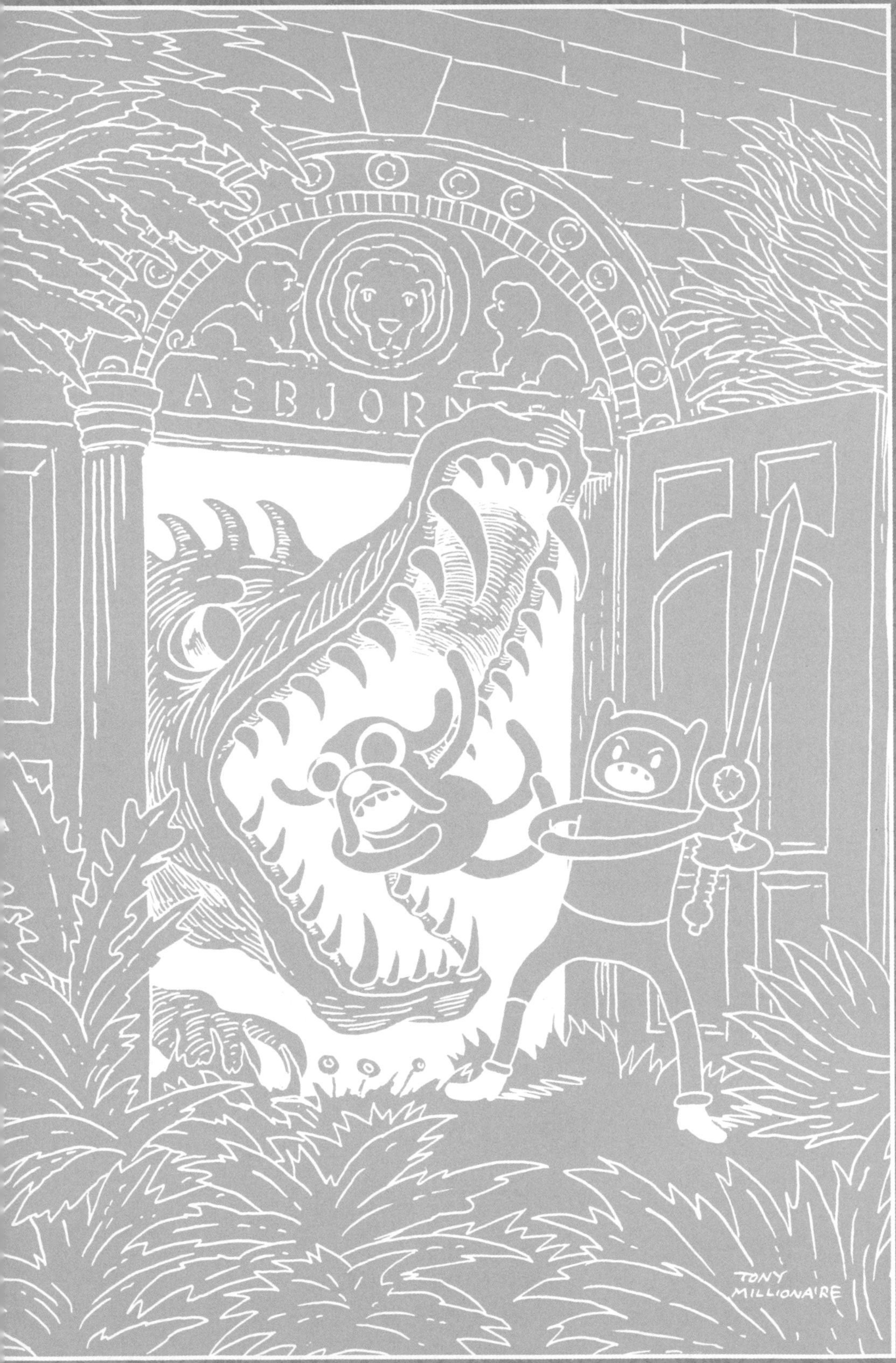
ASBJORN
TONY MILLIONAIRE

ISSUE #1 SAN DIEGO COMIC-CON EXCLUSIVE COVER
PAT MCHALE
WITH COLORS BY CHRYSTIN GARLAND

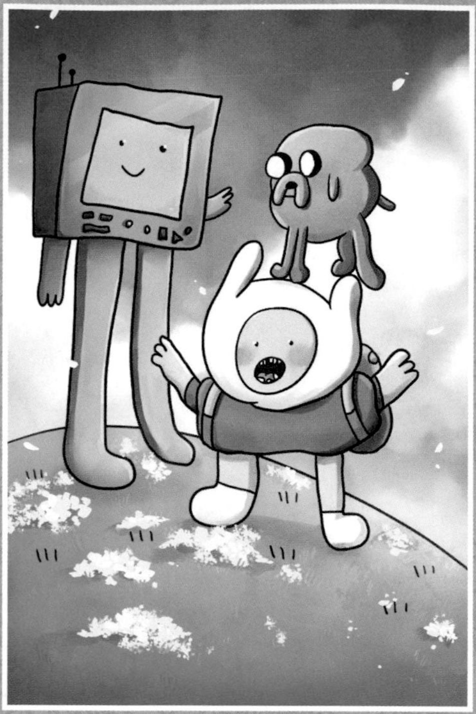

Issue #1 Fried Pie Exclusive Cover
STEPHANIE BUSCEMA

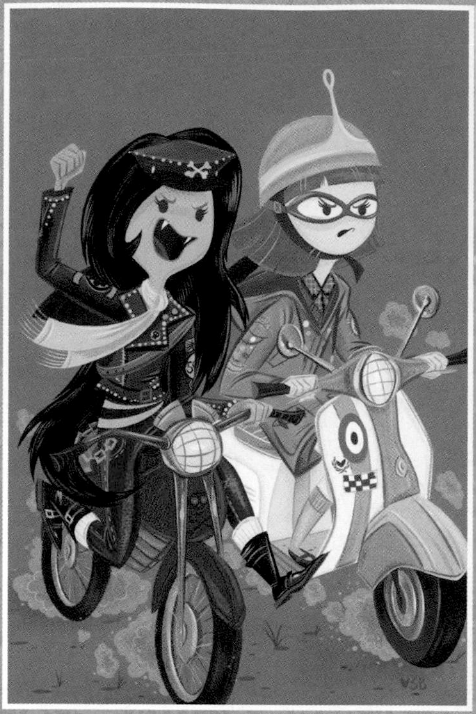

Issue #1 2nd Print Cover
LIZZ HICKEY

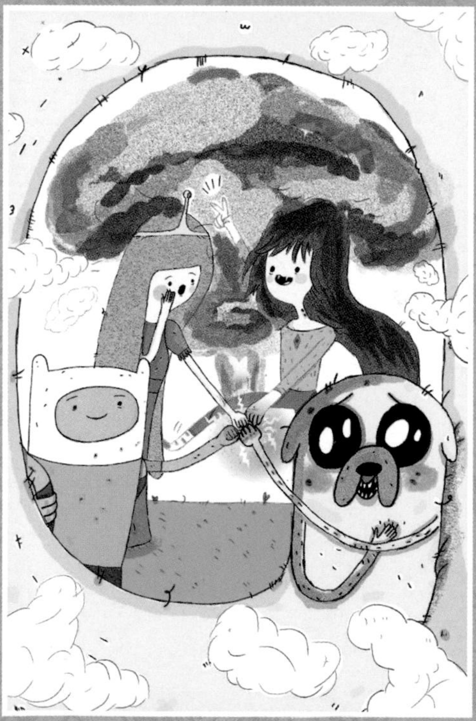

Issue #1 3rd Print Cover
ABIGAIL DELA CRUZ

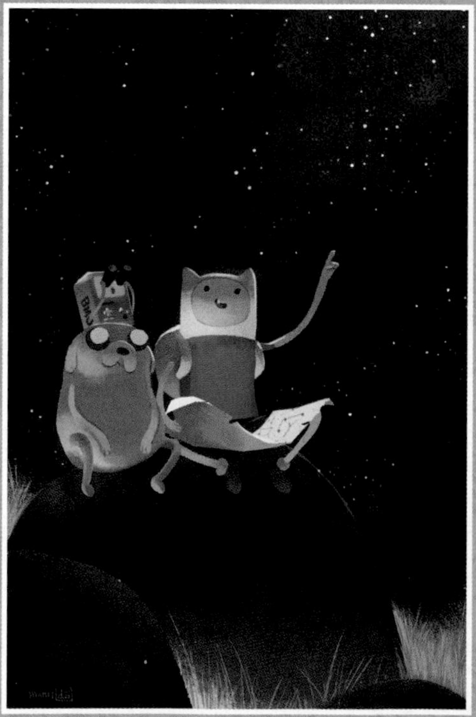

Issue #2 Main Cover

GREG SMALLWOOD

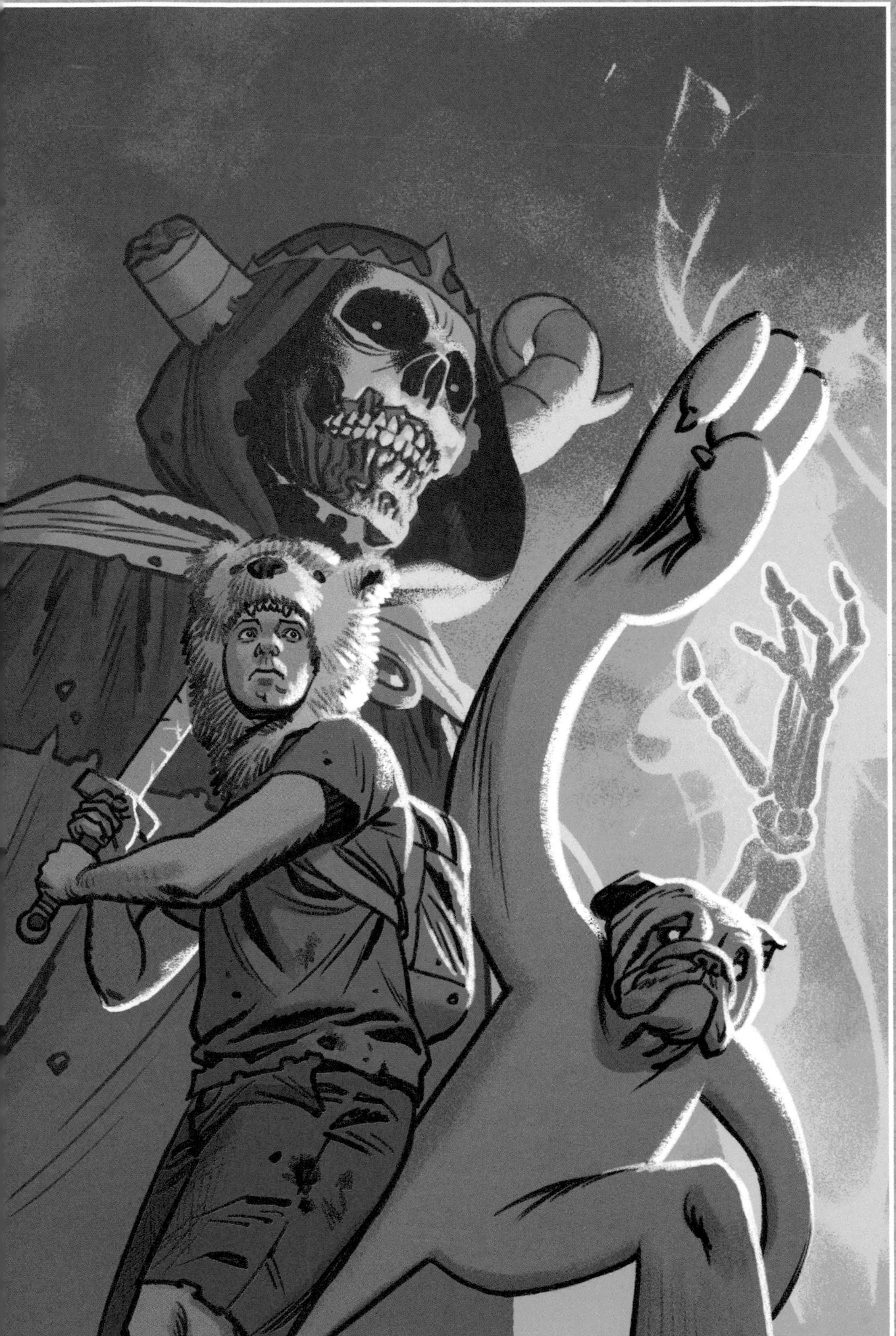

Issue #2 Subscription Cover

HELBETICO

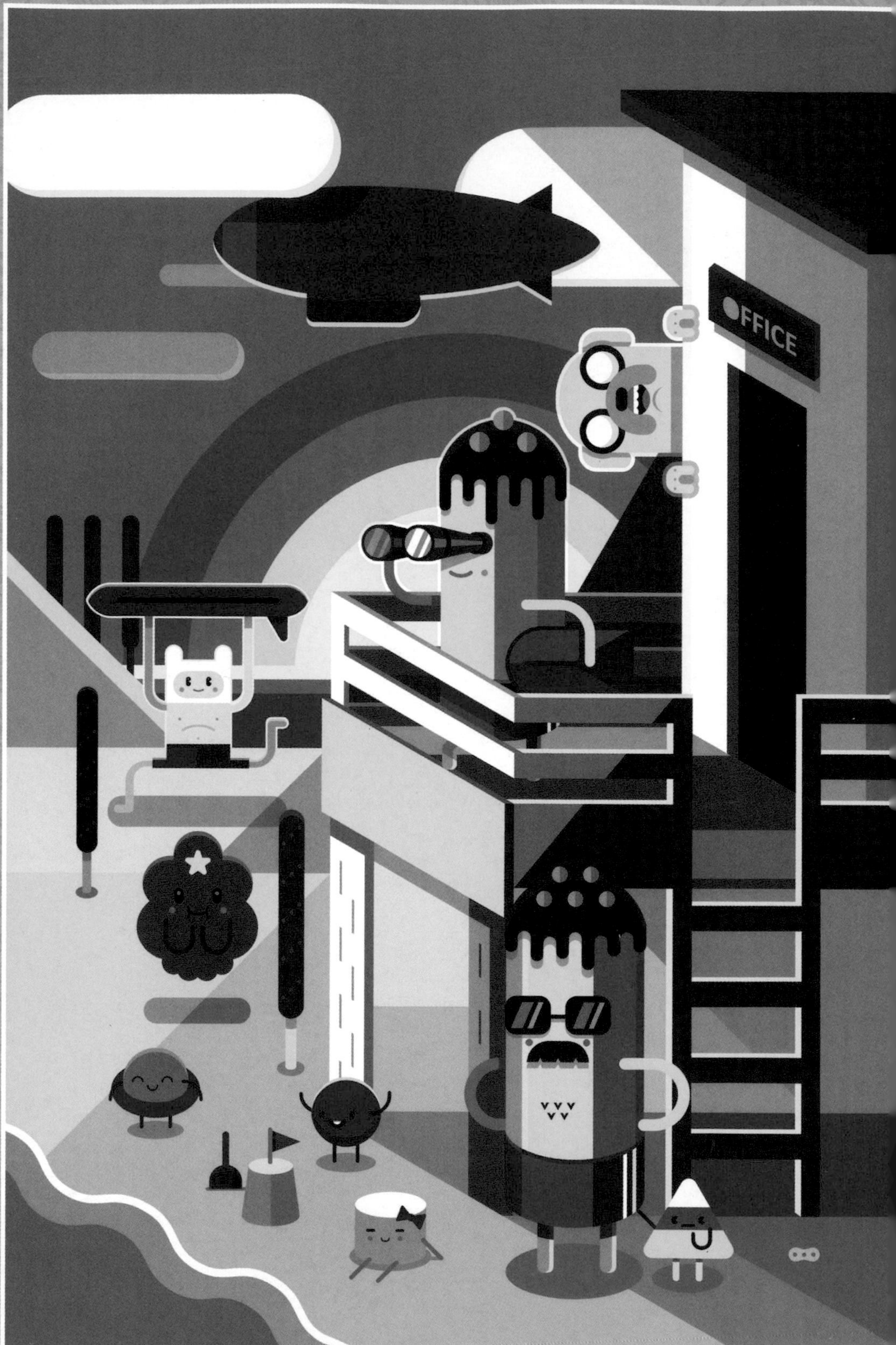

OFFICE

Issue #2 Variant Cover

CHRISTIAN CALAME

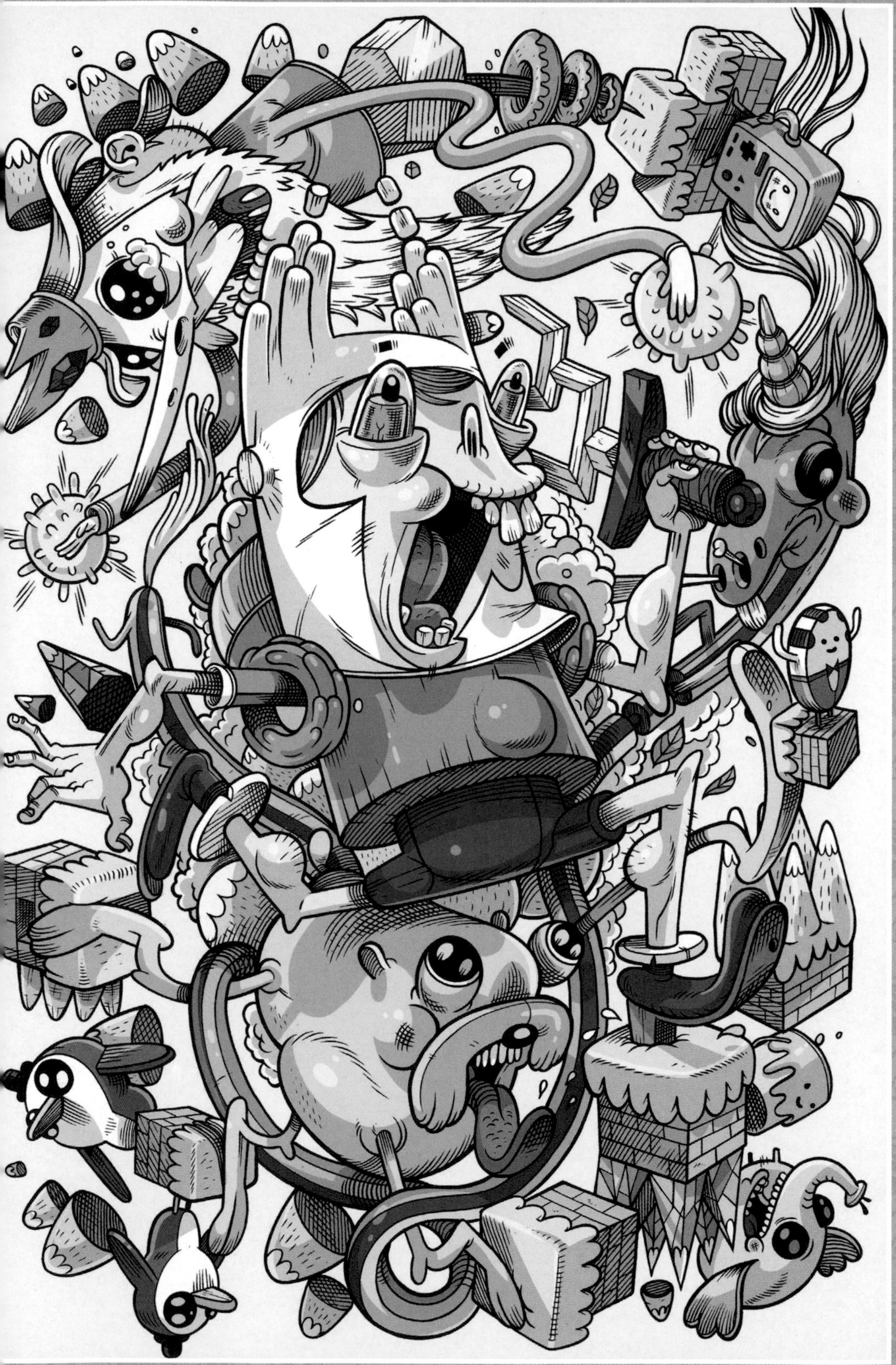

Issue #3 Main Cover

PHILLIP LIGHT

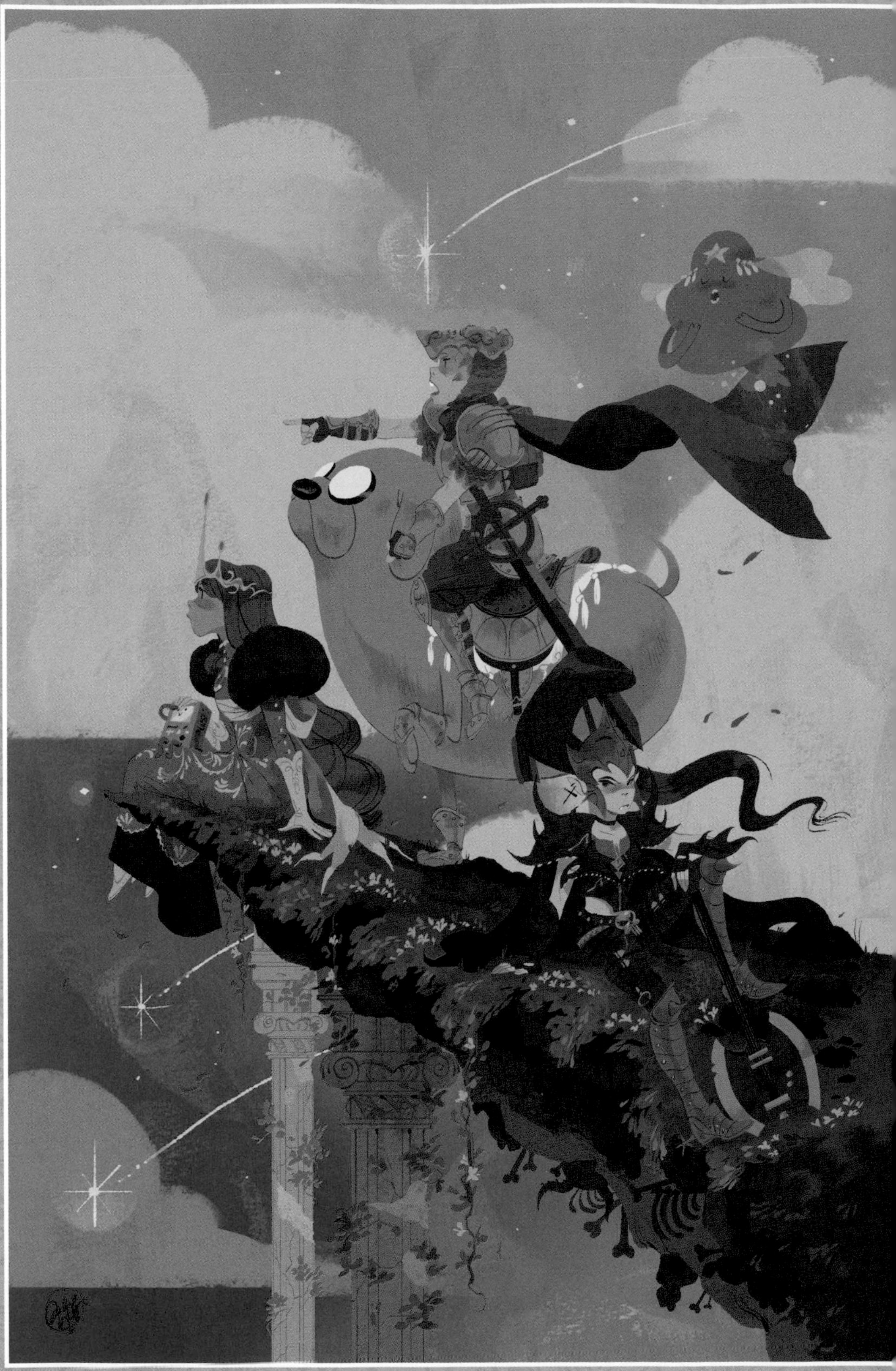

Issue #3 Subscription Cover

HANNAH ROSS

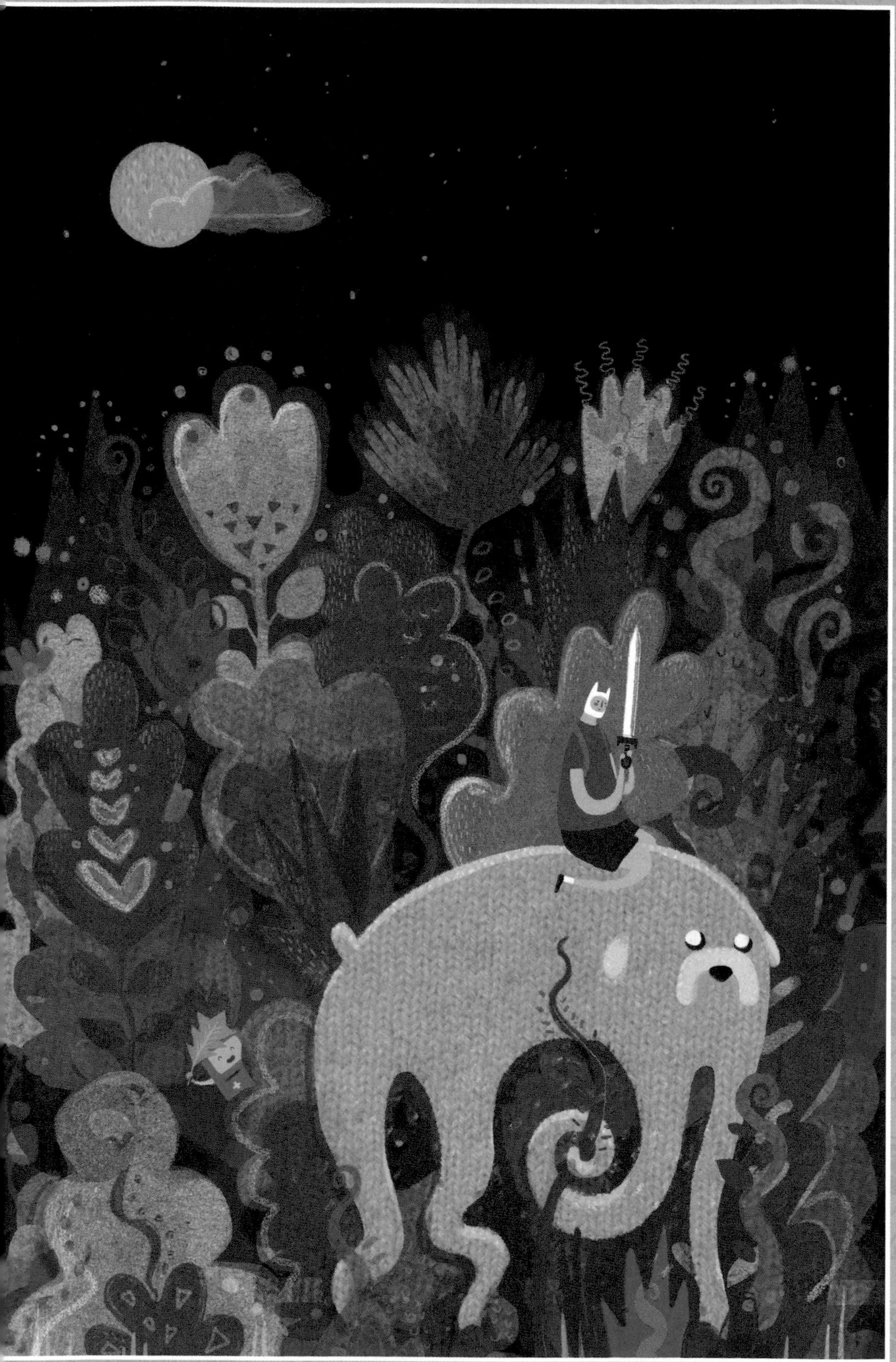

Issue #3 Variant Cover

A. SPARROW

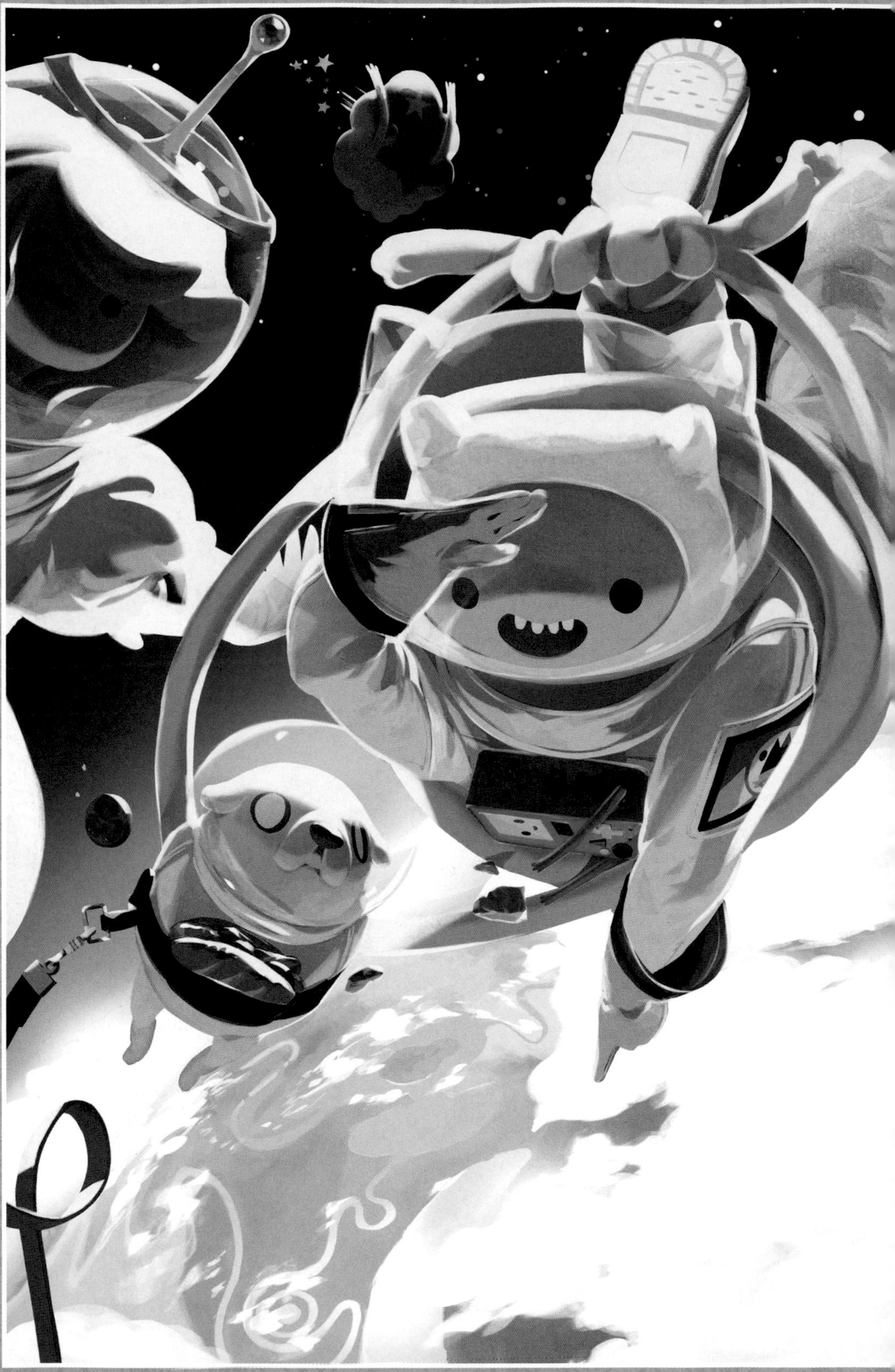

Issue #4 Main Cover
MARINA JULIA

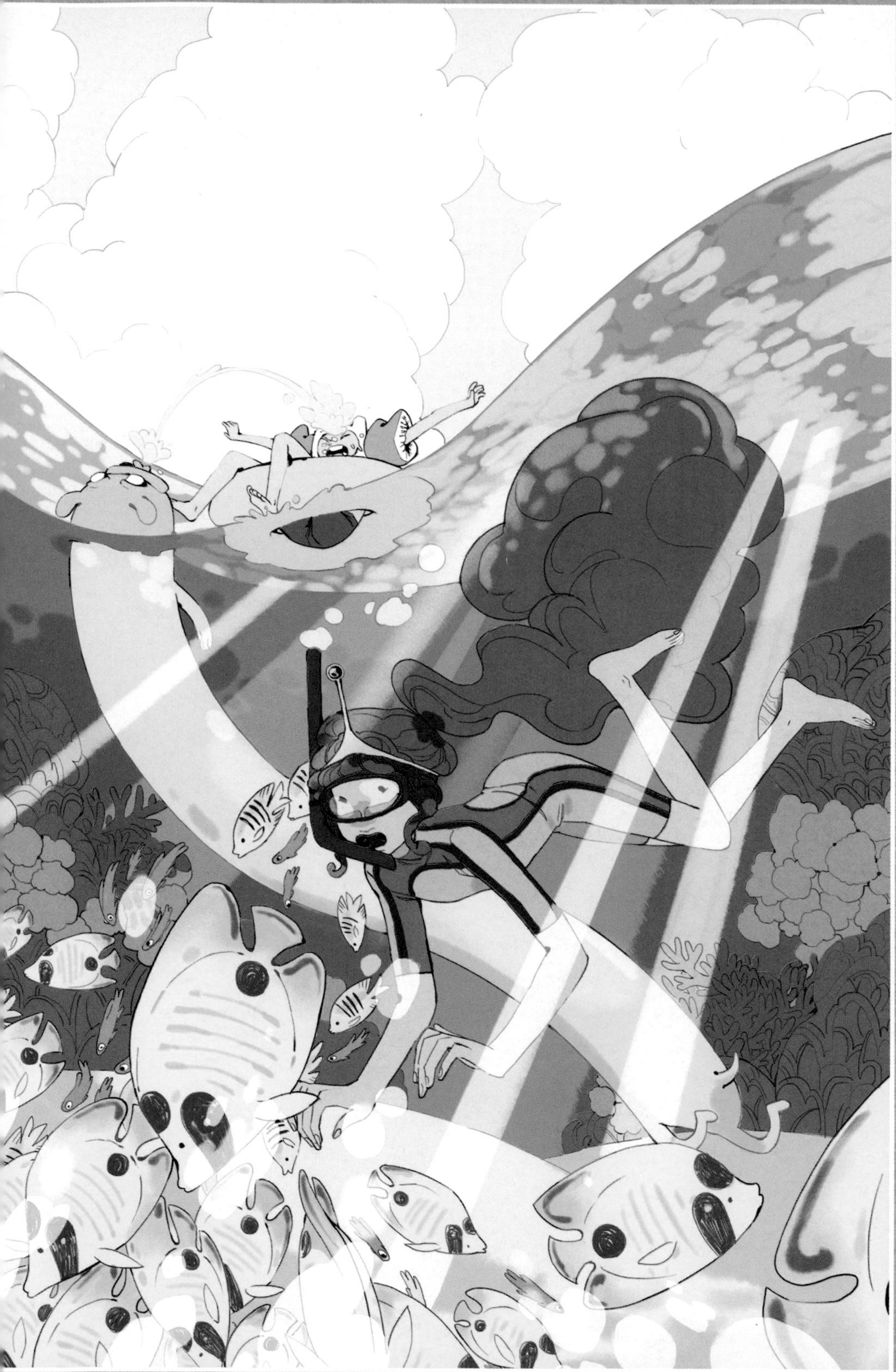

Issue #4 Subscription Cover

ANDREW GREENSTONE

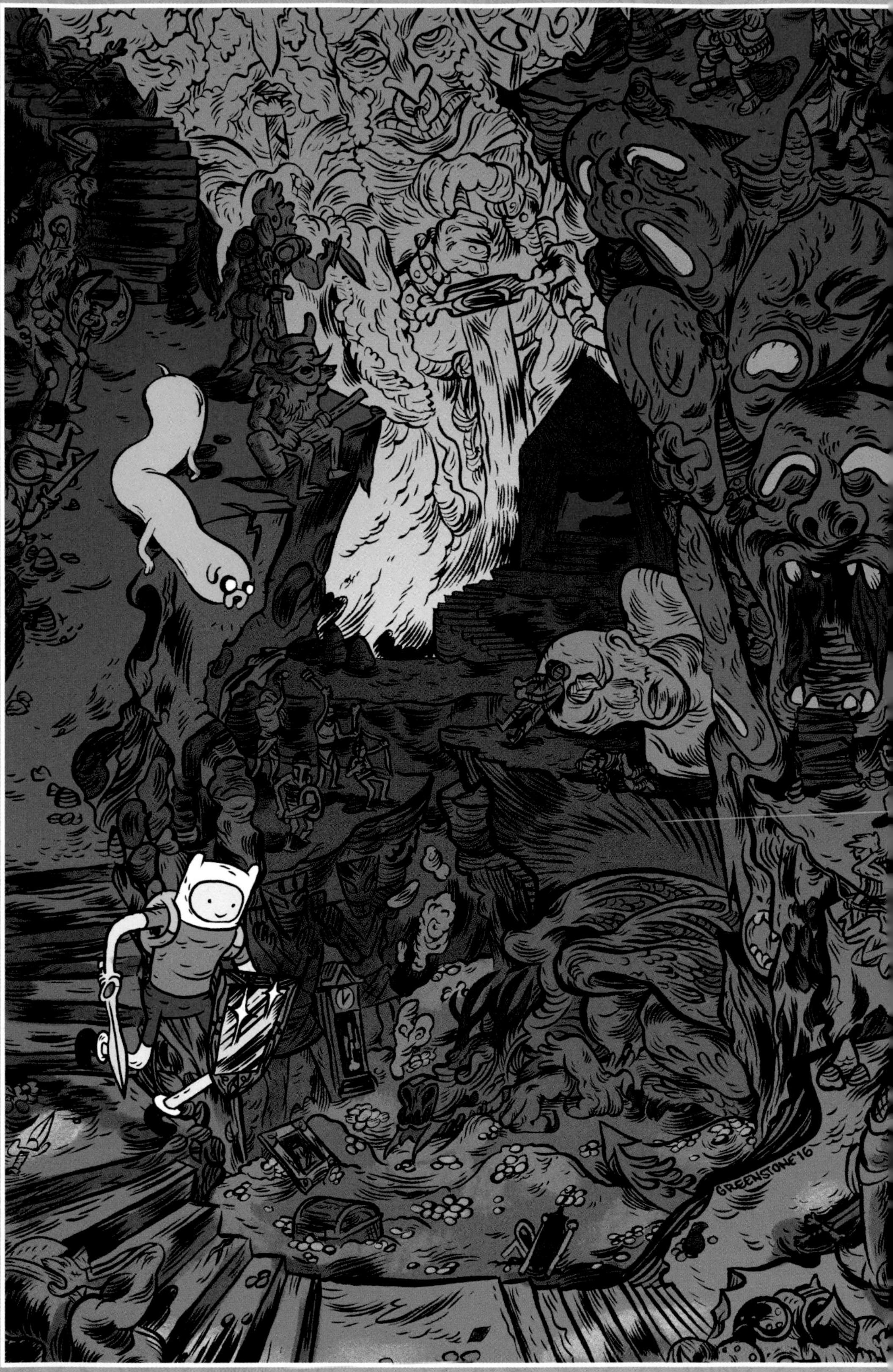

GREENSTONE '16

Issue #4 Variant Cover

ANTONIO SANDOVAL

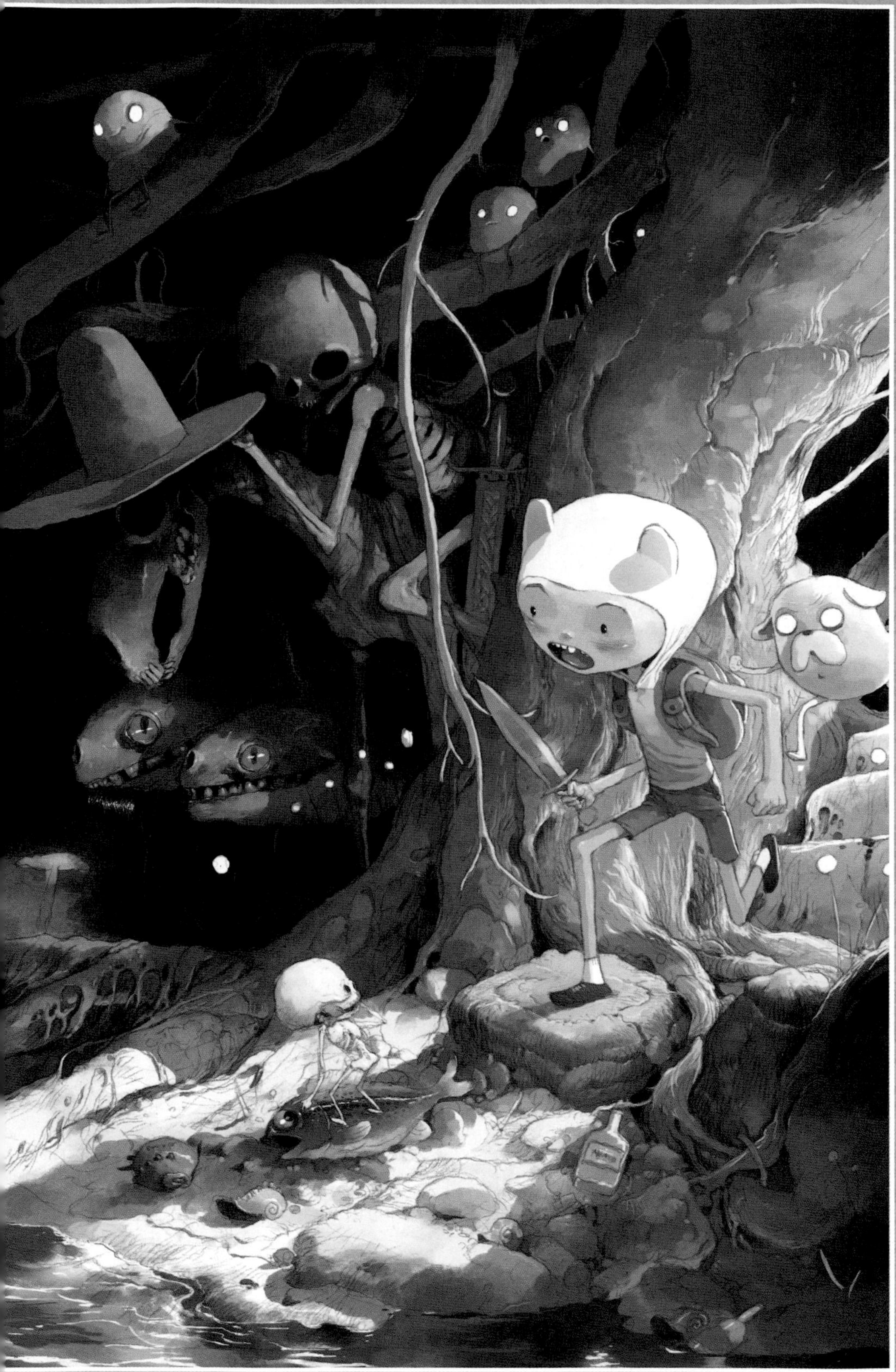